PRAISE FOR PORTRAITS OF DECAY

The stories in *Portraits of Decay* are terrifying in concept and execution. With his encyclopedic knowledge of horror history and incisive prose, Winter upends horror tropes with his wild imagination and dark sense of humor. For Weird stories exploring the depths of toxic masculinity and existential angst that are also captivating and thrilling, you can't miss his work.

— IVY GRIMES, AUTHOR OF *STARS SHAPES*

Portraits of Decay is horror at its finest. From heart-wrenching takes on vampires and kaiju to haunting studies of love, devotion, and grief, these stories will crawl under your skin, ready to reemerge and stay up with you on those long nights of self-reflection.

— EMMA E. MURRAY, AUTHOR OF
CRUSHING SNAILS

I0590279

A masterful, elegant, and fearless collection. Winter displays an exceptional amount of range in *Portraits of Decay*, but every story remains united by a sharp literary sensibility and a keen eye for the horrors of systems and selves. This isn't comfort horror—Winter's writing challenges and confronts while being executed with an incredible amount of control, skill, and style. Fans of Brian Evenson, Cormac McCarthy, and Chuck Palahniuk will feel right at home here.

— JOLIE TOOMAJAN, EDITOR OF *ASEPTIC AND FAINTLY SADISTIC*

Carson Winter's greatest strength as a writer is his keen observation of the human condition. Every tale in *Portraits of Decay* is a complicated web of circumstance and emotion, and at the dead center of each, of course, are people trapped inside. Carson is a master of weaving these webs, and then navigating the reader through them, and by the end of each one leaving them almost as wrought as the cursed characters whose dooms they just observed.

— ERIK MCHATTON, AUTHOR OF *STRAW WORLD AND OTHER ECHOES FROM THE VOID*

Who the hell does Carson Winter think he is? To just drop a collection like *Portraits of Decay*, one filled with stories harrowing, haunting, and heartbreaking, where each tale is conceived and composed with confident prose and ecstatic imagination...and it's his first collection? I'll tell you who *I* think Carson Winter is: a goddamn force of nature. Hold on tight to this book, dear readers. You're in for quite the ride.

No one writes like Winter. No one imagines like Winter. In a word filled with the prosaic, Winter's debut collection is one of a kind.

PORTRAITS OF DECAY

STORIES

CARSON WINTER

CONTENTS

A HUNGRY HOLE IN YOUR HEART

ANDREW F. SULLIVAN

Carson Winter does not tell uplifting stories. Rarely do his characters make it out of a narrative whole. Each one leaves a small piece behind. Minds shattered, bodies broken, souls eroded by the caustic world around them. To enter his world is to submit yourself to irrevocable change—minor or massive, you emerge altered. In his growing body of work, Winter embraces our fragile human natures with a gentle inevitability, a firm hand expertly navigating our spoiled fates. We were made to fail, to falter, to splinter off from one another. We were always meant to come undone.

But despite our flaws, Winter threads a deep earnestness through many of his characters, a desire to know and understand, a longing for connection disrupted by demons personal or mythical. It's rare to find this filament flickering within a lot of horror stories. These characters are not poisoned by irony or speaking at a safe remove. They exist within their circumstances, bucking against realities that no longer cohere, lashing out to find a meaning that has long abandoned them. The characters in stories like "The Harried Man" and "Canonical Victims" are acted upon, whether by the state, the world, or those they hold closest to their vulnerable hearts. They exist in a quietly tormented place, desperate to escape, but wary of what lies beyond. As they should be.

Some find their greatest fears bound up in others. That earnestness remains—a desire to be known fully, to be accepted, even loved. There is an ache within "The Museum of Lost Things" that has nothing to do with its own abstract horror but instead resonates through the tenuous connection between two lonely men, each fumbling toward some kind of friendship but unable to admit or address the full extent of their limitations. Horror offers a gate to that loneliness, articulated through ancient posters, mythical media, and a need to be right about something, anything really. People desperate to be taken seriously, to be acknowledged. They stumble through these pages with hands outstretched, forever grasping without seeing the vibrant beings all around them. Winter outlines lives couched in fear of reprisal, drenched in an anxiety of being truly known, and haunted by petty, inscrutable human motivations.

A recurring theme throughout *Portraits of Decay* is a struggle to record, to process, to define a stable reality with supporting evidence. Stories like "Zero Boundaries Podcast: Episode 182", "The Children of the Event", and "4633 Memory Stick (Phone Use Model 6A)" attempt to ground the strange and uncanny with our limited tools. Video evidence, chat logs, interview recordings, all of these methods can only gesture toward the shape of our loss. The need Winter exposes so deftly is one for certainty. No matter how great the evil, his characters cling to the unsustainable belief that if they can see the whole of it, they can overcome it. But mapping the interior will always fail when there is no stable sense of self. In Winter's world, your compass is a whirling trifle unable to provide any guidance. Your proof only brings about more questions.

Knowing as an act might be impossible here. It can only be gestured toward, never quite achieved. "In Haskins" knows this well. Masks are traded, lives are lived as imitations, but consequences last. Outcomes cannot be undone. "The Mushroom Men" pushes this further, asking us to stretch the borders of what we consider our reality, a corruption of the multiverse held together by grief. That same earnest humanity resonates again as our narrator attempts to justify his existence, unable to choose a self that can satisfy his needs. "They Always Kill the Dog" puts this in the bluntest terms, a desperate sacrifice to learn little and lose almost everything. Understanding is not a path to freedom; it is a hungry hole in your heart. It eats and eats. It will never be full. It cannot be satisfied.

The overwhelming anxiety of Winter's world is that of an observer, one unable or unwilling to act, forced to watch everything once known and trusted to fall away. Acting itself may not be enough. The world overwhelms, the universe undermines any attempt at comprehension. People wave fragments at each other, asking for meaning, asking for a brief moment of healing. The artifice is no longer stable. The world cannot hold its centre. The hidden places his character's attempt to document don't permit logic to define their boundaries or their needs. Still, they press on, still they search for small, honest moments of grace. Beacons in the miasma of his prose.

So, let us follow Winter into these volatile places, each page venturing further into his fragile, vicious realities. Let us see who makes it out the other side still whole.

WHO WE ARE

THE HARRIED MAN

I t was made out of paper. Brass tacks acted as hinges for its joints. When I found it, the thing was folded up; a flat, wild-eyed contortionist buried in my mother's attic. She passed two months ago and the house was a lot of things. *Smaller* was the word I kept coming back to. It was *smaller* than I remembered, because I hadn't run through its halls, tested its foundation with my bounding steps since I was a girl. But now, it was time to grow up, to reckon with the past, and now that my grieving had mellowed, it was finally time to finish what I'd started.

I found it in a *very* old box. Waxy, falling apart at the corners—something that might have carried cantaloupes years ago. In black marker, in Mom's handwriting —HALLOWEEN.

Of course, I remembered Halloween—its echo was only a day away—and with it came a curious mix of emotions. Growing up, everyone around me held the holiday in a rather simple regard. They liked it, or did not like it. They enjoyed candy. Or dancing. Or dressing up. Or watching scary movies.

The traditions were simple and universal: carve pumpkins, trick r' treat, tell ghost stories, decorate the house. And yet, when I saw the word HALLOWEEN I felt a deep discomfort, a roiling tide of bile churning in my stomach. I approached the box with dread and unsettlement. Halloween, for me, was anything but simple.

There were rubber bats and bags of recycled cobwebs. I tossed them to the side. Silhouettes of Frankenstein's monster and Dracula stared at me from their plastic, door-covering prisons. And then, at the bottom of the box was the Harried Man.

I remembered the name because I'd asked Mom why he wasn't hairy. She shook her head, pursed her lips. "Harried," she corrected. "Stressed, abused, picked-on."

And indeed, the man looked the part.

I pulled the Harried Man from the bottom of the box marked HALLOWEEN and stared into his terrified features. He was assembled of cardstock, printed in comic book colors. Not that different from the Frankenstein and Dracula that came before him. In fact, he had a strange sense of being too much like them. As if the Harried Man was just as iconic, but somehow simultaneously unknown. That was the problem with seeing the Harried Man. In some respects, it was like seeing nothing at all. A shape, a stranger. It was like having a dire revelation permanently stuck to the tip of your tongue. Because although the Harried Man wasn't a Dracula or Frankenstein, his design and shape made you think that he should be. And if he wasn't an icon in his own right, then clearly there was some mistake.

The Harried Man's face was that of illustrated terror. His mouth was agape, showing somewhat crooked and yellowed teeth. What was so specific though, is that despite this being a Halloween decoration—a cartoonish exaggeration—was that nothing about his design was so outlandish. The things about him that were strange and unsettling were only slightly so. The teeth, while crooked, were only normally crooked. Noticeable, but not uncommon. His eyes were red and bloodshot, shaded slightly yellow around the edges, great, dark bruises hanging under them like suspended half-moons.

His frame was thin and wiry, but true-to-life. The decoration, when fully unfolded, stood slightly taller than me. I watched as his legs dangled in space and I remembered turning corners in the house and seeing the Harried Man, holding my chest as I felt my heart stall and sputter as a child.

He was wearing a jacket with elbow patches, a striped tie, and an off-white shirt—one side of it untucked over what I assumed were brown corduroy pants. His hands were at his sides, his fingers gnarled with paralyzed fear.

I set the Harried Man down, folded him back up. We had a history. And sometimes history is better forgotten.

As a kid, Mom used to make me hang him up. Every year. "You've got to put him up," she said.

"I don't like him," I said. "He scares me."

"We still need to put him up."

I always acquiesced. With tentative hands I put a tack through the hole-punch above his head, standing on my very tippy toes to place him. His body hung limp on our door, always facing inside, never out.

When I asked my mom about this, she said, "Well, we wouldn't want to scare the children."

"It scares me though," I said. "I'm a child."

"Quiet, grow up," she'd say.

And so the Harried Man—our mystery decoration—hung unfettered.

And when November first rolled around, when our stomachs were full of candy and another year's magic had been put to the grave, Mother would take the Harried Man down herself, along with the lights, skulls, and other ghoulies and I would not see or think about the Harried Man for another year. One year I watched her do it, and it might have been my childish imagination, but I thought she was holding her breath. As soon as the Harried Man disappeared, her shoulders settled, her breath released.

Years later, in the attic that still smelled like Mom, I heard her words come back to me. "He likes to eat little girls, you know."

"What is he?"

"The Harried Man."

"Is he a monster?"

"Somewhat."

"I thought he was just scared."

"No, he does more than that. He eats children too."

All I could muster as a child was, "Oh."

Of course, Mom offered nothing more. Only the knowledge that the Harried Man seemed to be both the victim and the victimizer. No other explanation was given.

In the waxy box, the cardboard cut out stared up at me.

"What am I going to do with you?" I asked aloud.

The Harried Man said nothing.

"What are you *from*?"

Again, silence.

I sighed. The attic was filled with boxes. It would take more than a day to clean this up. It would take more than an uneasy trip down memory lane to relieve Mom of all her *stuff*. But that's what kids were for, right? Vessels for the dead; cleaners and housesellers and historians and proselytizers—all rolled into one.

Mom was buried but I'd bury her again. Orange and yellow leaves gathered in cairns along the sidewalk. Mom lived in a nice neighborhood—close to a school. Outside it was dark and it wasn't even five yet, children's voices gathered. Mom always said that she got lots of trick r' treaters.

Alone in the attic, I poked at the waxy box, daring the Harried Man to come to life and frighten me but he did not. Emboldened, and feeling like I'd broken new ground, I removed his corpse from the box. In the bottom, there rolled around a thumbtack, rusty and forgotten and fortuitous.

I went downstairs and tacked the Harried Man to the inside door, where he stood, ever-fearful.

On Halloween night, I returned to my mother's with a bowl of candy. I'd brought the rest of the boxes from the attic to the downstairs and began sorting items as darkness spread and the titters of children danced in from the street. It was true, Mom did get a lot of trick 'r treaters. More than I was prepared for. It felt like everytime I sat down I was up again to greet a new set of superheroes, vampires, and ghosts.

And each time I did, my hand hesitated for the doorknob as the Harried Man's terror-stricken eyes drilled into my own.

But the Harried Man was just a decoration. An obscure family heirloom. It meant nothing to anyone but my mother. In fact, as I settled back into my sorting mess, I played out scenarios in which I would throw it away, or burn it, or cut it up into little pieces and throw them into a great river that'd take them far away, rend them into tissuey oblivion, and then the Harried Man would be nothing.

I stole glances at him from time to time, my curiosity and childhood fear becoming repulsion, disgust. What does he have to be afraid of? Why does he eat children? That doesn't even make sense! He could not both be a monster and look like the victim of a monster.

A knock, three raps.

I jumped.

Holding my hand over my heart, I breathed deep. The sound of children.

The Harried Man swung slightly from his tack.

Maybe that's why he's so dangerous, I thought. *He's a predator that looks like prey. It's camouflage.*

I got up to open the door, this time refusing to look at the swinging, red-eyed malcontent. I pulled it open as fast as possible.

In front of me was a child holding a plastic orange pumpkin, its bottom filled with candy. I tried to keep my cool, tried to believe that the child was dressed as a professor, or maybe a salesman, or maybe some pop culture icon I'd long since lost touch with. But I couldn't ignore the dark circles painted under the child's eyes. When he said, "Trick 'r treat," it came out as almost a whisper. The child trembled, as if in great and terrible fear.

"Happy Halloween," I said, as I deposited a handful of candy into his pumpkin. "What are you dressed as?"

The child's eyes were bloodshot. I couldn't tell if it were contact lenses or if it was genuine.

He said nothing.

"Who are you?" I asked again.

Again, nothing.

I deposited two small candy bars in his pumpkin.

"Have a good night," I said, closing the door.

And I felt ashamed, really. I shouldn't be that easy to scare; yet when the door closed in front of me, I had completely forgotten about the decoration. And when his wild, fearful eyes locked into mine again, I jolted backwards.

As soon as I recovered, there was another knock.

I composed myself, pushing my hair behind my ears and forcing my best jovial smile. "Why hello there," I started.

Before me stood three children, two girls and a boy, dressed in the same attire as the last. Each of them wore the Harried Man's mask of terror, each of them were dressed in a suit and tie and corduroy pants. Their free hands were contorted into the rictus of the decoration.

Before they could say anything, I said, "Who are you supposed to be? Why are you all dressed the same?"

The children, in their horrific makeup, said nothing.

"Please," I said. "Tell me. Who are you? Where are you from?" My voice cracked. "Why are you doing this?"

I backed away from the door, closing it and turning sharply to avoid seeing the decoration. With my back turned, I waited for their footsteps to become faint. They did not though. There were no footsteps to hear. I stood in silence, waiting for nothing.

I rubbed my temples. "My god," I said. "You're being ridiculous."

I turned back to the door to open it and see the children and found only my mother's porch. Children squealed in the street, their parents waved to me—the Harried Woman—from the sidewalk.

I peered down the street, to see the orange blossoms of light in between the shouting, shoving, hungry blackness.

Six children, walking in formation, each of them dressed the same.

"Hey!" I yelled. "Wait! What are you?"

I ran out the door, down the front steps, onto the sidewalk. Children and parents alike stared at me, made way.

I sprinted down the street.

"Hey, watch it!"

"Someone must have gotten a trick with their treat."

I tried to explain as I ran. "No, no—they're dressed like a decoration," I cried. The end of the block came racing toward me, from street lamp to street lamp I ran. In between these bursts of orange light, they vanished again and reappeared again. But when I reached the end of the block, they were gone and I was breathing hard and the rest of the kids and their parents were looking at me strangely, wondering if I'd lost it.

One asked, "Ma'am, are you okay?"

"No—yes. I'm fine."

"You lose a kid? You need me to call someone?"

"No, I don't have a kid," I said. "Because he eats kids."

"What?"

"Nothing."

I walked back to the house. Buried memories were exhumed. It was time to look my mother's corpse in the face.

Inside the house, I stared at the Harried Man. I did not know what he was. I did not know what he did. I did not know where he was from. But he was there, on my mother's door, just as he always was this season. His eyes wide and slightly yellowed, his teeth to match. His uniform crisp. We stared at each other for a long time.

"I wish I knew you better," I said, not sure if I should say it.

Two boxes. One labeled KEEP, one labeled TRASH.

I turned off the porch light and ignored the pounding of tiny hands on my door. There were too many, much too many. They could wait. Or maybe not. Besides, I had a decision to make.

THEY ALWAYS KILL THE DOG

"They always kill the dog, honey."

You say it through clenched teeth, tears pooling in your eyes. One pretend cough later, your voice is strong again. Jason is crying, he has no reason to pretend. He's sad; this is the worst thing he's ever experienced and you want to tell him that, *no, no, no—this is just the beginning.*

But you don't.

You kneel beside him, in front of your new haunted house (aren't they all haunted?) and rub his back, determined to make the bad feelings go away.

The dog—you insisted on not giving her a name—lays in silence. No tongue panting, no tail wagging. You want to apologize to her. Maybe later, when Jason is in bed, you will. But what can you say?

I'm sorry I brought you here. I'm sorry they killed you. But you should have expected that.

* * *

Dinner is a somber affair. Jason won't stop asking questions.

"Why did they do it?"

You swallow. A memory of soft fur and dog breath comes to mind, and you wince and push it away. "I don't know," you say. "It's a warning, I guess. The house's way of telling people to stay away. Or maybe, they need to kill something small first so that they can kill something big. They work their way up."

Jason's lips quiver, he bursts into tears, and you put your head into your hands, shaking. "Please," you say. "Please. I'm upset too."

But he doesn't listen to you. Why should he? He's just a boy. He does what little boys do when they are confronted by something awful. Crying, he leaves the table. As he stomps up the old stairs, you listen carefully to the sound between his footsteps.

* * *

At night, you cry your eyes out. Long, heaving gasps into your pillow because you don't want Jason to hear you. One of you should be strong, it might as well be you.

The house creaks and groans and you stop crying. You look at the playback machine recording next to your bed. Carefully, you sit up.

You press the two upright parallel lines that mean stop. You hold your breath, and the old house sucks the air out of the room. It's a vacuum now, and you can't breathe. Empty lungs.

You rewind the tape. You listen.

The sound of your crying makes you want to cry more but you steel yourself. It passes and you hear the creaks and groans, the ones you desperately wish would speak to you. Between the house's thrashing there is a warble. It's always a warble, isn't it? It's never a clearly enunciated name, an articulate plaintive cry for help. You reason that they are speaking from afar, and those who speak from afar can't help but warble.

You zero in on it, an electronic distortion between creaks and groans. You replay it. You replay it. Volume up, you listen again—it's sharp, distinct.

On your laptop, the file looks like leaping daggers, stalactites and stalagmites in a frenzied dance. The noise is buried between these, hidden and nestled—a sound within sound. When you find it, you mouth an old joke to yourself. *Enhance, enhance.* You watched detectives do it in TV shows and it's exactly what you're doing. Isolating audio, removing noise, bumping clarity, turning treble and bass dials until a warble becomes a word.

When you press play, you think that this might be it. But as you hear the sound, your eyebrows raise. You question yourself. *Did I hear that right?*

It's not a word that bleeds out from your laptop speakers. It's a bark.

* * *

You call your husband and he says, "Honey—I mean, Ingrid. Ingrid, you have to stop this."

"You're not listening to me. You never listen to me."

He sighs. "Jason needs to be in school. He needs to be home."

"We're doing a project. He's my assistant."

"He's nine. He's a kid."

"They always kill the dog, Brian. Every time. Why do they do that?"

He ignores you. He sounds like he's having a different

conversation. "He must be so sad," he says. "I remember what it was like when I was his age."

"I think we've been examining this phenomenon through an anthropocentric lens, to a fault. I thought I was the main character here, that all of this was happening for me."

"I don't care if you stay," he says. "But don't bring Jason into it, please. I'll come over tomorrow and I'll take him home, where he'll be safe."

"He's safe with me."

"They killed the dog. They could kill him. They could kill you."

"You're not listening to me!" you scream. "They don't care about us. How many people have died? None. How many pets?"

Dead silence on the line. You listen to his breathing.

"I'll see you tomorrow," he says. "Tell Jason to pack."

The call ends. Real silence.

* * *

Jason sits in his room. All of his belongings are in a backpack. He has no bed, just a sleeping bag on a dirty wood floor. The windows are boarded up. The walls are covered in wilting wallpaper and obscene graffiti. He's still wrapped in his cocoon.

"I heard something last night," you say.

He turns over. His eyes are red and puffy. He nods curtly.

"I think she might still be here, somewhere. I heard her."

He nods. "She licked my fingers." He sniffs. "Not the same, though."

You don't know what to say to that, so you change the subject. "Your father is going to visit you tomorrow."

"He's coming to take me?"

"If you want."

"I do."

"If that's what you want, you can go. I'm fine being all alone. I don't mind at all."

"Okay," he says.

When nothing more is said between you two, you swallow and try to fill the silence with the rustling and whooshing of clothes and movement. You lean on the side of the door frame, trace a finger down the splintered wood grain, adjust the collar of your jacket.

Downstairs, paws scamper on the floor, the click-clack of tap shoes.

Jason sits up. His eyes widen. A smile teases the corners of his mouth.

"It's not her," you say. "It can't be." You're cautioning him.

But he rushes past you anyways. You follow him down the stairs, doubting yourself.

The sound of claws on wood sweeps through the house. Jason turns the corner into the kitchen and his face melts.

The kitchen is empty, but the sound of paws persist. He looks back to you and you can see rage burning in his cheeks. You want to reach out to him and tousle his hair and tell him that everything is okay, that they always kill the dog. But before you can do it, he turns away from you and runs out of the house.

Your heart breaks again and again and again. You want to chase after him, and you will—after you check the recording.

There's the same bark, now with a whimper and a plaintive howl. "Who are you?" you ask. "Why do you..." You don't want to say it, because saying it makes it real.

* * *

Outside, there are gray skies and wet wheat. The dog is still out there, mangled. Grunting, you find a shovel in a leaning shed. You start digging.

It's hard work, even for a small animal. It's not the sort of thing you ever imagined yourself doing. But in a funny way, that's the root of the problem too. So obsessed with death, so afraid of dying—but never getting your hands dirty with it. Never sitting with the heavy lump of sorrow in your chest. Never touching skin or fur after life has left it. Halfway through, you think about quitting. The dirt is hard and the clouds have taken on an indigo hue. A storm is coming. You wonder if the dog would've been barking, warning you. You're sure you can't go on. But you do.

When you go to lift the animal, you recoil. She is cold, stiff. Your heart breaks anew. Her final resting place is only three feet deep, but when you drop her corpse into the freshly dug hole, she seems to fall forever. When she lands, she does so with a heavy thud.

You turn away. You can't look.

"Why did you bring her?"

Jason is standing there, amongst the tall grass. His mouth is twisted in a frown. Behind him, sheet lightning flashes amidst the clouds.

"You always wanted a dog," you say.

"I really loved her, Mom." He sniffs, blinks. "Why did you bring her?"

You shrug, you can't look at him. "It's just research, honey. Sometimes, in research—"

"Why do you think it's all about you?"

You shudder at him dragging your thoughts into the light.

"We're all gonna die, Jason," you say, as if it's all you can say.

Your son grimaces. He clenches his teeth. He turns away

and goes back to the house. "Burying her won't solve it," he says. "It won't change anything."

Lightning flashes overhead, thunder roars. You know he's right, but you fill in the hole anyways.

* * *

The house leaks in rainstorms. There's no escape, not enough buckets and pint glasses to collect it. You're not sure where Jason is, he's avoiding you. Sometimes you shout his name, but nothing comes running. But it's a secondary thought. Really, you're trying to listen. To record.

You remember a lecture, something from school. Before Jason. It was about intelligence and how nearly impossible it was to quantify—especially through a human lens. We judge snails on how smart they are at being humans, when we should judge them on how smart they are at being snails. You think about this when you listen to the sounds and feel a sense of panic as you wonder if you're at the end of your rope. You do not know what is here, you do not know what it wants. You are an unfortunate prisoner of your own perspective and when you are helpless to your own thoughts—of your own decay, of your own impending cessation—you turn to Polaroid cameras and tape recorders.

And the barking continues. The slapping of tails on wood. The panting. The *smell* of dog-breath. It surrounds you and you wonder what it means, if anything.

"Why do you always kill the dog?" you ask the house.

The house says nothing.

You stamp your feet, ball your fists. "Take me. I want to see! I want to see!" Your voice is coarse and ragged with rage.

"Show me!" you plead. "I just want to understand."

It's then you hear it. A growl.

Jason stands in the doorway, off to the right, as if he's making room. As if he's standing beside someone. He reaches down and smoothes the air beside his waist. "Take her, girl," he says. "She wants to see."

The growl precedes the sound of snapping jaws. *Click.* Instinctively you throw your hand out in front of you. "What's going on?" But then, out of thin air, two of your fingers are snapped and eaten by the ether. You scream. Blood pumps in spurts from your phalangeal stumps.

You whip around. "Stop it! Stop it!"

More bites. More blood.

You fall to the floor. Hot stinking breath wets your cheeks. You look at Jason, your eyes like the moon. "Please."

Teeth clamp down around your throat. Something is shaking you. A scream dies on its way to your tongue. The bite crushes your windpipe.

When she releases you, you can't move a muscle. You stare up at your son.

"There's nothing for you to see," he says. "It's not for us."

Thunder. Lightning. Panting. Begging.

As the end approaches, hope blossoms in your heart. You pray he's wrong.

THE SPEAKEASY

"I was about your age when my dad took me. But you're what? Eleven now? Practically a man." I winked at Mitch and he nodded back. "These places aren't always on the up-and-up, if you know what I'm saying, but you know Jeb and Micah, right? They came over to the barbecue last August."

"Jeb and Micah," Mitch repeated. "Yeah, Dad. I remember them."

"They were good guys, right? They played with you, didn't they?"

"Yeah, they were cool," said Mitch.

"Old friends, those guys. These fights are how they make their living and if we told anyone, they wouldn't be able to feed their family. You remember Micah had that little girl? Cute blonde thing, right? Wouldn't want her to go hungry, would we?"

Mitch shook his head no and I mussed his hair.

"Good boy. Yeah, we don't want to take food from anyone's mouth."

"No, sir."

"And besides, if they didn't do this—those things would be out causing havoc. Biting ladies while they sleep, eating chickens. It just ain't right."

I twisted the steering wheel and took the exit that led us out of town, toward tall trees, black on the horizon. Beyond the I-5 corridor, I saw the familiar street signs, the dead grass, the quaint downtowns. I felt closer to home. We passed through and found old rolling hills and leaning sheds, ancient barns. I stole glances at Mitch in between every twisting turn. The kid was wound tight, like a coiled spring. I felt bad for him. He might have needed this more than me.

"We're close," I said. "Not too much farther. You see that treeline over there? That's the city limits. The town cops don't patrol that far. We're gonna go a little further than that, maybe a mile or two, and we'll be on Jeb's property. What a man does in his own home is his business."

The dirt road was tucked between pines, but I knew the turnoff by heart. Houses with crosses in the windows; silver door knobs—not a welcome mat in sight. My dad took me here until I left home. He'd sneak me beers and give me that cracked, don't-tell-mom smile. I always wished I could've gone with him one last time, but life doesn't play like that. You only have the now.

I passed a Wolf X-ing sign, made a turn, and followed it until I came upon Jeb's luxury cabin. He'd cleared trees in front of it to make a makeshift lot where a dozen other vehicles were already parked. I found us a spot and got out.

Mitch said, "Is the fight in the house?"

"No," I said. "It's just a short hike. Jeb's got deep property here."

Ahead of us, there were other pilgrims. Bearded men in flannels carrying coolers, fathers and sons.

"Jeb's dad started this. He was friends with your grandpa

—my dad. So, in a way, this is all kinda part of our history. All these other folks learned about it because people like Jeb's dad and your grandpa trusted them to keep a secret."

"I can keep a secret," said Mitch, a flash of pride coloring his words.

"I know you can, bud. You're a good kid."

He was loosening up a little bit, feeling himself. He ran up the trail ten feet ahead and waved me forward. "C'mon, Dad."

"I'm coming."

It was just like I remembered it. The smell of pine and earth mixed with the sharp tang of sweat. Dad always called this place the Speakeasy, and I guess that's what I would call it too.

Up ahead, barely visible, was the black barn—a large structure that used to be an industrial chicken coop. "You see it there, Mitch? Right up ahead."

Mitch squinted, his hand flat to his eyebrows. "Is that it?"

"Yep, that's it. That's the Speakeasy."

As we got closer, Mitch bounced up and down with excitement. He threw his fists in the air, wailing on an invisible opponent. "I can't wait," he said. "I've never seen a fight before."

Before long, we were amidst the energy of a rumbling crowd. Folks milled about outside and as we approached the throngs, Mitch stood closer to me. He'd taken a step forward, then a step back. That was okay, I could live with that. He was always nervous, shy around others. Ever since he was a kid. But that was okay, some kids are shy. They grow out of it. That's what I told myself.

"Look, Mitch, there's Jeb."

I pointed to the mouth of the barn and Mitch offered a meek wave. Jeb came bounding right over. He was a big guy, easily ten years my senior, dressed in a ball cap with a fish on the front.

When he saw Mitch, he offered him a handshake. "How's it going, young man?"

"Good," he said.

"Excited for the match? We got a good one tonight."

"Yes, sir."

"It's his first one," I said.

A smile spread like oil on Jeb's lips. "Well then, this is a special occasion indeed." His eyes darted to me and he winked. "I think that calls for some special treatment."

"No need to spoil the boy," I said.

He waved his hand. "Nah, we're not gonna spoil no one. He's just gonna have a special seat—don't worry, Dad, you can ride the VIP's coat tails."

"Oh, great."

Mitch looked up to me, unsure.

"He means we get a really good view."

"*Cool.*"

"C'mon, fellas. Let's get you settled before the riff-raff joins in. Need a beer or anything, Dad?"

"Yeah, I reckon I'll have a couple."

"Jeb's got you covered."

He led us inside. The smell pummeled me; I nearly gasped, there wasn't a breath of air left in my lungs. Mitch just ran forward, up the bleachers to our box seat while memories grabbed me by the collar.

"I don't remember *that* as a kid," I said.

Jeb said, "New addition. Sometimes we have sheriffs, mayors, bigwigs. You know. We keep 'em happy so they don't raise a fuss."

Mitch looked back at me and beamed. I was surprised that the barn was even large enough to accommodate two sides of bleachers, plus box seating. It's funny the way most things from your childhood look smaller when you see them again.

The Speakeasy was nothing like that. It was closer to the size of a hangar.

"You fellas sit down here, I'll grab your dad a six-pack and the show will begin soon."

Jeb made it away about ten feet when I asked, "Hey Jeb, where's Micah?"

My old friend turned around and shook his head. "Micah ain't doing too hot," he said. "He had an accident. Less said the better."

I put a hand on Mitch's shoulder, in case he was scared, but he didn't seem to hear Jeb at all. The dirt arena reflected in his wide, black pupils.

The arena was flanked by a wall, the front of the bleachers lifted above it. It was like a miniature coliseum—with two sliding metal doors on either side—built through the sheer ingenuity of people like my father, Jeb, and Micah.

Before everyone filed in, Jeb brought me six ice cold beers with a promise of a good fight.

I cracked one open as the Speakeasy crescendoed into a dull roar. I drank and then gestured the can at Mitch.

"When you're out here," I said, "you're a man."

He looked at the beer as if it were something from another world. Maybe it was.

"Go ahead, just a sip."

Mitch reached out and wrapped his tiny fingers around the can and pulled it up to his mouth. He took a meager swig, swallowing while keeping his face as straight as his lips would let him. He gave me a somber nod, as if he understood what this meant. That he knew he was now part of a secret club.

I was happy to have him.

* * *

On each side of the Speakeasy, great wide doors opened, bringing in fresh air to the makeshift arena. I could hear the beep-beep-beep of two backing trucks. Mitch stood up from his seat like a meerkat, hoping to get a look at this development.

Sure enough, a U-Haul appeared in the maw of both open doors. Jeb's farmhands secured the space around the trucks. There was no light at all, except for the inch of blue sky appearing from where the tops of the U-Hauls nearly met the upper frame of the barn door.

Electricity whirred and several work lamps that were haphazardly nailed to the rafters lit the place up with a hot orange glow.

Jeb walked out to the middle of the arena and said, "We got a good one for you tonight!"

Applause erupted, men screamed in rapturous excitement.

"Sounds like some of y'all got money on this fight."

Laughter from all around. I squeezed Mitch's shoulder and lifted the beer to my lips for another long drink.

Jeb raised a hand and the crowd fell silent. "Most of y'all heard about Micah. He's a friend of mine, probably a friend of a lot of you all as well. He got in an accident last time and that's why we're doing this here. This is for a good cause. All of you who put down your hard earned money for tonight's show are putting money directly into the pocket of Micah and his wife as he gets closer to recovery..."

More applause. I hung my head. I hadn't heard about Micah's accident; I'd known him since I was a kid.

"But, just because Micah can't walk no more, doesn't mean he's out of the game." Jeb pointed to the box across from us, on the other side of the arena, a black rectangle. I squinted my eyes and I could make out a faint shape.

Another work lamp illuminated and suddenly the man I

knew as Micah was bathed in light. The crowd all turned at once. When they saw him, they averted their eyes.

He was wrapped from head to toe in crisp white bandages. His head leaned to the side, his lips parted slightly, and I could make out that he had some plastic tube going from his mouth to somewhere in the wheelchair that carried him.

"Micah, we love you, brother," said Jeb. He waved toward a farmhand and Micah's light extinguished. "We'll be passing the hat around later, so to speak, in case any of y'all want to give a little more."

I noticed Mitch was still staring across the barn's arena, to the black box across from us, no doubt eyeing the charcoal gray silhouette of the horribly injured man.

"He's gonna be okay," I whispered.

Mitch broke his gaze and stared down at his shoes.

Jeb's voice echoed through the barn. "I ain't gonna keep you folks from the show any longer. Give us a minute to get to safety and then we'll open the trucks and let these two sons of bitches go at it!"

Cheers.

As promised, Jeb ran to the side of the arena, hurried through a door, and disappeared into the crowd.

After a moment of extended silence, of anticipation, the farmhands approached the trucks' locking mechanisms. They turned to each other and yelled, "Ready?" "Ready!" before counting to three, flipping the locks, and running like madmen to safety. Mitch leaned forward. So did I.

All I could see was blackness, but that was the most exciting part. As a kid, I'd look into the dark mouths of the trucks, wondering who would come out. Wonder, that's really what all this was about. Disneyland. Magic. Memories. That's all I ever wanted to give Mitch.

You could hear a pin drop. The entire barn held its breath.

And then Mitch heard it, footsteps on metal. He edged up further on the chair, his ass barely balanced on the front lip, his eyes wide like a puma's.

Out came a bloated corpse. Flushed everywhere. My dad would've called him ruddy. His pupils shined like a predator's, two silver dimes embedded in his skull. He could barely walk; he was confused. It was daytime, and usually these ugly bastards don't come out till night. Jeb kept the arena dark enough though, dark enough for a fight.

The thing turned to us and gave a mindless hiss, pure venom. A reflex to stimuli.

Mitch whispered, "Look at his teeth."

"Deadly," I said. "They can do some real damage."

The corpse had long, but sparse hair that sprouted from a crown of baldness. His lips were cracked and withered, pulling back to show his red and torn gums.

On the other side, we heard shuffling footsteps. Mitch swiveled away from the vampire, to see what would come from the other truck.

"Oh my God," said Mitch.

"A fine specimen," I agreed.

A large, mangy looking wolf with paws as large as a bear's wandered out from its U-Haul. It reared onto its hind legs to walk, where it became obvious that its limbs were disproportionate. One arm was as long as an ape's, the other was the size of a man's. One was clawed, but with fingers, the other had become a stout paw. It hunched too, walking oddly, dragging one canine foot. Its spine twisted in a painful spiral. I could make out the vertebrae pressing out from its hide.

"Why's it covered in scars?"

I shrugged. "These things aren't easy to work with, champ. You gotta keep 'em in line."

Mitch took this knowledge in quietly, his mouth opened.

The two fighters made their way into the ring with a sort of dizzy perambulation. The vampire on one side, all endless hunger. The wolf on the other, corporeal rage. When they saw each other, they stood still as the drugs wore off, staggering slightly.

"They're enemies," I said to Mitch. "Like cats and dogs. They'll start any second."

And just as the words left my mouth, the wolf fell down to its knees, eyes rolling back into its head.

The crowd erupted. First in surprise, then in anger.

Jeb's voice came through on a megaphone. "Hold on now, everyone. This ain't our first rodeo. Give us a second for technical difficulties and we'll be right back."

"Is he gonna be okay?"

"I don't know," I said honestly.

"What are they going to do to him?"

Four men rushed out into the arena, two of them carried white crosses the size of their torsos, the other two carried bull whips.

I pointed to the vampire. "Sometimes these fellas here need a little blood to get into it."

The two men whipped the wolf as it laid on the muddy arena floor. Two, three, four cracks each and the beast's lolling head gained something akin to alertness. It stood, and the men began to clear the arena, the cross-bearers the last to leave.

The corpse stuck its nose in the air.

"These things are like sharks," I said.

"Sharks?"

"Mindless. All they care about is blood."

And the wolf was bleeding alright. I could see the blood matting down its fur, could see the old violence overtake it.

Its twisted body eyed the corpse and let out a low rumbling growl. It was going to start now and I felt like a child again, because this was all any little boy wanted to see and I got to share it with mine.

The bloodsucker clicked his teeth together, the long fangs hanging outside of his lips. He launched into a half-jog—a stumbling action that was ferocious, but somehow more akin to the toddling steps of an infant rather than a fierce jungle cat. The wolf leapt forward, an agonized groan escaping its muzzle. It swiped toward the vampire, barely missing the bloated corpse's papery skin.

The vampire lunged forward and caught the wolf's human-ish hand in its mouth, no doubt relishing the warm trickle that was crawling down its throat. The wolf yelped and swiped the vampire's face away with a thick, furry paw.

The corpse went sailing, eight, maybe ten feet back.

Mitch's mouth opened wide. He covered his mouth with tiny hands. His eyes were so bright, so alive.

The crowd cheered and he cheered with them.

I leaned over to him. "Who are you rooting for?"

"The wolf," he said brightly.

"I always liked the wolves too." It was true. Maybe it's just part of boyhood. For a lot of us, our first friend was a dog. Of course, we all knew the other side too. Sometimes there'd be a poor boy who came out at night when he heard the chickens screaming from the coop. And he'd stumble back inside with his entrails on the outside. And in a month—if he made it a month—he'd leave in the middle of the night and not be seen again, until a bullet popped his heart or he ended up here. But even then, it was hard for a boy not to romanticize the wolf.

The corpse got up, but he didn't just get up—he was stiff like a board, rising on his heels to his feet. Half the crowd screamed in delight, the other half booed. To celebrate the corpse was to celebrate death—the biggest bad guy of them all.

"It takes all types, I guess."

The vampire locked eyes with the wolf, who was now rushing toward him with hungry, snapping jaws.

"Get 'em!" screamed Mitch. "Tear his guts out!"

Yeah, kid. You tell 'em.

But then the wolf stopped dead in his tracks.

An odd calm came over the Speakeasy, a serene strangeness as we tried to parse what was happening.

The wolf stared into the vampire's shiny dime eyes and swayed back and forth while the corpse held him there under his mesmeric gaze.

Someone yelled, "Blink goddamnit!"

"Snap out of it!"

The vampire took no pleasure in this, because it was a pleasureless being. It did nothing but consume. It slept in grave dirt and drank blood, rarely seen even by the farmers here. It simply raised one hand and beckoned the wolf and its mangled skeleton forward.

"No," screamed Mitch. He stood up, shouting into the arena. "No, no, no!"

I grabbed him by the shoulder, my heart breaking for the kid. "It's okay," I said. "It's not over yet."

But it was.

The corpse sunk his teeth into the wolf's neck, tearing out long strips of sinew and flesh, as fresh blood bubbled out of the wound.

The wolf gurgled between short, rapid breaths. Then, it fell to the ground. When it did, the vampire went with it, laying on top of it, continuing to gorge himself. Mitch's hands dropped to his side, color drained from his face and I saw the beginning of tears in his eyes.

"It's okay, champ. It's okay."

"He's dead," he cried.

"These things don't always go how we want them to. Sometimes the good guy loses. There'll be others, Mitch."

He bowed his head as the vampire lifted his red mouth from the wolf and let out a monstrous scream of triumph, before moving lower, to the wolf's abdomen, to peel it apart with his long nails.

The wolf wasn't moving now. It just laid there as its guts were torn out, as the crowd began to throw popcorn and beer cans into the arena.

Mitch said, "Dad, I want to leave."

"No," I said. "We don't get to leave." Seeing his wet eyes provoked a sort of stark disappointment in me, rage. "Watch the fight. We came here to watch the fight. This is the fight."

Mitch recoiled and I grabbed him with both hands and forced his head to see the wolf's shaking leg, the vampire's bloody maw, and the blood pooling in its midsection.

"We don't get to walk away from things we don't like to see. I taught you better than that," I said.

Mitch swallowed a sob and I finished one can and started another.

"Besides," I said. "The fight is only half of it. You can't have the fight without having the rest too."

Mitch sat like a statue, marble, as the vampire tore the wolf limb from limb, drinking every last drop of blood, until it would be as fat as a tick fixing to burst. Across from us, in the other box, I saw the outline of Micah, bandaged. Jeb had just entered the box with an envelope. He must have bet well.

When Jeb's megaphone-enhanced voice arrived, it was time to leave. The corpse was shepherded by men with crosses back into the U-Haul truck. The remnants of the wolf were dragged out from the center of the arena, to somewhere beyond.

"What are they gonna do with him?" asked Mitch, his voice shaking.

"Feed him to the pigs, most likely. Come on," I said. "Get yourself together. I don't want any of these people to see you like this."

He nodded and wiped his eyes.

Outside, the men gathered and there was camaraderie again. Stories swapped, hugs shared. Men discussed the fight with the imprecise words of Sunday morning quarterbacks.

"The wolf was a tall one—I heard it used to be that Mullens kid."

"But who could've guessed the vamp had that hypnosis shit up his sleeve? Most of 'em don't."

"Jeb said he had to cross state lines for that one. Was out living in the Cascades. Heard about it from a small church."

Mitch followed a couple steps behind me. "Hurry up," I said. "You're dragging ass."

He jogged up beside me, but still kept three feet away, just out of arm's reach.

Just as we were about to hit the trail, out of the pool of chatting men, Jeb came to us, a boyish smile on his face. "Enjoy the show?"

"Like old times." I suddenly became self-conscious of Mitch's sullen face. "This one here was rooting for the wolf. A little disappointed, I think."

Jeb nodded knowingly and got down to Mitch's level. "Can I tell you a secret?"

"Yeah," said Mitch.

"Those vamps scare the shit outta me, excuse my language. But this time, he did us a favor."

"How's that?" I asked.

"That there wolf is what got hold of Micah, tore him to bits.

I like to think this was karma. See, Mitch? That wasn't a good wolf. That was a bad wolf. The sort you hear about in stories."

"You hear that, Mitch? It's good that the wolf is dead."

"That it is," said Jeb.

"Okay," said Mitch, his voice a whisper.

Jeb patted him on the head and stood back up to look me in the eyes. He shook my hand and asked us to return when we could. I told him we'd be back, but Mitch seemed distracted. He kept looking back toward the Speakeasy.

On the way home, he stared out the window the whole time and didn't say a word. I talked with him, I tried to at least, but after a while I fell silent too. I took each bend in the road with a sure hand. He'd remember this. Wheat and pines surrounded us, gray clouds blanketed the horizon. These small towns and fields made up my history, their frequencies rattled in my bones, roared between every word I ever spoke. He'd remember this. I looked over to Mitch as we got onto the high-way, trucks and cars whizzed by while he swallowed another sob and tried not to look at my reflection in the mirror.

Please, remember this.

THE MUSEUM OF LOST THINGS

To whom it may concern:

Last night, I sat on my couch watching found footage horror films until midnight. When I woke, the *Blair Witch Project* was running itself in yet another repetition. The characters screamed at each other, got lost, cried. They did this ad infinitum. And in each cycle, they asked the genre's most sacred question: *why are you filming?*

I couldn't shake the feeling that my subconscious was taking the wheel. I'd been through something horrific. I was watching scary movies. I was processing. I was studying characters whose primary motivation was to document—to decide if that pull I felt inside myself was its kin.

What happened with Hank was worse than anything. Making it a story cheapens it. But, I'm a cheap guy. I'm gross. Sad. Confused. And I'm watching scary movies.

I don't know what happens after the camera falls to the ground, blasts static, and goes black. But, I do know that if I don't document any of this, it might as well have not happened at all.

We all have our comfort food. And as a writer, as a person in trouble, I reserve the right to tell my story however I want.

So, yeah, here I am. I'm staring into the camera. I'm thinking about found footage.

* * *

The camera rewinds, we see everything through jittering static bars —an effective anachronism. Three months pass and when you first see me, I may as well be invisible. It's black and white, grainy. I'm at a bank, standing behind the counter. Customers walk backwards and disappear out the door. The rewind stops, and we've returned to normal speed. A man walks in. He comes to me. There is no sound in the security footage, but you can see us talking. The timestamp reads 4:56 p.m.

* * *

Hank was the first person to ever recognize me—not that I ever expected to be recognized. In the world of horror blogging, I was a medium-sized potato, which is to say: in the world of actual writing, I was no one at all. I wrote informal essays on mainstream horror, piecing together the zeitgeist through slashers, reboots, remakes, and Blumhouse. But in spite of my relative insignificance, Hank paused when he saw me—gasping, even—like I was some sort of a celebrity. He asked if I wanted to grab a beer sometime. I was standing behind the counter at the bank, watching the clock, and said, "Why not now?"

An hour later we had drinks at a nearby taphouse. And in another half hour, our conversation had sputtered to a halt. We'd talked movies, but really, that can only take you so far. We agreed that *The Thing* was a classic, just as we agreed on a dozen other films. Our enthusiasm for agreement was dwindling. Hank was a classicist who enjoyed Hammer Horror and Universal flicks, but I admittedly had more modern tastes, so once again, our conversation lost its steam.

To fill the silence, I mentioned off hand that I might have to do more UFO features, as the release schedule for upcoming horror films was somewhat anemic. This was a part of the blog that I didn't particularly like doing—the paranormal write-ups—but, in spite of that, they tended to be the pieces that got the closest to going viral. The way Hank's face lit up, I realized I'd hit upon a topic of interest.

"So, do you believe in any of it?" he asked.

"Believe in what?"

"Unexplained phenomena."

"No," I said. I searched for a clock on the wall, wondering if I could make up a reason to leave.

"None of it?" His eyes widened. "UFOs? Bigfoot? Government conspiracies?"

"No," I said. "Well, maybe the last one."

He was smiling, but he didn't find any of it funny. "There's shit out there, man. I've seen it, you've written about it."

"Everyone wants their government to be spying on them," I said, trying not to make my boredom obvious. "It's a dystopian disenfranchisement fantasy. Reality is, by its very nature, unexciting. In response to this, we try to make it fit the fictional narratives we admire."

"Okay," he said, "Sure. But what about the stuff we don't admire?"

I almost had a retort, but as soon as I opened my mouth, he started again.

"There's stuff out there that you don't want to be true—but it is. Girls get trafficked into sexual slavery. Kids get left in hot cars and die," he said, almost casually. "Men and women toss chunks of poisoned meat over fences to kill family pets. People *kill* people. These are things we don't want to believe happen, but they do."

I drank my beer, pretending his fervor hadn't unsettled me. "Bad things happen," I agreed.

"Yes, but if the things that are bad really happen, they aren't phenomena, right?"

"Sure," I said.

"And if they don't happen, what are they? Myths? Legends?"

I shrugged. "I guess."

"But the moment we discover they did happen, it's no longer a myth."

"Real things are real and unreal things are myths—yes, got it."

He stopped for a moment, looking down into his glass. "Can I show you something?"

"I'm not buying anything," I said, feeling stupid as it came out. Hank was no salesman. He was too soft, too earnest.

He slapped a twenty on the table and put his hands up like a magician reassuring a mark. "I think I found something, a phenomenon. Maybe you'd like to see it. Maybe you can write about it."

I could've said no. I probably should've. I don't believe in much beyond what I can see. But the way he said it made him seem so sad. Hank looked at me with those big, innocent eyes and I didn't want to disappoint him—he was a fan, after all. So, I told him I'd go. It was the beer talking, at least a little. But, to tell the truth, it was also because I felt special. Hank wanted to show *me* something. He thought *I*, above anyone else, would appreciate it. My narcissism was in full-bloom.

We left the bar and Hank led the way. I trailed behind him, hands shielding my glasses from the rain.

When he turned down an alley, I almost doubled back. *No, man, fuck this, I'm not going down an alley with you*—but just as my faith faltered, he turned and waved me forward. "Just a little further," he said. His face was that of dumb oblivion. Hating myself, I trusted him.

The alley sliced through a block of four-story brownstones; dumpsters lined the slick asphalt. On the other side of the alley, I could see an orange street lamp strobing against the charcoal blue sky.

"C'mon, it's here," he said.

I broke into a lazy jog to meet him in the center of the alley. The brick gave way to a steep stairwell, going down. Hank shook his phone, producing a flashlight. The steps were gray concrete, flanked by a metal railing covered in chipped paint.

He looked at me expectantly. "This is it," he said.

"It's a basement," I said. "Storage."

"You're half-right."

Which half?

He took a step forward and put his hand on the railing. I followed behind him, stopping at the top step, watching my new acquaintance disappear into the darkness. Over the sound of rain, I heard a hinge creak from the blackness. The steps illuminated, wet and slippery and bathed in white fluorescent light.

Hank's silhouette said: "C'mon, wait until you see this."

And because I came this far, I followed him to the cracked door.

Down a dark alley, down dark steps, into a bright room.

I stood, bewildered. This wasn't just a room, it was a lobby. Velvet ropes guided us to an unattended service desk, pristine in its absence.

Hank turned back to me. "Weird, right?"

"What is this place?"

He didn't answer, instead forging ahead, navigating the velvet ropes. I followed him, feeling a creeping dread as I did. It was too perfect, too clean; it looked human, and yet, there were no people; there were no tills, there was nothing to suggest we were supposed to be here.

"Are we trespassing?"

"I don't think so," he said.

At the end of the velvet ropes there was a door. He motioned to a small spinning wire rack filled with pamphlets. "Take one," he said. "A souvenir, I guess."

I did as he said and looked at the oddity in my hands with disbelief. Its header was written in the digital cursive of an amateur graphic designer. *Welcome to the Museum of Lost Things! If you enjoyed your visit, please consider donating!*

"A museum?"

My question was rhetorical, of course, it was right on the pamphlet. Looking around, I couldn't imagine it as anything but. It indeed did have all the makings of a museum. But a small one, surely. Displays lined the room in neat rows, each with a central artifact and a placard.

Hank forged ahead as I traipsed behind him.

"Look at this one," he said. "Notice anything?"

I found him staring at a glass case. In it was a miniature boat. I didn't have much in the way of nautical knowledge, but the placard beside it said that it was a steamboat. *Lady Calabasas 1892.*

I mouthed the name, shrugging. "I don't get it."

He pointed at the printed index card beside it.

"Okay," I said, "I'll play." I hunched over and read the card aloud, feeling as if I were a weary father checking the closet for boogeymen. "'From 1890 to 1892, *Lady Calabasas* was a member of the *mosquito fleet*—small steamboats used as trans-portation among Oregonians along the coast. These boats were smaller than trade ships, but no less stunning to see in person. *Lady Calabasas* was—'" I cleared my throat, looking at him. "What is this?"

"Keep reading," he said.

I took a deep breath and skimmed along the itinerant facts of its historical captain, James Sval. Beside the model ship were several grainy black and white photos—families staring blankly into the camera as Captain Sval waved farewell to land.

"'Tragedy took the *Lady Calabasas* when a storm swept the ship out to sea. While the ship remained intact, its travelers did not."

Hank winced. He was waiting for me to say something, but I wasn't sure what I was supposed to say. Finally, he said, "None of it happened."

"What?"

He rushed over to another display. This one was a photograph of a woman labeled *1930*. She had a child on her lap, she wore an apron. Behind her was a rusted cylinder, maybe a boiler, that melted into stark shadows. Beside the photograph was a wooden handle ending in a sharp rock, connected with tightly wound twine. The label read: *tomahawk*.

Hank read, quickly—as if he'd already read it a thousand times over. "'Mary Whishaw, pictured here with her son Calamity 'Cal' Whishaw, worked as a seamstress throughout the early 20th century. She was known by friends and family as Merry Mary for her jovial spirit and penchant for tawdriness. Cal Whishaw was her only living child, and for a long while the only known—until a razed storefront in Mary's neighborhood led to the discovery of a mass grave. It seems to many that Merry Mary was not that merry at all—and as her dalliances spun out of control, so did she. Authorities counted seven infant corpses, all disposed of in the rotting floor of an abandoned grocer. Merry Mary was sentenced to death by hanging."

As Hank stared at me, looking at me for some sort of answer, I dwelled on the image of purple faced infants with crushed skulls. I thought of the rats that chewed on their silken flesh, a shrill scream their first and final contribution to reality —before Merry Mary slammed their fragile bodies into the foundation, amongst a nest of cracked skeletons.

All I could say was the obvious. "That's messed up." Then, disgusted, I became defensive. "Why are you showing me this shit?"

"I didn't do this." He motioned to my pocket. "Look it up, do it."

None of it happened, he'd said. I took him at his word. I looked up 'Merry' Mary Whishaw, Calamity Whishaw. I looked up local child deaths. I searched for the last voyage of the *Lady Calabasas. Nothing.*

I felt as if I were being forced to reconcile two great opposing forces—the immaculateness of the museum with the eels coiling in my stomach. I was ready to run. And I would've, if Hank hadn't looked so sorrowful, so confused, so fucking normal.

"I just thought you might know about it," he explained.

I turned for the door. "I don't know shit about this."

On one of the walls was a bookcase filled with documents —some in elegant cursive, some typed. All of them were under the raised bronze lettering that titled them *Manifestos.*

Hank walked after me. "I couldn't keep this shit secret," he said, continuing his explanation. "It's too weird."

I found the door to the lobby, beside it, a sign: *Thank you for visiting!* Above was a map covered in red pox-like dots—*See if we're in your city!* I passed it without a second look. When I got outside I breathed deep, thankful for cool air. The rain had stopped and the city smelled clean. I left the alley and hit the sidewalk and slammed my back to a brick wall and tried to process what I'd just seen. A full museum—exhibits, dioramas, and history—filled with fiction.

Hank caught up with me, wearing the same hangdog face. "Hey, hey—I didn't mean to trap you like that. I'm sorry," he said.

"How did you find it?"

I winced as I waited for him to say: *it found me.*

"Just the right place at the right time, I guess."

I exhaled.

He reached into his jacket and pulled out a smoke. "I was playing location scout and needed an alley. Wandered down the wrong one."

My ears perked up. "Movies?"

"Commercials, mostly."

"Right," I said, breathing slowly under control.

"What do you think it is?"

"Maybe it's some sort of performance art."

"I've thought of that," he said slowly. "But I've never seen anyone else go in."

We were silent for a moment. Above, rain started to fall again in a fine mist.

I had one last question. "Why me?"

For the first time, Hank's loose sullenness hardened. He threw his cigarette to the ground, extinguishing it with the sole of his shoe. "I like your blog," he said matter-of-factly, "and I wanted to meet you."

And that was that.

We parted ways and exchanged numbers. The strangeness of being sought out by a stranger was dwarfed under the shadow of the Museum of Lost Things. Compared to the *Lady Calabasas* and Merry Mary, Hank was a trifle.

* * *

I saw him again a couple times, and we'd talk about the
Museum, but we kept the conversation light, easy. He was
nervous, overeager and easily wounded, but he liked to talk,
and he sure as hell liked me. If I posted a review (or when I was
feeling especially self-important, a retrospective), Hank would
call me to discuss it at length. He'd pick at my word choice and
challenge my conclusions, offer obscure counterpoints, but it'd
always end with him swelling with joy in some way.

I came to realize that we were both outsiders looking into
the world of film, hoping desperately for someone to call on us
when we raised our hand. I had my writing, which I desperately hoped *Fangoria* would notice; and Hank was waiting to
get called on to some sort of prestige horror flick. He was a
writer too, I found out, with a stack of original screenplays
read by no one but himself. We joined hands and did what we
did best: vomit our thoughts onto a page, then throw them out
into the void.

We were like minds. We could talk about movies, books,
and even the real-life phenomena I continued to dismiss. Hank
always had a friend of a friend who was gutted in the woods or
abducted by aliens. It was the same sort of dialogue you could
imagine having in a tent with a bunch of nine year olds. Everything was real, everything was magical.

Before long, we had decided that the Museum of Lost
Things was some sort of viral marketing pop-up that didn't
take off. "There must be a hundred of those things," Hank
suggested, and I said, "Sure, why not?" Time had taken the
sting out of the scorpion. What once felt like a waking nightmare, was now merely odd. Funny, even.

Hank went off as a production assistant for a shoot in
Northern California and our texts and phone calls grew less

frequent. I was starting a new job. Weeks passed and life went on.

The last time he called me, we hadn't spoken in a month.

The call was short, caked in static, but the first words out of his mouth were: "I went back."

The rest was a garbled mess of run-on sentences. He kept saying he was sorry, and I kept saying, "Sorry for what?"

When the call ended, I felt an overwhelming sense of despair. I called the police to let them know that I had gotten a disturbing call and that I thought my friend might be in trouble. But I had no last name, no location, just a phone number. And when I tried calling him back, it was disconnected.

It was winter and I couldn't afford to turn on the heat. I shivered myself asleep, dreading the worst.

The CCTV camera footage shows the bank. Customers do business. Our humble narrator processes transactions. Time flies in fast forward, then stops. I, or the person that looks like me, walks out to refill papers at a self-service kiosk. The camera jumps, and suddenly I am two feet to the right of where I was. Nothing else happens.

I felt the loss the most when I pressed publish on an editorial about the lack of iconic monsters in modern horror. I was thinking about the over-influence of H.R. Giger, but I was also thinking about Hank.

My life kept moving forward, but Hank was an unforgettable bookmark. I'd gotten a new job, I got more serious about my writing. I lost my girlfriend. But there was always Hank at the back of my mind.

He loved the old school. *Them!, Rodan, Dracula*. He once told me the greatest monster of all time was Oliver Reed in *Curse of the Werewolf*. I wrote about how the age of iconic monster designs were far behind us, that in the quest to make everything look alien, that nothing was memorable. This was, in a way, a calling card. I knew if there was anything to make him raise his head out of the dust, it'd be this. I even put a big old one-sheet of his favorite wolfman as the header.

But, of course: nothing.

Angry and hurt, I was putting off the inevitable. I remembered his first-last sentence. *I went back.* He said it in the same sad, plaintive way he said everything.

The radio silence regarding my monster story was deafening. I felt smaller than ever, the very definition of an outsider looking in. Pathetic. So, I went downtown, first just to grab a beer and drown my sorrows, then, I began to retrace my steps. There was nothing else to do, really. My ambition had been sapped, not just for Hank but for myself too. I was just going to get drunk.

I arrived at the same taphouse—not through any urge to recreate that first meeting with Hank. No, it was just the only place I knew. I went there and had two beers and planned on talking to the bartender about why everything I ever tried to like tasted like shit. But the place was busy, he barely had time to charge my card. My legs were restless. I checked my phone to see if I got any comments, shares, anything at all in response to my story. Nothing.

So, I stood up.

I was just walking. I didn't know where I was going. I pretended well enough.

When I stood at the edge of the immaculate alley, when I looked down its dark corridor, I pretended it was just a happy coincidence. *Oh, wow, who'd've thought I'd end up here, huh?*

Then, I was at the stairs. *Maybe just a quick look-see.*

And in a moment, I was running down them, disappearing into the black, groping in the dark for the door, pushing helplessly until it gave way and light stunned my eyes. I remembered how easily Hank found it, I wondered how many times he'd been there.

I cowered behind my hand as the light struck me; these were the last moments of blissful ignorance, and as my eyes adjusted I knew it was all coming to an end. I could turn around and never come back, I could tell myself that the museum no longer existed. It was gone. A viral marketing pop-up, just like I said.

But it was still there.

And it was gorgeous.

Nothing had changed. The Museum of Lost Things remained in perfect stasis. I followed the velvet ropes while questions rattled. *Who changes the lightbulbs? Who writes the placards? Where do the pamphlets come from?* I tried to imagine construction workers hauling materials up and down the stairs. *Did they have a radio? Did they listen to music while they worked? Where did they take their breaks?*

As I passed through the doors, past the pamphlets, I realized that I couldn't imagine the museum being built, only existing. And for some reason, the thought made me sick to my stomach.

"Hank?" I called, remembering why I was here.

My voice sounded dampened and hollow, totally alone. With it came the realization that everything people make is draped in some sort of figurativeness. We use simile and metaphor, we create proverbs and analogies. Sarcasm, in its pointed irony, becomes precision. Hearing my own voice in the caverns of the Museum of Lost Things was repulsively literal. It was a reminder that language is the product of people, and that here, I could not see *people* in any of its warm humming ambience, its literature, or its curative design. It was a place of absence, documenting absence.

I staggered on shaky legs, looking for some sign of the friend I almost knew. But there were only exhibits—cairns of information arranged as sacrifice to some unseen eye. They all worshipped at the altar of the massacre, as if these were the self-congratulatory first steps to mass extinction. To my right was a loving depiction of a commuter bus unpeeling itself as its driver guided its nose into a too-small train tunnel. It rode on the tracks until it reached its natural end, and as the doors were sealed shut by the crumpling of its metal, the honking scream of a locomotive sounded to its trapped passengers that their time had come.

All varieties of weapons were celebrated—knives and pipe-bombs; AK-47s and revolvers. A man who killed his family by weighing them down to the bottom of the pool was memorialized with a full diorama as well as statistics on blood-oxygen levels for each victim's size and relative terror. The man, a friendly looking suburban father with a mustache and a lawn-mower, waved in a photograph.

Then, there were the school shooters. Placards fetishized where they found their weapons, which gun laws allowed them to carry and which they had to circumvent. Big quotes in leaning italics danced across the wall. *"He was always kind of a loner." "We tried therapy after his father and I split."* In the glass case, there were drawings of torture contraptions, poems written in heavy scratching ink, and video installations of the would-be killer speaking directly to the viewer, detailing their future actions. Beneath the video, there was a colorful diagram showing where chance and circumstance forced the perpetrator to deviate from their plans.

Then there were bombers—whose displays were invariably

accompanied by lengths of twisty blackened metal. And then: the poisoners, who lived their last moments doling out punch to friends, family, and coworkers. The last questions they heard were the people around them questioning the brand of juice. *It's a little bitter—not bad, just a little bite. Is it cranberry based?*

And none of them existed—killers and victims joined fully in some cosmic cycle. I felt myself growing weak, tired, over-stimulated. I was ready to leave, but I knew there was more, that something in this place was calling to me, just as it called to Hank.

On the outer edges, closest to the furthest wall, I found it. It was a humble display, with just a fragment of the murderous spree that inspired it. Three shell casings and a bank state-ment, the last processed before the intruder entered, opening fire like a madman. Stills from the camera were too blurry to make out, but the informational placard said the perpetrator's name was Henry Laramie. I looked closer at the picture and recognized the same carpet, the same faux-Greek pillars that rose to a stunted ceiling beside the front door. I cocked my head, not quite believing what I read, what I saw before my eyes.

This was *my* bank. My old job. The canvas for a massacre.

I looked at the timestamp on the photograph and realized that it was either my last day or the day after, I couldn't be sure. I might have arranged an early day. It wasn't so long, only a month, but my memories seeped into each other. And of course, it was around the same time I got that last call from Hank.

I went back.

Hank is short for Henry sometimes, I thought with a shudder.

In dignified Times New Roman, the dead were engraved in

48   CARSON WINTER

bronze. I looked for someone I knew, but was left scrambling
for connections. *Elliot Grandmont?* Was that Elle? *Michael Carr?*
Maybe that was Matt, maybe I misremembered his name; they
were both common.

None of them jogged my memory. But that was *my* bank,
and I should've known every single one of them.

Among the names was that of Henry Laramie, who ended
his life moments after the last teller collapsed.

"To read Laramie's manifesto, please see the Manifesto
Library," I read aloud.

I turned my head and saw the great exhibit at the south
side of the underground museum. Lamps shined on the wall,
illuminating it with a kiss of warmth. Like a library newspaper
stand, the shelves were shallow and the covers looked you in
the eye. Each was laminated, with a hole punch at the left
hand corner that housed a protective wire that secured each
page to the wall behind it.

They were organized by act. *Mass Murder-Politcal-H, Bomb-
ings-Apolitical-W, Infanctide-Cult-D.* When I reached Henry
Laramie (*Mass Murder-Apolitical-L*), I closed my eyes and
thought about keeping them shut. I could still turn around,
leave forever. I could be content in not knowing.

But, that wasn't me. I wanted to know.

I pulled the single typed page and the wire made a zipper
sound as it gave. I held it with two hands in front of me.

It read:

Funny how life happens, right?

*To a certain degree, we all have expectations. Like, when we're
young we have a vision of our lives.*

*When I was a kid, I used to walk really fast—because of
metaphors. I thought that when I passed kids in the hall that I was*

setting a goal post. I was faster, I was better, and now that I had gotten to class earlier, the rest of my life would fall like dominoes in some grand butterfly effect. The disappointing thing is that of course, that's not the way it happens. The slowest walkers can go on to do great things and the fastest walkers get fucked over sometimes.

Maybe not bad. It wasn't bad for me. I shouldn't let people think it was. It was okay, most of the time. But when you want great, anything less just hurts like hell. It becomes uncontrollable and suddenly mediocrity is all you see—in yourself, in others. I know all of these things to be true: I am the one that is wrong and I am the one that will hurt people.

If you can't tell, this is more of a letter than a manifesto. I won't say who it's for, but I hope that it finds its audience. I would say, but names are a dangerous commodity around here.

How weak are we? How sad and pathetic? Living through power fantasies disguised as disempowerment fantasies—it's the same urge of self destruction they call the call of the void. L'appel du vide, as the French say. Think of when you're driving and you can't help but want to twist the wheel and slam into oncoming traffic. It's the same thing: eternal predator, eternal prey. Forgotten somewhere, remembered elsewhere.

It's a choice, it's a balance. It's concrete, even if it's erased. Like a pencil sketch that gets rubbed raw and laid over with a new drawing. Still there, still there.

Best regards,
H

As I let go of the paper, the elastic pulley whirred and brought it back into the bosom of the Museum of Lost Things. I backed away, adrenaline coursing through my body, rickety legs propelling me through the doors. On the way out, I saw the donation box—someone had left a fiver.

When I reached the velvet ropes, I ran. Up the black stairs, into the alley, onto the street, straight to my car. I turned up the radio and tried to sing songs I'd never heard before, and I thought about all the songs I've heard but since forgotten, all the songs I sang that were never there. I drove fast and kept thinking about Henry Laramie—maybe Hank, maybe not.

And then, when I got home: I sat, I settled. I thought about everything that happened to me, and realized nothing had. I tried to remember my old coworkers. My memories felt dreamy, hazy—large swaths of characterization performed in thick brushstrokes. My manager was a curt middle-aged woman. Elle was very pretty and nice. Matt asked me if I wanted to play poker once. I dwelled on these facts, tried to make them real, but every so often, a new image would infiltrate, an implant or a recollection, I couldn't tell.

Then, a violent scene:

Screaming, crying; a gunman passing me without a second look, sparing me. Shots fired, bloodshed and carnage. The smell of iron. A woman pleading, my heart galloping. Just a sketch, a cast of characters erased, new ones pencilled over their faded outlines.

Maybe. Or maybe not.

I don't want to be forgotten. Like, Hank, I am a sad man with bones to pick, with dreams unrealized and an unfortunate deck of genetic cards. All I want is a record, something to say I was here. I won't sign my name because names are dangerous. But if I release this in the wild, it'll survive; even if everything catches up to me, even if I do something stupid.

* * *

I'm staring into the camera, my face fills the frame. Quietly, if you listen, you can hear cars in the background. You realize I'm outside. Around me, around you, a thousand tragedies perpetuate themselves in silent infinity. With this realization, after a moment of lingering, we cut to chaotically shaking footage. We can't tell what's happening, but it ends as soon as we realize people are running.

* * *

Sincerely.

CANONICAL VICTIMS

I heard him before I saw him. A stop-start scream that *chk-chk-chk*'d like a stuttering lawn sprinkler. Full-throated, punctuated with glottal stops, high-pitched. "Ahh! Ahh! Ahh!"

I was in a coffee shop, curled up in warm neon. Rain fell so hard it looked like the white lines in a comic panel. I turned my head from my book, tucked my hair behind my ear, and adjusted my glasses, all very calmly, because I was practiced at being an urban adult. I didn't want to appear surprised or concerned when I looked out the window, across the street, and saw the man holding his throat.

As blood coughed out from between his fingers, I saw movement behind him. Instantly, in a detached, intelligent manner, I thought, *Oh, that must be the murderer.*

I took a drink of coffee and raised a polite finger to the waitress. "Excuse me," I said. "I think that man might need help."

The man fell to the ground, knees first. He reached out with a desperate hand, as if he was trying to ask us to do something, which annoyed me somewhat. What could we do besides what we were doing?

The waitress had already dialed the police. There was nothing left to do. We weren't doctors.

Red and blue lights flashed through the heavy rain, sirens wailed. Police cars screeched to a stop.

I sat and waited, drinking my coffee, which the waitress topped off, thankfully.

When an officer came in, he looked at me first. I smiled at him and folded the top corner of my book and closed it.

He cleared his throat. Then, said, "Miss, did you see what happened here?"

I nodded. "Someone cut his throat."

"Did you see who?"

"He took off down the alley."

He paused for a moment and scribbled my comments on a notepad. Outside, they threw a sheet over the corpse.

"Could you describe his scream?"

* * *

I went out the next night knowing there was a murderer on the loose. Most of us did, because death was part of living in the city. My friends and I spoke about it at length—the murderer, not the death.

"You saw him?"

"Sort of," I said.

"What victim was this?"

"The sixth, I think."

My other friend chimed in. "The sixth *canonical* victim. There could be more."

"There will be more," said another.

We laughed at that, even though we weren't supposed to.

When I walked home that night, I was drunk, but carefree. Really, we all were.

My heels clicked against the sidewalk; I passed the alley and held my breath.

* * *

I was pulling the stuffing from a gash in my couch when I heard a knock on the door. Quickly, I covered the white fluff with a fleece blanket. "Hello?" I called.

"Police."

I unlatched both locks and opened the door a crack. It was the middle of the day and I was wearing sweats and a ratty shirt. I felt exposed, foul. There was something coldly professional about the two officers in my doorway.

"Ma'am, we have some questions."

"About the man?"

"Yes."

"Okay, go ahead."

They asked me a series of questions involving the timeline. They asked me if I saw how the man's throat was cut. I did not. They asked me if the man said anything to me. He did not. They asked if I could describe the killer. I could not.

"Is that all?" I asked.

"No."

"Okay, shoot."

"Are you sure it was the man who screamed?"

I thought for a moment. "I assumed it was. Maybe I was wrong."

"Did you see his mouth move and did sound come out?"

"I didn't see that, no."

The two officers shared a glance. "Okay," said one.

"Stay safe," said the other.

And then they were gone.

* * *

At the coffee shop, where I drank my own reflection in the silky surface of black espresso, I considered the place where the dead man fell. I replayed the events in my head. In some way, as a witness, I felt connected to the comings and goings of this murderer. I was part of the story now and I was reminded of it constantly. People were asking me about what I saw and I had very little to say. It didn't feel right.

In the newspaper, an anonymous witness—me—described the attack dispassionately. I ran my hands through my hair and thought about pulling some out when I read that. *No, that makes me sound cold. I'm not cold,* I thought. No cop or reporter asked me if I cried into my pillow the night after, or if I was scared to walk alone. Of course I was, but also, you become acclimated to these sorts of things. It can come off as cold in print, when really, it's just familiarity.

In front of me, I had five other newspapers. I worked my way backwards.

* * *

Number 5

This was a woman. I found that comforting, in an odd way. It wasn't at night, but the early morning. She was walking her dog. I liked the night and didn't want to be fearful of it. I laughed to myself at first, because there was at least one good thing that came from her death. Her throat was slit and I touched my own throat when I read over the description. The knife went quite deep apparently.

Number 4

A man walking home alone at night. Disappointment reared inside me. His throat was slit, but they do not know how. I don't know how you can not know that. The newspapers said, with some desperation, "Please, if you know anything, do not hesitate to share."

I sighed. I already said all I could.

Number 3

This one died in a church tower. She was a nun and she was praying. There was a certain sentimental charm to that, because I didn't know anyone who prayed. I certainly didn't. The paper printed a picture of her blood-stained habit.

Number 2

The Frantic Man, The Bleeder. This one had nicknames. The paper hadn't confirmed that his sliced neck was part of a pattern. Therefore, there was a certain perverse joy in the article. He was found in an abandoned building. He nearly painted the peeling walls with his blood. Brilliant spatter marked his frenzied pace through the quiet room where his life ended. I had to admit—the room was stunning.

Number 1

Finally, number one. The original canonical victim. I liked this one the best because it seemed the most regular. Here was a woman in her own house, killed by someone she most likely knew. They confirmed that it was a blade that cut into her throat, which was a relief. Trace amounts of metal were found lodged in her windpipe. She died in her bedroom, which is where I'd like to die as well.

This was also the only murder with a witness—her two children. They waited in the bathroom tub while they listened to her mother's scream from the other room.

I put the paper down and shook a chill out from my spine as I imagined its stop-start rhythm.

* * *

"How many victims now?" asked a friend.

"Still six," I said.

"Incredible."

"Yes," I agreed.

She looked at me like she had something to ask, but avoided the question. For a while, we spoke about our jobs, our apartments, but never about death. Eventually though, it came out. "Are you going to look for him?"

"Why would I?" I said, but I knew I should've asked what she meant.

"You saw his work. You witnessed him."

"Well, yes. But that doesn't mean anything. I was just in the wrong place at the wrong time. He probably didn't even realize I was there."

"That can't be true. He must've."

I realized now that my friend wanted it to be true. That the story was better if the killer had seen me, had marked me in some way. I played along. "He might've looked back once, just a glance. I think we locked eyes."

She put down her drink. "No."

"Yes," I said. "I'm sure of it."

"You're so lucky," she said. "That's quite a story."

"Yes," I agreed.

In the bar, there were hundreds of men. When I looked to see their faces, they all seemed to look away. I bit the flesh on the insides of my cheek. My friend smiled wickedly, like, *see?*

* * *

I called the police to ask about the children, the children of the first woman—the one who died in her bed.

"Hello?" I said into the receiver. "I wanted to ask about the children, the children of the first canonical victim."

There was a long pause, and a click. "How do you know about the children?"

"They were in the paper."

Another pause. "Right," said the voice. "Right."

"Are they okay? I wanted to visit them, talk to them."

"We can't discuss that with you," said the voice. "Is there anything else?"

"Well, no."

Dial tone. I found the sound grating, vicious—like all sounds.

* * *

My friends agreed that I should do what I could to strengthen my bond to the narrative. We didn't talk about death often, because we weren't as young as we used to be. We talked *around* death now. We talked about murders and car crashes but avoided the acknowledgment of *the end*.

At night, I visited the crime scenes of those canonical victims and strengthened my narrative. Sometimes, I tricked myself into hearing the clicking heels of Chelsea boots, the groaning breaths of a mad man, the whisper of a razor halving rain drops. But every time I turned around, there was nothing.

* * *

I found myself back inside my favorite coffee shop. I was curled up by the window, reading a book that was not about death. I was the only patron at that hour. The waitress seemed more interested in whatever was in the backroom. Her giggles traveled through the walls, she spoke rapidly to a friend, coworker, or lover.

So entranced she was with her conversation, that she did not appear when the door chimed. I looked up from my book very briefly. It was a man, short with round glasses. His hair was thin and spackled to his forehead from the rain. I nodded to him, because he looked at me, and then he nodded back.

The waitress said, from a distance. "No, no—that can't be." But she said it while laughing.

The man walked toward me and I felt my heart stutter—a stop-start rhythm.

He smiled wanly and sat across from me in the booth. Every one of my muscles went rigid. Dark circles formed a purple outer ring to his full moon spectacles.

I said, "Who are you?"

He shook his head, like that was an answer. Then, he opened his mouth.

A scream. Shrill, staccato. A woman's scream coming from his lips. His face contorted as if he had become the mask of death from which he stole that awful noise. Instinctively, I recoiled, scrambled out of the booth. "Ahh! Ahh! Ahh!" the scream spritzed from his mouth like a second language. And as it did, my neck opened with a secret pair of lips.

I thrashed, clawed at my own throat. I could not scream. I was on the floor, kicking and screaming my own scream—a single long vowel.

From the other room, the giggling stopped. The waitress came bounding out, just in time to see the man leave. I looked at her, like, *help me.*

But she couldn't help, she wasn't a doctor. She called the police.

I tried to remain calm. I stretched and didn't think about the man. She would be worried, this waitress. She didn't sign up for this. As I bled onto the cold tile floor, I attempted a smile, to calm her. That's what I would've wanted. I wouldn't want to think about death. I'd want to think everything would be okay. She looked out after the man, who disappeared into the night, and became a part of the story. I waved my arms at her, to make her look back at me, to refocus her, just in time for the end.

IN HASKINS

Everyone, both the young and the old, went about their lives as usual on the day of the Mask Festival. The downtown streets were covered with colored leaves and Mr. Burkett still waved at children and swept in front of his storefront. Mrs. Farley still clucked to Mrs. Durant on how the new teachers at the old school would not and could not teach their children anything. And the policemen still ate lunch at the Morrison Deli on Main. Normality ruled with benevolent routine. But still, as the leaves fell, and the stage was erected, the people of Haskins braced quietly for their most insistent tradition.

At the fairgrounds, Jennifer arrived early to help set the stage. Her eye sockets hung loose and rubbery around her blue eyes. She was the first Jennifer to have blue eyes. The mane on top of her head was coarse and tawny. Flies buzzed in her stomach and she was thankful she was Jennifer because Jennifer always had to stay busy. Cindy was already there, cross-legged and cutting orange leaves out of construction paper, looking prim and sweet in her blue dress.

She nodded to Cindy as she found a pair of scissors. When Cindy did not return the movement, Jennifer decided that her eyelets must be misaligned.

"Hey," she said, gaining her attention.

Cindy looked up from a pile of construction paper. "Good morning," she said between ragged breaths. She always complained of being overheated. "Are you excited?"

Cindy's voice was low this year, deep. She was tall and muscular, but Jennifer always gave her credit for her commitment to Cindy's primary traits—innocence and geniality. They were best friends.

"Yes, in a way," she said.

Cindy's scissors made ripping sounds as they ate through the construction paper. "Are you worried?"

She was talking about Rance and Rance was a key aspect of Jennifer. They fit together like pieces of a puzzle. Jennifer was a cheerleader and Rance was the high school quarterback. He had a shock of blond horsetail hair on the top of his rubber scalp. His mask was loose and shook back and forth like a great Jello mold when he spoke. They were to be married the day after the Mask Festival.

She froze for a moment. "No," said Jennifer, wondering how much of herself she should share. "Rance and I will be very happy."

"Of course."

"We'll be very happy," she said again. Because right now, she was Jennifer, and that is something Jennifer would say.

The stage was decorated with cornucopias and browning sunflowers—symbols of the season. Orange and brown paper leaves decorated the backdrop, frozen in mid-fall. The people of Haskins shuffled in quietly, some enthusiastically. Others came with an expression of boredom, of toe-tapping impatience. Haskins was a small town, but it contained all sorts.

Jennifer snuck down from the stage as twilight struck and the big sky above the small town glowed with gold and crimson ribbons. The people were drinking their ciders, wiping the grease from the lips of their masks as they devoured turkey legs through the slits that made up their mouths.

She found Rance sitting on a hay bale, his legs resting on a large pumpkin with a blue ribbon. She said his name and he reacted in mock exaggeration, pretending to fall from his spot. Rance had always been a jokester—for the last three dozen years, at least. Before, he was cruel—a bully—but time had softened his demeanor. He was now something of a class clown. Even in Haskins, times change.

"There she is, my beautiful." He stood up and touched her waist. He was shorter than her and the way he looked up into her eyes made him seem like a child looking up at the stars in the night sky. She could see him, his eyes behind the rubber curves, big and brown, pointing up to an endless sky with infantile delight.

They mashed their faces together, crumpling into each other as their masks folded into sweating slabs of rubber. Their tongues found their way out of their mouth-slits, tasting each other's flesh.

They held on for as long as they could. Rance found his head on her shoulder. He would not say what he wanted to say, but she could hear the choke in his voice all the same. She could divine his meaning.

She pulled apart from him and looked down, grabbing his half-drank cup of cider for a sip. "We're getting married tomorrow," she said.

He swallowed, a noise that seemed to echo behind his mask. "Yes, I know."

Behind them, past the tents and merchants, folks began to gather. A horn blared.

"Could we just—"

She stopped herself. It was not Jennifer speaking.

Rance sniffed and took her by the arm. "We should head up," he said. "They'll start without us."

They pulled each other through the crowd and stood to the far side near the stage where they could see Mayor Granger adjusting his cufflinks. He preened in the expected manner, debuting a new suit with extravagant embroidery for the occasion. Mayor Granger was always wearing the finest clothes.

"Alright, yes," he began. "Okay, well, here we are. This is the Mask Festival. The Festival of Masks. An old tradition, a very old tradition, indeed." Mayor Granger's speech ran out of steam before it began, as it often did in the last year, so instead of continuing, he straightened his silk tie and smiled. "Let's begin," he said, finally.

Through the wings of the stage, two farm boys with rubber jowls pushed a wooden cart with a large pumpkin on top of it. Granger clapped his hands and let out a nervous sigh. The two boys hoisted the pumpkin's top off together, struggling under its weight.

Jennifer and Rance held hands as they watched Mayor Granger close his eyes and reach into the pumpkin. When his hand came back with two slips of paper, the festival began.

"Connie and Delmont," he called. "Please come up to the stage and make your exchange."

A small woman with a snug mask trotted up on stage, she carried with her a wicker basket of flowers. She curtsied before the audience. On the other side, a mechanic in overalls with long black hair stomped with heavy boots to the center of the stage. They turned to each other and bowed, then walked to the rear of the stage, their backs to the audience. With both hands they removed their masks, then, without looking, held them out to the other. The new

Connie's mask was so tight that her features seemed to pop out of the eyelets. Delmont was slight and wiry, but the wearer had begun to learn his movements, raising his feet in great destructive arcs. The crowd cheered and the new Connie skipped heavily back into the crowd and disappeared.

Before long, Mayor Granger's name was called too. His change was extravagant, of course. He danced to the back of the stage and when he came back his voice grew more resinous, his stature more assured. The old Granger disappeared into the crowd wearing Jim Brown's face and drinking sweet liquor with Jim Brown's loud friends.

Jennifer held Rance's hand until he had to leave for the stage. He met with Susan Hickens, a girl a year below them, and they swapped faces. When Rance came back to Jennifer, he was taller. Susan held her face in her hands as she was embraced by her family. For just a moment, Jennifer saw her look back at her, the black holes of her eyes an implacable enigma. She was always known to be shy.

The new Rance put his arm around her—in a way that was so unlike the old Rance that it made her skin crawl. She told herself that it was okay, that they were to be married and that this was a perfectly apt display of affection. It was only that— Rance used to hold her hand. He did not usually wrap his arms around her casually, she was used to feeling his fingers between hers. She wriggled out of the embrace and grabbed his hands, demonstrating the protocols of their relationship in a discreet way. His hands were rough and large. He turned his head toward her, bright hazel eyes hidden behind eyelets. She thought she detected a nod of understanding. He held her hand and watched the stage.

Mayor Granger dug his hand into the pumpkin and came out with two slips of paper. He squinted his eyes, one hand tugging a finger into his eyelet, spreading it so that he could read. "Cole Drewson and Jennifer Maisey. Come on up!"

Her heart shivered, palpitating in erratic bursts of electric anxiety. She unhooked her hand from Rance and felt a chill. She looked at him briefly, to see his eyes, but they were not the eyes she knew. She seemed to float to the stage, dragged along by an inevitable leash. Mayor Granger took both of their hands and raised them. He was adding to the spectacle, he was making decisions. She reflected that this was indeed in line with Granger's character, and she wondered why no one considered taking the hands of those on the stage and raising them before. It added a sort of spectacle to the event, and historically, Mayor Granger was spectacle incarnate.

Granger joined their hands and for just a moment, she felt as if the hand in hers was Rance's. The Rance *she* knew. But the palm in hers was sweating and Rance never sweated from his hands. She and Cole walked to the back of the stage—an eternity—and she looked straight ahead as she took off her mask.

Cole was doing the same beside her.

She wondered if he felt the same rush she did when she removed it. *I'm still Jennifer I'm still Jennifer I'm still Jennifer*, she thought. Her face was naked and she was still Jennifer. She panicked. Her heart kicked her sternum. She did not feel any different. She liked being Jennifer. She was still her. Jennifer was who she should be, and why now should Cole get to be Jennifer? Why now should *she* have to be Cole?

She tried to catch her breath and reach some sort of compromise with herself as Cole pulled off his own mask and held it out to her.

Her body failed her. It had become too accustomed to the ways of Haskins. She reached out with her own mask and they exchanged without looking at each other. She pulled on Cole Drewson's face and felt the sweat and stink of another human and she began to pray—that she would *be* Cole, that she would forget what it was like to be Jennifer, what it was like to love Rance, her Rance.

They both turned around and Cole Drewson waved weakly to the audience and went down the opposite side of the stage. Jennifer found Rance and they put their arms around each other and embraced.

In the back of the fairgrounds, Cole found himself in the men's room, staring at his new face. Long jawed, with a mustache. Stubble dotted his chin. A trucker hat covered his black hair. His creases were long and deep like knife cuts.

Behind him, a boy he could not see left a bathroom stall and walked out the door. When he was alone in the surgical teal bathroom, Cole whispered his old name.

The next month was a period of adjustment for everyone. Cole woke up in his new home and learned his old habits. His wife, Pauline, was a quick study. She would cower in fear whenever he entered the room, although she would do so in a pathetic, approval-seeking way.

Cole was more lethargic, less vigorous in his anger than usual, but he made his threats, he spat between the lips of his mask and cursed. He drank the same beer, although he had not been able to drink as much as he used to. Most nights, when trying, he fell asleep in the white light of the television while Pauline stepped lightly out the front door to meet their neighbor.

When he'd wake, he'd go to his job at the plant, where he learned to speak crudely with the other men at work. His tone was high and girlish but they accepted him with backslaps and unhinged laughter.

He did not feel like Cole, but he did appreciate that the others felt like he was playing his part. Cole was a difficult role, he demanded a certain physicality that was difficult to match at first. And although, behind the rubber of his face, he still felt like Jennifer, he was beginning to appreciate the inherent violence of his new identity.

He'd begun to get comfortable slapping Pauline when he was angry. The first hit had been a surprise to them both, but it was very much in line with what Cole would do. She looked up at him, having fallen to the floor and rubbing her cheek, and she looked almost appreciative.

"Don't look at me like that," he muttered.

The incident happened after he came home late. He told her he'd gone to the bar, but really he'd gone down to the old high school to watch the football game. He'd brought a bottle with him. It was gone by the time he got back. She only had to ask him where he'd been and it was enough. It took only a second for his rage to show its face.

After, of course, he felt sick. As Pauline hid the rest of the night, he became preoccupied with the dimensions of his mask. He drank until he fell asleep.

Cole was not known as a sports fan, but it was certainly not so out of sorts for a drunk and a wifebeater to enjoy football. Cole considered this to be an aspect of the Cole character he could develop. What are games but an excuse to drink? What violences could he commit to Pauline when the home team lost? At first, it seemed strange for Cole to go see the local team play every Friday, but then as his work friends came around, it didn't seem so strange at all. And besides, if Rance could now put his arms around Jennifer rather than hold her hand, why couldn't Cole like football?

"You like that cheerleader? The one with the legs?"

Cole shook his head. He did not care for the cheerleaders.

He was not looking at them. His eyes were always on the crowd, looking for a young girl with brown hair that always fell in front of her mask. But Susan Hickens was shy and he didn't know why he thought she might decide to come to the game.

He took off his hat and rubbed his mane of hair. He punched the side of his head impotently.

"Y'okay, Cole?"

"Yeah, fine. Watching the game."

Rance, the quarterback, completed a thirty-yard pass and the crowd erupted in unhinged ecstasy. Cole put his hand on his head and said, "I'm gonna head out. I wanna go fishing in the morning."

His friends booed and waved their bottles in mock-disapproval, but fishing had been another recent addition to Cole's canon, and he was allowed to leave. He balled his fists in the cuffs of his coat, cursing under his mask, stealing glances at the field. *They were going to be newlyweds*, he reminded himself. He got into his car and rubbed at the rubber covering his face. He rubbed it into himself, tried to make it melt into his flesh.

When he got home, he greeted Pauline by cracking her jaw.

She threw her hands up in front of her, but her eyes showed the same twisted sort of glee she always shared whenever Cole played his part well. She braced for the next hit and when she got it, her head snapped back into the cupboard behind her.

Blood flowed from the slit of her lips. He heard whimpering from inside of her mask. Cole stepped over her body to get a beer from the fridge.

She got on all fours, she was trying to stand. "Cole," she started.

He wound up and kicked her in the ribs. She dropped back to the floor, moaning as she gripped her sides.

Cole stood over her, sweating. In a shaky voice, he said, "Don't ever call me that again."

When she tried to speak again, he stomped down on the back of her neck until he felt something crack.

"I'm sorry," he said. "I'm sorry."

Her legs were shaking, twitching.

"It's just—I'm not Cole."

They stopped moving, and because he was supposed to be Cole, he could only do what Cole would do, so he stomped his boot down hard once more; again and again until her spasms ceased.

Cole had never killed anyone before. There would be side-eyes and gossip, as Haskins generally appreciated its townsfolk to maintain the status quo—but Cole was always a violent man. This was as true an ending to Pauline's story as any, he told himself.

He placed his head against the wood of the pantry and tried to think. *Yes, this was a fine ending. True to character. People had died in Haskins before. Not many, but it has happened.*

The body would be discovered eventually, perhaps by a mailman or a friend of a friend. He would be locked up when it was discovered, but he felt no real urgency regarding these truths. He would perhaps have days, maybe weeks to continue on unfettered. Cole sat down beside Pauline and stroked away the hair on her mask. Blood leaked through its nostrils. It was not a pretty mask: it was far too large on her, as most masks were.

Cole wondered what would have happened if he had been Pauline. If Cole would have killed him in the kitchen, if he would have been so sniveling and grateful as the world blackened around him. He yanked on her hair and saw a bit of skin, real skin, beneath. The idea of it was so alluring, so mysterious. He pulled again to free her head and he pulled until Pauline's face was limp in his own hands, stretched into a long liquid yawn. Cole turned her head, the head of a young man with light brown hair buzzed short. His face was covered in bruises, a kaleidoscope of greens, yellows, browns, and purples. Cole took off his own mask as well and rubbed his fists into his eyes. This is not something Cole would do, he realized, crying harder. He was not Cole.

* * *

After work, he and his buddies went to the game like they always did. Such was their lot. They all drank, but by now Cole was used to drinking. They didn't realize he was drinking less, but then again, it didn't matter how much he drank because drink pervaded his being. He smelled perpetually of whiskey. And no one questioned whether Cole was drunk because of course he was. He's Cole. And just as everyone assumed he had been drinking, no one asked about his wife. Because Cole never talked about her anyways. It just wasn't done.

"You lookin' at those cheerleaders, Cole?"

"Too old for me," said Cole, his voice flat. "I like 'em young,"

His face was pointed toward the announcer's box. He was squinting as his friends howled.

"Oh yeah? How young?"

"Real fucking young."

They liked that. They screamed in joy. And as they screamed, he squinted his eyes to see the shy girl with brown hair keeping score a world away.

When the game ended, he waved them off. "I gotta go fishing in the morning," he said.

The crowd was clearing out and he disappeared within them—several hundred rubber faces adorned with wigs and eyeglasses. The girl was climbing down from the announcer's box and he started to quicken his pace. Susan was unassuming, her back turned toward the fence, ready to slip out unnoticed now that her obligation had finished. Cole jogged lightly, not so fast as to draw attention—just the pace of a man eager to get home.

She passed through a split in the chain-link fence and began walking down the sidewalk with her nose in a book. Susan was always reading. Cole followed, a block back at first. If anyone was watching, they'd see him fumbling with his keys, looking for his car.

Susan lived near the school, the ward of bookish parents with large rubber noses and glassless spectacles. She spent most of her time at home and she was no doubt eager now to return. Susan portrayed this well when she first heard Cole shout her old name.

"Rance," he said. "Wait."

She stopped, moving her shoulders as if she were breathing deep, frightened. She turned at a glacier's pace, her mask turned downward toward the pavement.

"I've got to get home. It's late."

"It's not late," said Cole.

"I've got to go."

"We were supposed to be married."

"I'm Susan," she said. "We don't talk. You're too old to talk to me. I'm just a girl."

Cole ground his teeth, sweat dripped into his eye. He thought of Pauline and her face of mashed cherries. "I want you to come home with me tonight, Rance."

"No—I really can't—"

"It's Jennifer. I'm still Jennifer, Rance. Please, come with me. This is me speaking, I want you to come with me because I still love you. We're supposed to be married."

"Rance and Jennifer are getting married next year, the day after the festival. Not us." Her voice quivered when she said it.

Cole was a fast man, quick—a coiled spring. And when he bound toward Susan, she froze. That was a very Susan thing to do. She was not good under pressure and she was so much smaller than Cole.

He wrestled her to the ground and did what came most natural; an open hand pressed to her mouth, then a stranglehold around her neck. He felt her soft, sweating flesh. "Please," he said, whispering through her nostril holes, "come with me."

* * *

Like in any small town, a death causes an uproar.

A dead girl on the side of the road, bleeding out her mask.

And just like in any small town, time marches on.

* * *

"You don't usually have people over, is that true?"

The two had never been here before, a fact they seemed self-conscious of—still, they remained as chipper as they could, considering. They pointed at the elk's head on the wall and asked Cole if he hunted. They complimented Pauline on the furniture, their aesthetics as well as comfort.

Pauline bowed extravagantly, an ironic affectation. "The house was such a mess before. We're trying to be better about that."

Through the kitchen doorway came Cole, holding a tray of cocktails. "Please, help yourself, plenty more where that came from." He lowered the drinks on the table and poured himself a glass of club soda.

"You're not drinking?"

"Oh no, I'm a monster on that stuff. I'm turning a new leaf. I found God, I guess. The grain spoke to me. The seeds were sown. The old scarecrow came home to tend to the blackbirds in the field. All that jazz, you know?"

Pauline rubbed his shoulder, she kissed the back of his head. "He's been doing really good. Great."

There was a moment of silence, a pregnant pause. Pauline reached a hand out to their guests—a man and a woman, with large noses and glasses. "Awful what happened to Susan."

The man nodded solemnly and Cole huffed in sympathy. Snow began to fall and the gray light outside penetrated every inch of their humble home.

"Haskins isn't perfect," said the woman. "But then again, no place is."

They stared at each other, through each other for a long moment. Pauline's brown eyelets shined like glossy caramels by the fire as she took Cole by the hand and held it ever so tight.

WHO WE WISH TO BE

WE CAN ONLY GROW IN
THE DARK

The whole class, outside in the early morning chill, kneaded their tiny hands with neurotic intensity. Felicia cut in beside Mara and began to whisper.

"There's nothing we have to worry about," said Mara. And as if to prove it, she looked up at the great black shape in the sky.

Felicia shivered. "Mara," she said. "*Don't.*"

But Mara kept staring upward, her eyes focused on the shape. "I'm not afraid of it," she said simply. "Orphans don't get scared, it's our superpower. But you're only a half-orphan, so maybe you—"

The bell rang and Ms. Harris ushered them in with unusual urgency. "Hurry," she said. "Quick, quick!"

Felicia looked to Mara, but Mara only shrugged.

A television had been wheeled to the front of the class.

The children were seated hastily and after a long, taut pause, Ms. Harris clasped her hands. She wrung them together so tight that blood drained from her knuckles. Her hands looked like bones. "Well, class," she said. "This is a special day

—this is the sort of day that none of us are adequately prepared for." Another pause. "We just don't really know what to do. Of course, it's good that you're here—to be safe—but well—well—" Again, she struggled for words. It was unlike Ms. Harris—a tall and taciturn older woman, who knew schooling like the back of her skeletal hands—to be at a loss. "Something has happened. There's been an incident. Many people are dead. This was an attack, we think. That's all we know. I think that about covers it, yes. You're going to remember this day for the rest of your lives."

Ms. Harris turned the television on and sat wordlessly at her desk. Felicia closed her eyes. For a moment, she considered raising her hand, asking if her Mom could come and pick her up.

Maybe Mara could come too.

But when it blinked to life, she was allowed no escape.

"We are in the dark here, just like everyone," said the news-caster. "The White House hasn't scheduled any press confer-ences. We just know the object—or device, if you prefer—crashed."

Another voice cut in. "Well, let's not jump to conclusions. We don't know that it was a crash. We're applying too much of our language and worldview to properly articulate the event. This object, device, or yes—*ship*—didn't necessarily crash. It fell to earth, causing minimal damage to its environment, and then broke apart. We, from our own understanding of our own ships and our own physics, will say that this looks like a crash. But until we know more, it is only a resemblance."

Felicia felt a hand touch hers, gently, surreptitiously. Folded paper slipped into her palm. Ms. Harris was looking out the window, at the sky, her eyes wide and red. As the men on the television continued to dissect the possibilities of the crash, or not-crash as it were, she unfolded the note carefully.

To: Felicia
From: Mara
Skip?
Check Yes or No.

Felicia stuck her tongue out the side of her mouth and beneath "Yes or No," she added "Maybe." She drew a red circle around her addition, looked to see where Ms. Harris' attention was drawn, then passed the note back.

She stared straight ahead, to maintain her ruse, to not draw attention to herself. It was a secret she learned from Mara. *Don't go looking around with googly eyes like you want the attention.* Mara said that if you act like you're guilty, they'll never leave you alone.

The newsman touched his ear. "I'm getting word that we need to go off the air. I'm sorry, but they've given me the signal. We can't talk about this any longer. We need to go off the air." He looked like he was going to keep talking, keep saying: *we need to go off the air,* but before he could repeat himself again the television let out a short siren, then switched to a blue screen that read: *We Are Sorry For the Inconvenience.*

Felicia smiled because the message was sort of funny, like something they'd say at the grocery store. She wanted it to be funny. Sometimes laughing just makes everything easier. She let out a weak chuckle, a pale shadow of relief, low enough that no one would turn to look at her.

Ms. Harris pulled the blinds shut. *That's better,* Felicia thought, not quite sure how it was better, only that it was. The television was wheeled away by a tense custodian and the students cringed as its wheels screamed on rusty axles.

"I'm afraid there isn't anything to do today," said Ms. Harris, still staring at the covered windows. "Use this time to read or draw quietly."

For the next two hours, the class worked itself gradually

from dead silence to a deafening crescendo. Children wondered aloud if this meant war. They spoke with shaky voices, trying to make sense of the insensible. Ms. Harris allowed this, perhaps, because it *was* a special day. Because there would be no other day like this in the history of their lives.

Felicia and Mara sat huddled in a corner drawing violent deaths. Mara drew dead women who looked like her mother with knives in their stomachs, their necks garroted with piano wire. If anyone asked, she'd say she saw it in a movie. She drew killers who looked like her father. Whenever Felicia brought this up to her own mother, she was only told: *Mara's going through a tough time right now.*

Yeah? But I went through a tough time too.

Yes, honey, I know. But this is worse.

They drew dead people until the bell rang. Ms. Harris exhaled long and hard, as if she'd been holding it the whole morning. "Alright, lunchtime," she said. "Please, be cautious."

* * *

"So? Are you gonna do it?"

The two girls walked together, away from the cafeteria, to the empty baseball field, where no one stood for fear of what could fall on them.

Felicia shrugged. "I don't know," she said. "Should we do it today?"

She kept looking up. The black shape had moved considerably since she last saw it. It was now touching the far edge of the sun.

Mara shook her head. "You're always afraid."

Felicia pushed her friend. "Am not," she said. "I just don't know if today's the right day."

"You'd rather go home to see your *mom?*"

This thread existed between them, and when Mara was in a mood, she couldn't help but tug at it.

Felicia dodged the subject. "What do you want to do anyways?"

Mara quickened her pace, to where the wire fence met the edge of the baseball field. Felicia figured she was doing one of her *Mara-things*, rattling her chains and brooding, but she was actually pointing. "You see that there?"

"What?"

"The Church."

"Is that a church?"

"That's what the older kids call it. I think it used to be one, a long time ago."

Felicia squinted, following Mara's finger. She could see it, on the edge of downtown. It didn't have a pointy steeple like the churches she knew. It might as well have been a used car lot, or a convenience store, or an old bank. She was happy to talk about this old building though. It was a welcome distraction. "Why do they call it the Church?" she asked, too eagerly.

"I don't know."

"So, why do you want to go there?"

Mara turned to her, eyes alight. "I had a dream about it."

Felicia nodded. Mara had more dreams than any girl she'd ever met. For someone who couldn't bring herself to start an essay, she wrote more about her dreams than Felicia ever did on assignments. Felicia was fascinated by Mara's peculiarities, emulating them when she could. She wanted to study them— to know them so wholly that they felt like her own.

Mara cleared her throat, as she always did when she talked about her dreams. For her, dreams were a religion, a looking glass to a fairer world. Felicia waited patiently for Mara to complete her ritual, to affect her teacher's voice.

"I dreamed I was in bed. I didn't think it was a dream at first, you know? I just thought I woke up in the middle of the night. The window was open and I was cold, so I got up, but it was a dream. I went to the window and looked up at the sky, and everything looked different. Like yellow-greenish, like there was pollen everywhere in space and it was falling down to earth. Weird, right?"

Felicia tried to sound unbothered, to not look up. "Yeah, weird. Was that it?"

"No. As it got closer, it started to, like, form together. The pollen—no, the *spores*—somehow I knew that they were spores. They all started to form together. Like long strands of hair. And they all gathered like they were attracted to each other. These long hair strands of spores twisted down from the sky and they went to six different houses, to six different kids."

"Like Santa, kind of," said Felicia.

Mara grinned fiercely. "Not like Santa at all." She looked up to the black thing in the sky that had just begun to eclipse the sun. She looked at it too long, too steadfastly.

Felicia's stomach dropped. She tried to refocus her. "What about the Church?"

Absently, Mara said, "I opened my mouth and the spores went down my throat, I could feel them buzzing in my lungs like a swarm of bees. My bones felt sticky. Everything in me felt weird and heavy and not-real, but I knew it was a dream because I wasn't hurt. I just felt different. And connected. I felt connected too. To the six other kids. All the spores in my body made a picture of the Church in my head, I bet they did for the others too." She stared off into the distance, smiling. "So, I want to check it out."

The bell rang in five short bursts.

"But you said it was a dream."

"It was."

"And?"

Mara jogged ahead, away from the school, off to the sidewalk. "I don't know," she said. "But it's better than this, right?"

Felicia saw her friend disappear ahead of her. She looked back to the school. They were already lined up, with more oppressive whispers and more white knuckles. Ms. Harris was counting them, but halfway through she stopped using her fingers and just waved them in tiredly.

"You coming?" called Mara.

Felicia looked to her friend. She wondered what she was going to tell her mom. *Surely one skip won't ruin me,* she thought. *I've earned it, all things considered.*

Her eyes followed Mara.

This wasn't for me, Mom, she practiced, *I did it for Mara. She needed me.*

She ran to catch up, her heart skipping as it did. She wanted to be excited. *This should be exciting,* she thought.

When they were down the block, and the chatter of students died with distance, Mara's face was bright and cheery.

The Church was down at the end of Main, past downtown, stretching to the outskirts where the road merged into the two-lane that led to the countryside.

She looked up to see the black thing that was moving at a glacier's pace. It had partially eclipsed the sun now, covering half of it. It was only lunchtime but everything around her looked dead and empty and dark.

She couldn't avoid it any longer. "Is that one of the things that crashed?"

"Who cares?"

Felicia swallowed. "I just wanna know."

"It's just gonna give them what they deserve. It won't matter; not to us."

They trekked on and soon the empty stores became empty lots; empty lots became rocky earth and weeds; and then, when the sidewalk cracked and became nothing but earth and pebbles, there was the Church.

"This is it."

It was a rectangular building made of rotting wood. Now that she was closer, she could see the specks of white paint that clung to its exterior. It stood lonesome and decayed on the furthest reaches of town, in the middle of a large dusty lot. There were windows to the Church, but they were all broken. Like eye sockets without eyeballs, the Church stared blindly at the road that passed it.

"Can we even go in? I mean, is it open?"

"It must be. Remember my dream?"

"Where are the others then?"

Mara laughed. "I might be early," she said. "Or late."

"Are you sure we should be doing this? Today? People might be worried. I think something big—"

"Do you think they cared when they put me in a foster home?" she snapped.

Felicia stopped. "I'm sorry," she said. "I didn't mean to—"

Mara shook her head. "Forget it. Let's check it out."

Above, the black shape drifted further, muting the sun's rays. The whole town was silent; the crunch of earth beneath their sneakers seemed to Felicia the loudest thing she'd ever heard. She imagined the sound reverberating up to the sky, where the black shape listened. The thought unsettled her. Whatever was up there made the hairs on her arms stand up, like static electricity.

The door to the Church was old and thin and it flew open when Mara pushed it. She squealed in delight at the loud clap it made as it slammed into the wall. "Wow," she said, more to herself than Felicia.

The place could've been a church, the same way any building could be called a home. There were no features that made it feel like one place or another, just a large white space with paint-flecked pillars. There was a red couch with patches of fabric missing, yellow foam spilling from its wounds. There were beer bottles, empty, lined against the far wall. The smell of stale urine and salt permeated the air.

"It's not what I expected," said Felicia.

Mara crossed her arms. "It's exactly what I expected."

Felicia didn't want to know what Mara meant. "We've seen it. It's just an old building," she said, making her voice light. "Just a dumb old building."

But Mara kept walking. "It's just like my dream," she said. She turned to Felicia, raising a finger to her neck, tracing the path of her esophagus. "I can feel them."

Another voice, soft and young, came lilting through the floorboards.

"You had the dream too?"

It sounded like the voice of a little boy, a child, not too much younger than them.

Mara stepped on tiptoes, her hands cupping her ear. "Who's there?" she asked.

The voice, as cold as river water, said, *"My name's Tommy. But there's others here too."*

Mara searched for the source of the voice. "Am I the last of us?"

A new voice spoke up, a girl this time: *"We've been waiting for you."*

"What does that mean?" asked Felicia.

Mara turned to her friend, her hands outstretched, beckoning. "C'mon, Fee," she said.

Felicia started backward, to the door. "What does that mean?"

A voice, from the floor, another girl. "*She's not supposed to be here, you know.*"

Felicia looked to the floor. She closed her eyes and for just a moment, she thought she could hear them breathing from the shadows.

Then:

"*Is she here to help us?*"

"*You should come down here.*"

"*Yes! Come down here! It's so much better in the dark!*"

"*Do you hear them too? Do they talk to you?*"

"*We're going to live forever; they said they'll take us to see the stars.*"

The voices all came at once, excitable, babbling over each other like old friends. Mara looked down at the floor. "How do I get to you?"

"*The door!*" said one of the voices, and then they were all shouting it from the floorboards. "*The door! The door! The door!*"

It was just a square cut into the floor on hinges. Felicia thought it looked like one of those trap doors magicians use. It fell open, whooshing in the blackness.

Mara was at the opening before Felicia could even speak. Then, she was climbing in, disappearing.

"Mara, wait," she said, finally. "You don't know what's down there."

She took a step toward her friend, Mara's head was all that remained above the floor. "I was hoping you'd go with me."

"*She can't! She wasn't chosen!*"

"I could choose her, maybe. I bet we could turn her if we wanted. Or maybe she could just help us. We could protect her."

There was silence, jabbering from the black basement.

"*Can you trust her?*"

"Of course I can trust her," said Mara. "She's my best friend."

"*Okay, okay. She has to stay up there. She can't see us until the sun goes out.*"

Mara nodded. She looked at her friend. "It won't be too long. That's part of the whole deal. I have to go down there and wait for a little bit." She sounded apologetic. "I want you to wait for me. I want you to see what's coming. For the first time —for the first time—things will be different, I guess."

Felicia could only guess what that would mean. One black eye and Mara considered her an equal in suffering. Her friend took another step down toward the basement and she could hear the other children breathing, excited, waiting. "*Welcome, Mara!*" they squealed.

Outside, the sky darkened. Felicia stood alone in the Church, frozen in place, listening to the children beneath the floorboards. They were tittering, speaking in rapid excitement.

"What are you waiting for?" asked Felicia.

One of the children answered. "*The dark.*"

"Oh."

"*It's going to happen!*"

"*Finally.*"

"*We're just waiting now.*"

"*We just have to be patient.*"

"*It's happening everywhere, you know? It's all kids too.*"

And now Mara's voice was amongst them, bright and fluid. "*I'm going to go back to my house after this,*" she said. "*Then, I'm going to go back to school.*"

Felicia paced above. *I shouldn't be hearing this.*

She looked out the blinded eyes of the window and was disturbed to see that the sun was almost gone. Twilight's last seconds trapped her. The air was gray and cold. And now, the silence had been broken.

An image flashed in her head.

"*Felicia, am I doing it?*"

Felicia staggered above the children. She held her hands to her head.

"*You're doing it! You're doing it!*" the other children squealed.

She was running through the night, down the streets of another small town. The darkness let her grow in a way the sun never could.

Felicia felt like she was going to vomit. "Is this you?" she asked.

She fell down to the floorboards and Mara whispered through them, her words like honey in her ears. "*No,*" she said. "*This isn't me. Not yet.*"

A family huddled together, a bald man with a gun. "Get out of here, get out of here," screamed the father. Muzzle flash. A brief, sharp pain. But nothing. Teeth. Screaming. Blood. Iron in her mouth.

Felicia gasped.

Another scene.

This time, they were together, as one. She could feel Mara guiding her. Pulling her along.

They were in the same home.

The mother and father were in pieces, their bodies torn limb to limb. Their blood ran down Mara's throat. They stepped forward, their head skimming across the ceiling.

"Oh God, Mara, please don't. Don't hurt them."

The kids were hiding under the bed. Mara knew this somehow. And because Mara knew this, so did Felicia.

"*I would never hurt them.*"

Mara reached out to touch them, the same way she reached out to touch Felicia.

Suddenly, Mara could see inside of them. Felicia wanted to turn away. She saw them cowering, but on a different night, from a different monster.

"You see? They're just like me."

The children were quaking, yes, and Felicia could see that it was true. She looked to the other room, breaking from Mara's vision for only a moment, to see the dead husband and wife. Their bodies intertwined in frozen panic. Intestines crawled out of the open wounds in their stomachs. They were white like chalk. Felicia wondered if Mara had seen her mother like that when her father had cut her throat. She wondered if she'd felt a thrill of resolution when he put the shotgun under his chin.

The children scratched at their cigarette burns. Felicia did not know whether they were real, from the present or the future. But Mara talked to them, anyway. "It's okay," she said. "You're safe."

When Mara released her, she realized her head was resting in her own vomit. She had blacked out. Other beings danced within her skull.

"Are you sure you want her, Mara?"

"I don't think she's like us."

"She wasn't chosen. Not everyone can be chosen."

She stopped, listened. Tried to stand.

"You saw it too."

"Her dad went to jail. What did your dad get?"

She was unsteady, but on two feet. She went to the window.

"He only hit her, just once. What did he do to you?"

A low hum.

She put her hands on the windowsill as the children of the eclipse weighed her merits. She looked up to the sky. The black shape had overtaken the sun almost completely, leaving only a tiny sliver of yellow. Her heart dropped. She wondered if the televisions had come back on, if the news had started to report again.

"Mara?" she said.

The children quieted.

"Yes, Fee?"

The Church seemed to insist upon her, for some sort of action, for some sort of resolve. "I don't know what to do," she said, and she realized her voice was shaking.

"It's different down here, with others like me." Her voice was soft and loud, it felt like her lips were right up against the bottom of the floor. *"They're right, I think. People like us, we can only grow in the dark. You... you—I don't know, Fee. I needed a friend to be there with me, because I was scared. But, now that I'm here..."*

Felicia backed away, shivering. A lump was caught in her throat, her eyes were wet. "Okay, Mara," she said weakly. "Okay, I'll go." She felt silly for crying, despite the sour fear that sloshed around inside her. She didn't want to stay with Mara, she realized. She just wanted Mara to *want* her to stay with her.

She backed out of the door and ran, hot tears stinging her red cheeks. The hum grew louder as the last bit of sun was swallowed by the shape in the sky. She raced down Main, past the empty storefronts, feeling a sense of awe as she did. Whatever was up there demanded the forsaken.

The afternoon had been devoured and now she could see a thousand stars jumping as she ran harder and further from the Church. She realized where she was running just as soon as she got there. A safe place, imperfect as it was. She ran up the front steps and swung open the door and didn't stop to breathe until her mother took her in her arms. "Are you okay? What's happening? Why aren't you in school? We're supposed to be quiet, Fee. Shh, we're supposed to be quiet."

They sat on the couch in darkness, holding each other's hands. The lights had all been turned out. Down the street, there was the laughter of children. It sounded like the high keys of a piano, bright and mellifluous.

"They shouldn't be out," said her mother.

Felicia held her breath and looked out the window.

As her eyes adjusted, she saw a face in the window. Bright red hair collected in a savage mane, fungi gathered in chips of barnacles across her face. She was tall now, her head reaching the top of the window frame. She had grown so much that her eyes seemed abnormally small for her head, like black pin pricks. Her open mouth revealed dozens of sharp, translucent teeth. In the dark, she had the faintest glow, a greenish aura that pulsed slowly.

I'm sorry, she thought.

The words appeared within her, just as if they were her own: *I know.*

There were screams down the street, punctuated with the flute-like melody of a child's glee.

Felicia gripped her mother's hand tight, and they huddled together as they heard the children play.

ZERO BOUNDARIES
PODCAST: EPISODE 182

[**E**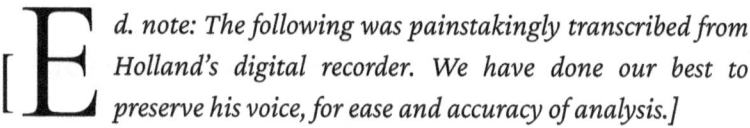*d. note: The following was painstakingly transcribed from Holland's digital recorder. We have done our best to preserve his voice, for ease and accuracy of analysis.]*

[...]

Alright, so, I think this is rolling. Well, wait—fuck. Yeah. Okay. We're on, I'm recording. Can I even say rolling anymore, is that allowed? Does a digital recorder *roll?*

Whatever your verb preference, this is episode one-eight-two of Zero Boundaries, *the* premiere paranormal urban exploration podcast; and this time, we're going live! Well, almost—I'm recording live on the scene, but you guys will hear it whenever it hits iTunes or whatever. Losers.

. . .

[*Ed. note: Zero Boundaries is no longer available online for the greater listening public.*]

Right now, speaking from my digital recording device, I'm parked at a campsite on the edge of Olympic National Park in Washington state, and I'm about to go on a week long hike in an attempt to piece together a mystery that won't stop unraveling. And because I'm *in the field*, so to speak, I'm going to be recording all my thoughts.

And what mysteries does this lush, green, beautiful forest hold?

Hundreds of missing people, for one. But make no mistake, that's only where the story *begins*. To pass the time on the trail, I've brought all my research with me. Throughout the next week, I'll lay out everything I know about the Black Pilgrimage, while—drum roll—I'm actually walking it. I take my first steps on the trail tomorrow morning, until then, this is Zero Boundaries.

[...]

I've been hiking for about, oh, let's say three hours now. I've just been kinda enjoying the scene, really, it's one of those things you have to see to appreciate. Sun is out, air smells crisp and clean, I don't think I'll mind roughing it in these parts.

So, just a recap for all those who don't know how this works. I'm going to be recording this episode in the forest itself, I have a couple fully charged batteries for my recorder, and I'm assured I could record a hundred hours straight if I wished. If you remember the Detroit episode where we spent the night in the haunted factory, this is gonna be kinda like that, except way more ambitious. I'll explore the mystery, kinda go through the facts in my downtime and report anything I see or hear. It'll be fun, and hopefully—spooky.

To complete the experience, I also brought a camera and when I get home I'll post some stuff to the Zero Boundaries blog, just so, you know, you can get the whole *picture*. Yeah, I know, I know, I'll be here all week—literally. Double zinger.

[*Ed note: Blog no longer exists. Unfortunately, to our knowledge, no pictures have been recovered yet.*]

But anyways, let's get to why I'm here. The Black Pilgrimage. What paranormal investigator Kipler Roshe called "an unacknowledged holocaust, the most prolific serial killing in the history of the human race." A deadly trail that some say is the Pacific Northwest's Bermuda Triangle; discovered in part by non-profit Missing But Not Forgotten, a foundation intent on solving missing persons mysteries, with the help of a large and active community user-group. The site's flagship application, The Missing Map, was used as a tool to help keep track of high-risk areas and to highlight the possibility of a human trafficking ring operating in the United States. A couple of users local to Washington, noticed the high density of dots in and around the perimeter of the forest and from there, the ball started to roll.

Who were these people, who all so suddenly vanished? Well, at first glance, they had no connection to each other at all. They were normal people who lived quiet lives both online and off, flew to the Northwest, headed off towards the forest and were never heard of again.

One of the most interesting pieces of evidence, in regards to a sort of anomaly, is this blog post by Jeff Koons, a man who allegedly sat next to a woman named Marcy Pollock on a plane ride to Seattle. Koons found out the woman was missing a couple weeks after his flight, and came forward to reveal his recollections in hopes they could help authorities.

He writes, "She was quiet, kinda tense, maybe a little sad [...] I tried to lighten the mood with her a couple times and chatted a bit. I asked her if she lived in Seattle, and she said, 'No, I'm just going home.' I took that to mean she grew up there, but moved away. The wording stuck with me though."

[*Ed. note: Holland misquotes Koons' blog post here. In the original post, Koons writes that she says, "No, I'm coming home." There are no known records of Marcy Pollock having any connections to Seattle or the Northwest.*]

The last places the missing are seen are often at gas stations, campsites, or sometimes on the trail itself. And to be true to the case, I've made all the obvious stops in the obvious places. Some listeners have suggested, in preparation for our Black Pilgrimage episode, that someone who works at one of these common sites is scoping potential victims. If this is true, I've left a strong enough trail for anyone to follow. They know where I'm going, the only thing I didn't tell them was my real name and what I was doing here.

[*Ed. note: This was Holland's first misstep. The pseudonyms he left at various hotels, restaurants, gas stations obfuscated his comings and goings. He intentionally chose bland names like Robert Brown*] *or Jeff Williams, names found at other registries in the area, thus widening the search when it could have been more focused.*]

According to my map, I've made it to my first real stopping point today. Time to set up camp. Tomorrow, I'll tell you about the little mystery that's guiding my journey and how it connects to the Black Pilgrimage. Peace out!

[...]

I'm eating breakfast now, and I'm eating the good shit. Baked beans cooked over a campfire, authentically smoked-in flavor. The night was quiet, I heard a couple of animals but nothing too Blair Witchy. Slept pretty decent, but I'm a city boy, and I reserve the right to be torn up from a day of hiking.

Anyways, I said yesterday I was at my first real stopping point. Which means I should probably talk about the Map.

If I were to describe it to you, you'd think it rather unremarkable. This is the McAllister Map, this is what is leading me onward.

For fifteen years, the McAllister Map has been passed around on the internet as a lesser known piece of internet folklore. Some users of sites such as 4chan and Reddit recall seeing it posted occasionally, dating from around the early millennium onward. Much of its rather limited popularity came from its unnerving visual factor. Basically, if you look at it, and I'll be posting this to my blog along with any other pictures I come up with, you'll see that it looks pretty creepy.

But, initially, anyways, that was the problem with the McAllister Map— it didn't have any real staying power. It didn't have a name or a purpose like Slenderman, therefore never experienced the same sort of growth. Back then, the names floating around were sillier and more decidedly horrific, like Satan's Eye, or Worm Waves. It wasn't even widely acknowledged as a map back then, not until a user from a forum dedicated to unresolved mysteries commented that the map was of Olympic National Park. From there, one map was connected to the other and the fervor began.

Internet researchers pinpointed the first sharing of the map back to 2001 in the golden age of online piracy. It was posted to an anonymous and now defunct image board at 9:36 pm October 12th. There were a couple comments, all of them lowercase, misspelled, and not altogether too interesting. But, someone who saw it there, downloaded it and then included it in a file titled creepy.exe. It was not actually executable, but simply an image gallery. Most agree that the title was likely written by a kid who thought it sounded 'techy.' The file contained a host of typical creepy images, one of which was the McAllister Map. Creepy.exe became a starter kit of sorts for kids on the internet, and this is when the image started to spread, albeit modestly.

But once the Black Pilgrimage became a specifically North-west phenomenon, the Map took on a new weight as users noticed similarities. The comparison took minutes to make, and pretty soon commenters were pointing out that both depicted Olympic National Park, and more disturbingly, the entry points on the McAllister Map correlated with the largest congregation of dots on the Missing Map. People began to wonder how it came to be, what it was, and when it was made.

Well, the first clue was the map itself, not what was drawn upon it, but the original untainted map. Users matched it to a road map published in 1952, stocked in gas stations and convenience stores across the United States. On the blotch of green that is Olympic National Park, the black lines were drawn, probably in marker, designating a number of trails that all led to the same spot, in the shadow of Mt. Olympus. The McAllister Map is a black and white scan of that map, the scan's distortive quality highlighting its sinister undertones with the ragged, stark aesthetic of horror movies like *The Ring, The Grudge,* and earlier, *Seven*—this coincidence, along with the growing mystery surrounding the Black Pilgrimage, cemented the McAllister Map as more than just a map, but something innately *sinister.*

The plot thickened when a man named Buck Pfarrer claimed to have the original download on an old computer, saved on a whim from the original image board. Pfarrer said, in a now lost, but endlessly screenshotted MySpace post, "My friend saw the picture of the map and sent it my way, and when I saw it, I was immediately thirteen again. I remember seeing it, not thinking much of it, and then saving it. But back then, I saved everything. The map was weird and kinda cool to look at. When he told me that it was becoming a big deal, I had to dig out my old computer."

Pfarrer did the mystery a huge service by finding the original download and uploading it, and an even bigger service by exposing its metadata, revealing the file to have been uploaded by a Louis McAllister. All it needed was a name, and the McAllister Map became canonized into internet folklore.

We're going to switch gears before we get back to Louis McAllister, but remember that name, because it's not the last time you'll hear it.

[...]

. . .

On each trail, or Veins as they've started to be called, are smaller dots—internet commenters call them bloodclots. Charming, right? Well, I've been hiking for a while now, and I think I've found my first bloodclot. Should just be over the hill here.

So, no one actually knows for sure what these represent, but as we get deeper into the tangential material surrounding the Black Pilgrimage, the McAllister Map, and *The Damned Abattoir*, more theories will present themselves. The general consensus is that they are pit stops of some sort. Either way, we're about to find out for sure very soon.

[*Ed. Note: Holland mentions* The Damned Abattoir *but never speaks about it at length, save for a few allusions. It is not yet clear whether Holland acquired a copy, or is using what he has seen online as a reference point.*]

[...]

Holy shit.

I—

Oh my God.

This is amazing.

I can't—

[inaudible]

This is... incredible. So. Here. Let me try to describe this. I'm looking at the Vein I'm following, and this is the first of two bloodclots before we reach the end of the Map. I can't even— I'm seriously so excited right now. This is real headway, no one has seen this before and lived to tell the tale. Alright, let me take a deep breath. Fuck, fuck, fuck! This is awesome.

So, I was walking up this hill. It was super rocky, but still, let me tell ya', beautiful, gorgeous. Green on everything. Even the moss here is fluorescent. I get to the top and the trail tells me to steer left down the other side of the hill, which leads to a small valley. Down in the center of the valley, which is maybe, let's say about two-hundred feet of flatland flanked by heavily wooded hills, there is a structure. Man made, definitely; stone, but overgrown with vines and moss. It looks like an arch, kind of Stonehenge-ish, you know? I'm not an expert on this stuff, so I'm going to take a lot of pictures, because I want to know when this was built, but I'm going to guess sometime in the last hundred years.

This is amazing, and it's getting dark. I'm gonna camp here for the night and gather some more data to take back with me.

[...]

Alright, it's morning. I'm still alive. No devils whispering in my ears, although I'm pretty sure someone did walk through my camp last night, but I'm thinking it was probably just another hiker.

Freaked me out a little bit when it happened, but what are you going to do? I'm in the woods, people hike. Just for the record, I didn't see the hiker, but I did hear him and I can see his footprints right now. I'm taking some more pictures for the blog, uh, just in case.

Just to be clear, I'm not fearful for myself right now, I'm more concerned that I'm documenting the latest victim to fall into the Black Pilgrimage. So, hopefully, that's not what's happened here. Either way, time to break camp.

[...]

On the trail again, saying goodbye to our first bloodclot. Looks like my trail is taking me in a different direction than the footsteps of our fellow traveler. Am I a pussy for saying I'm relieved. Yes?

Fair enough.

[...]

Changing gears here, another piece of the puzzle. More fodder from message boards of days past. Remember when discussion boards were big? Before all discussion was centered in Facebook groups? It's a thing of wonder, really.

I'm on the trail right now so forgive my foot-stomping in the background.

This next thing—I actually knew about this before I ever got into this Black Pilgrimage stuff. Way before. A Zero Boundaries listener tagged me in a story and I thought at the time it was a cute mystery—small potatoes, but still—intriguing. It was a video pulled from a local news broadcast out of Bismarck, North Dakota, a little fluff piece surrounding a seventy-three year old blind woman who paints. They talk a little about her art, why she chose painting, her struggles with her disability, and her can-do optimism. Meanwhile, they cut to some folks who I assume are from the Bismarck art scene and they all have some really nice things to say about her painting technique.

Nice, right? It's a fun story that you could probably see *your* local news running too. The paintings are no great mystery, they tend toward the abstract and are almost purely expressionistic—she is blind after all—but they do have a very raw quality to them that makes them appealing. Well, there's one scene in the video where the interviewer is standing in Abby's studio and they're talking about her art. They go through a couple of her paintings and she talks a little about them. In the background of the studio, we see all these paintings hanging on the wall, and this is where whoever uploaded the video zooms in and digitally circles a single painting. You can barely see it, and the video itself was produced around 1996, so the quality isn't quite up to snuff in the first place, but you can see, pretty clearly, that this painting in the background is the only of the set that *isn't* abstract. It's a mountain, surrounded by forest, and it's tucked into the corner of her display.

Well, this definitely raised an eyebrow for me at the time, but I shrugged it off and moved on. I mean, there's the obvious answer here: Abigail Zdor wasn't always blind and she painted the nature scene back when she had sight. Boom. Case closed.

Except, that's not correct in the least. Abigail Zdor was born blind due to Leber's Congenital Amaurosis, an inherited disease. She has never known sight.

[*Ed. Note: It is possible Abigail Zdor possessed limited sight throughout, or early in her life. Holland seems confused, or is sensationalizing Zdor's story. However, it is still a remarkable feat for her to have painted this piece. Either way, it is suggested that her sight is in parallel with* TDA.]

. . .

With that in mind, new questions emerge. Did she actually paint this? Was it purchased? Would a blind woman purchase someone else's art? Does she personally enjoy art or does she just like the way it allows her to express herself? One of our users went online and did some research. FreshJack13 found a great number of her paintings on a BigCartel site run by her surviving family. Abby died in 2004 and wanted her paintings to be sold cheaply to people who would appreciate them. Well, what do you know, the mountain painting wasn't there, and for good reason too: it was sold four years ago.

You gotta give credit to FreshJack13, because he goes a lot deeper than your average researcher. He found the painting online, a high resolution scan and a title. But where did he find it? A deep web message board called The Abattoir. The painting? *The Red.*

[*Ed Note: Abattoir user Doug Jackson has claimed to be FreshJack13, and has submitted screenshots of emails sent between himself and Holland as proof.*]

But with a clear scan we can see a lot more detail, in fact, as soon as we posted a mini-episode mystery of the scan we knew we were onto something a lot bigger. Almost instantly, our Northwest readers chimed in. The painting was of Mt. Olympus, the mountain I can see right now, looming, and if I'm being totally honest, I'm fairly close to the painting's perspective, about a day's hike from the next bloodclot.

It's chilling to see it like this, because the deeper you get into the Black Pilgrimage, the more things connect, never exact, but they have a way of falling into place.

The painting, why is it called *The Red*? There's no red in it, it's just motel art— albeit more ominous. The reason is another of those puzzle pieces, one that never quite fits into place, but another question to inspire endless debate.

But, let's deal with The Abattoir first. Hidden on the deep web, discovered by FreshJack13 from a lone link in an occult forum that's been dead for about a decade, is an old school message board centered around a mystery. Well, that's not quite the right way to put it—it's populated by *devotees* of a mystery.

Anyways, the—
[*inaudible*]

[...]

Alright, first big accident of the whole trip. Talking to myself, tripped. That about sums it up. If I'm correct, I'm still about two days from the end of the journey, with a bloodclot on the radar for tomorrow. I'm just torn up right now, I fell down into a, uh, I don't know, a ravine? Is that right? I guess so. Hit a lot of trees on the way down, I might've twisted my ankle, which is the majority of the pain I'm feeling right now, but hopefully, it's not actually sprained. I managed to get myself back to where I tripped and a little farther, but I'm still about a mile short of where I originally wanted to stop.

It's still light out, and it will be for another three or four hours, but I'm going to set up camp and try to rest my foot. Peace out.

[...]

· · ·

[*Rustling noises, footsteps. The sound of voices, individually inaudible.*]

[*Ed. Note: Sound file available in* Primary Documents Forum.]

[...]

[*Ed. Note: From here on out, Holland starts to sound fatigued, possibly dazed from the encounter he had the previous night. This could also be a compounding of factors, including exposure to the elements and potential injuries. From* The Damned Abattoir: *"They walk and they shamble, through the woods like a flock of sheep. They walk all day and they walk all night, and I smell like bourbon and brains."*]

I don't know what to think anymore. I was afraid to leave the tent this morning, you know? I didn't want to get out of my fucking tent.

I'm taking pictures of the footprints, all that kind of stuff, I know I need to, but it's hard, because right now I'm not sure—

I'm just going to keep doing what I'm doing. But, make no mistake, they were here. I can see the footprints, about ten of them, and they were all around the tent, and they were talking to me. But I don't know what they were saying. Would it be cowardly to just convince myself it was a dream and move on? I'm kicking myself for turning on my recorder at all...yay, Zero Boundaries Podcast, the premiere paranormal—

[*Holland trails off and says nothing for forty-three seconds*]

This is a lot harder than I thought it was going to be. A lot harder. I'm going to eat something, and then I'm going to the next bloodclot. God help me, I am a stupid man.

[...]

I'm a little shaken up still. It's hard to describe how I'm feeling, because, well, I've never had to feel anything like this before. I'm isolated. Like really isolated. If I wanted to get back to civilization, I'd probably have to hike a good fifty miles.

I mean, it all fits together, right? That's what makes a good mystery, is that at the end, you can see the pieces fall into place? Well, right now, I'm wondering, you know, what if this isn't a good mystery? What if this is a bad mystery?

I'm getting tired, I've only been hiking for an hour, and I'm tired. I'll try to push through, God, where were we? Oh yeah.

[*Seven seconds of silence, papers shuffling*]

The Abattoir is a forum on the deep web, a scary term for the internet that isn't part of search engine databases. Imagine all the websites you go to being on a... map. Wait, sure, a map. Not *the* Map, but a map, like a road map. Uh... it's all documented, you can trace the lines, outline it with marker if you want, make stops along the way. But, now imagine some cities haven't been put on the map yet, and to get there, you just need to *know* how to get there. Well, that's the deep web. That's The Abattoir, it's not cataloged and you won't find it on any maps, but it's there. And this is where we start to go deep, maybe too deep if you ask me.

The Abattoir is a dedicated forum for everything related to the Black Pilgrimage. If we'd found it a long time ago, we'd have saved a lot of legwork. But the truth of the matter is that it has to already be known. It's like the chicken and the egg, how do you find a way to know something you're already supposed to know?

God, I feel like I'm going to be sick.

You know all those women who write to serial killers? The ones who fall in love with them? The Abattoir is a lot like that. The masthead is made up of the faces of the missing. You'd think, like, maybe it's like, for remembrance. They're trying to help the families, or something. But look at the name: The Abattoir. Do you know what an Abattoir is? Do you?

It's a slaughterhouse, man.

[*Ed. Note: It is possible that Holland is congested here as the tone of his voice changes. Some users claim to hear sniffling too, after "...the masthead" and later, "...eloquent user speculation." Users are split on whether the congestion is emotional or viral.*]

This is the slaughterhouse. The forest, a giant meat grinder.

They have threads upon threads with thousands of pages of eloquent user speculation. We were talking about *The Red,* right? Well, they know all about it. They've deconstructed the technique, have a rough timeline of when it was painted, and they know who bought it.

Remember McAllister, the kid who uploaded the Map, the one who gave it its namesake? Well, guess who bought *The Red.* Go ahead, fucking guess. Another McAllister, the Second this time, his father.

It just keeps going deeper. You can ask yourself why, you can ask yourself why so many times, but it never comes together.

Everyone wonders what they're doing now, who they are. But you don't need the Abattoir to figure that out.

At the age of fifteen, Louis was found guilty for the murder of a twelve year old girl. Before that, he was known as a quiet kid with a good family. That's right, ask anyone who knows them, the McAllisters are a good family. But then again, most of these people aren't on The Abattoir, right?

[Ed. Note: Most users remain anonymous.]

Louis was quiet, his mom and dad were around a lot, they were decently upper middle class. But, Louis would sometimes act out in school, act goofy to get attention. Some people thought he had undiagnosed ADHD. And then, one night, he lured a younger girl out of her house, and killed her in the forested area of a nearby park. Details are vague, of course, but someone in the police department came up with the fact that he pulled out her eyes, cut off one of her fingers, then buried them nearby.

[Ed. Note: Another parallel from The Damned Abattoir: "I buried pieces of her along the trail, in the hopes that her flesh would act as seedlings, and: grow."]

Louis McAllister III is in prison for life. His family has spoken out against his actions, have condemned them vehemently, and have offered nothing but support to the family of the girl. Still, still—there isn't a week that McAllister II misses a visit with his son.

I'm looking at the Map now, and I'm getting close, really close. Chillingly close, I'm in spitting distance of the perspective from *The Red*. It's like I'm seeing the painting right now, it's unreal.

[...]

The ground, it's quicksand, I guess; I'm at a loss for words. I'm looking up, right now, at Mt. Olympus. I feel sick, I feel tired, I feel out of my element, and right this second, I am seeing *The Red* in a way no high def scan can ever represent. But, the ground, it's like a marsh.

I'm at the bloodclot, the exact same perspective Abby Zdor painted. Jesus fucking Christ, the exact same, it's—I don't know what to say. There's no structure, nothing man-made, just this marsh and the view.

I can't tell if I'm underwhelmed or terrified. I don't know what I can say about any of this anymore. All I can think about is the fact that I'm starting to warm up to the idea that I might not make it out of here. Is that too dramatic to say? Maybe. Maybe. I might be stuck here, I might be the—

[*Holland exhales, slowly. Theatrically, even. Some users believe Holland had already prepared this line before he entered the forest and is now using it, regardless of his dire situation.*]

I might be the latest Black Pilgrim.

I don't even know what to think about that. I can see it now, my face, my smiling face will appear in newspapers, they'll take quotes from my friends, they'll ask my family what I was like growing up. All this will be published, then it will be forgotten. And the only place I'll survive is on The Abattoir, they might even put me on the masthead. They'll plot my course and imagine my terror at what I might've seen, what might've happened to me.

You know, on The Abattoir, they have a forum called The Goodbye? You know what they post there? Well, it's right there, right there in the name. It's just a natural extension of the hobby. Once you start researching the Black Pilgrimage, eventually, you'll want to take the trip yourself. Once you read the literature, once you see all the facts—the mystery becomes too great, and when it's time, when you finish your tattered copy of *The Damned Abattoir*, when you've discussed the disappearances until you've memorized all the canonical victims, when you've seen *The Red*, when you've read about the McAllister murder, when you start changing your desktop backgrounds to pictures of the forest, when nothing else interests you:

You say Goodbye, and venture onwards, as a fellow Pilgrim.

[...]

The marsh—
    [*inaudible*]

[...]

[*Ed. Note: The dull roar in the background makes the audio difficult to hear, but as user BEDLAM2 suggested, it is clear that Holland is reciting the last lines of* The Damned Abattoir, *where the narrator, in free verse, gives himself over to an unnatural, living structure, most often referred to as the Tower.*]

Bricks mortared,
    sealed and stuck with
    dice and pin-ups
    We build, we build,
    forever.

[end of transcription]

Ed. Note: Tape was found twenty-four miles in, following the McAllister Map's trajectory, starting from Vein 4 with some minor deviations. The above was transcribed for ease of analysis. Lester Holland was never found by authorities, but this recording was found and sent in by listener TheLast_45. Please do your due diligence and keep these materials off the greater web.

All materials are presented to you by THE ABATTOIR.

LOST FUTURES, DEVOURED PASTS

I did not think there was anything wrong when I woke up that Saturday morning. Rose was in bed, snuggled against me, and I was snuggled against her. I'm an early riser though. I get restless. My bones hurt in bed. She never understands when I tell her that. She says, "How can your bones hurt? You're just lying there." But they do, so I rolled up out of bed and put on my jeans, bra, and T-shirt and quickly did my makeup. Rose and I have been together for three years, but I still prefer to do these things when she sleeps.

Every so often, I'd peer out from our shared bathroom and watch her. Sometimes, she'd toss and turn and talk in her sleep and I'd say, "Hey, Rose, are you up?" but get nothing in return. Not even a snore.

I had a cup of coffee in hand and a pot of chamomile tea on its way to boiling (milk and honey in waiting, but never added —Rose liked to do that herself), when I heard her scream.

She had the blanket covering her, hitched up to her neck. Her eyes were wide and her mouth gaped. Blood flushed her cheeks. There were tears. She was sniffling.

"Rose? Are you okay?"

"Who are you?"

"Is this a joke?"

"Who are you?"

My guts twisted. "What's going on? Are you asleep?" I felt silly asking her that, but it was the only thing I could think of that would explain this reaction. A nightmare, some sort of waking nightmare.

"No, no, no. I'm not asleep." Her eyes darted around the room, searching. "Where am I?"

"Rose, wake up." I kept my voice steady, I was used to doing that. I worked at a mortuary and always had to be the one to mix business and sorrow. The ability to ask someone for their credit card while they're screaming at God, "Why, why, why?" is a learned skill. No regular person should know how to do it.

"I'm not asleep." Her eyes narrowed. "I remember you."

"I should hope so."

"From a long time ago."

"Last night."

She shook her head. "Longer."

"When?"

"I don't know. I wasn't here before." Panic seeped into her voice. "I haven't been here in ages!"

I saw no other option than to play along. Slowly, I asked, "What can I do to help?"

Her head turned toward me—sharp and sudden. "I want you to answer my questions."

"Okay," I said. "Sure. Whatever you say."

She looked around the room. "I need to get dressed. Can you give me some privacy?" She pointed to the dresser. "Are those my clothes in there?"

"Yes," I said.

She nodded. "Give me a minute."

I did as she requested, departing to the kitchen where I reheated her tea and laid out her milk and honey just as I always did. When she came out, she wore a sundress.

"I have tea for you."

"Thank you."

Rose sat across from me, looking at the cup, the milk, the little translucent bear half-filled with honey. "I remember this," she said. "We used to be together."

"We still are," I said. My tone was more hopeful than I anticipated.

"I have questions."

"Ask them."

She did. The year, the date, the fundamentals of our relationship—I answered each, gamely suppressing insult. Sometimes, there was a glimmer of recollection. She would nod her head and give me a half-smile and say something like, "Oh, yeah, I remember that." The questions came at a steady pace, and then slowed down. I thought, for a moment, that everything was going to be alright. What do they call it? A brain fart? Yeah, that's what this was, just one long rumbling brain fart.

But then she'd discover a new thread and the questions would start again. Now, it was her childhood. Did I know her as a child? No. Did she ever tell any stories about herself as a child? Sure. Could I tell her one? I did my best.

"I haven't been here, I said that right?"

"Yes, you said that. Where have you been?"

"I died not too long ago. I was sixty-eight."

"You don't look dead."

"My name was Dorothy Rogers."

I resisted the urge to ask her if I should call the hospital.

"I had a different life. I wasn't married to a woman, I was married to a man. He died before me, his name was Lenny."

"*Rose*," I said, emphasizing the name I knew her by. "You said you remembered me. How could you remember me if you were Dorothy? I've never met a Dorothy in my life."

"Because when I was a little girl, I had a dream. It's been so many years and I can't remember all of it, but I can remember parts of it. It all happened in the space of a blink and I can remember *you* or parts of you."

"What do you remember?"

"I remember you bringing me tea. I remember us going to New York, people watching. Snapshots. That's it. Just snapshots."

"Are you trying to leave me? If you want to leave me you can go."

"You don't under*stand*," she said. She was getting angry, I could tell. Whenever she got angry she'd stress her final syllable. "You see me here, right now, in one unbroken piece. But I'm not me. Or rather, I'm not only me. I've lived two lives. I have two people inside of me, in two different times. Except now, one is dead. I think I used to come here when I dreamed. Maybe I went back to Dorothy when I dreamed here."

This was getting absurd. "I need to call a doctor. We have insurance. You never asked that, but we do. Something's wrong with your brain."

"I don't need to go to the doctor," she said. Her eyes glimmered with tears. I always felt bad that I thought she was prettier when she was crying. "I need to tell you about how I died."

I grit my teeth. "Alright then, tell me."

"I lived in a house in Missoula. That's far away from here, I know, but I grew up there and never left. I had friends there. I met Lenny there and he was the sort of guy that's easy to fall in love with. Lenny and I were good together. He worked as a librarian."

Watching Rose talk about another lover made me want to

lash out. But I withheld any reaction, only nodding for her to continue.

"Lenny and I retired pretty handsomely in a nice house on the outskirts, closer to the woods. Lenny made sure books lined the walls, up and down. It was like living in our own private library. I liked to read, but Lenny loved it. We'd spend our mornings sunning on the back deck with our coffee and tea, listening to the birds while reading.

"But Lenny wasn't well. I think that's what happened. Lenny wasn't well and he was starting to act strangely. He started writing. I always was bothering him to start a book but I had also always expected him to let me read it. But he kept it hidden. He began writing in our basement. He would go on nighttime walks. He said to me, 'I'm having trouble sleeping.' in that gruff sort of voice he always put on whenever he was trying to complain without complaining. I think he always felt a little effete because he was a librarian and that was seen as a woman's job, so he made up for it in other ways. His voice was one of them.

"I was alone in our house one night, sitting and wondering what was going wrong. I was scared for his health. We were in our sixties, but that's not *that* old. We still had time, I thought. Three weeks later, Lenny died in his sleep. I woke up next to him and he was cold. He was usually so warm. I used to call him my furnace. To feel him like that revolted me. I didn't like it at all. Here was my husband, dead, and I couldn't stand to touch him. It makes me sad just to think about it."

She read the grimace I wore on my face.

"But you don't want to hear about that. Who would? I remember you too. A very long time ago and I think Lenny was bothered by my memories of us here. I learned to shut up about it and pretty soon those memories were gone, like they never happened. They slipped away from me, the way dreams do. Now that I think about it, I think that's why I read so much science-fiction growing up. I always had crazy ideas about the future, but it was because I lived it, I suppose.

"When they took his body away, the house was lonely. Quiet, like a cave. My voice and footsteps echoed. I didn't want to stay there anymore. It was *our* place. But now, it was only mine and that didn't seem right. I'd read everything there was to read about death and grief, including morbid statistics about how when one person in a couple dies, the other is sure to follow.

"I filled my time by going through Lenny's things—his favorite books that I told him one day I'd read but never got around to. I devoured them. I tried to place myself within Lenny as much as I could. When I ran out of things to read, I watched his favorite movies. And when I was finally ready, I read his secret book in the basement.

"His writing area was relatively small. Just a desk and a lamp. He wrote on a typewriter and when he wrote it made that clack-clack sound. It was a love-hate thing. Some days it gave me a little burst of joy, the way you feel when you hear children playing. And then sometimes I'd get pissed off—the way you get when children are playing too loud. Now though, I was happy to just see it. He wrote the thing and it was his life's work. For better or worse. That idea made me uncomfortable, because I wasn't sure if it *should* be his life's work.

"I made the decision that it would only be for me. Upon reading the first page, I discovered that was exactly what it was."

Rose spoke quickly, eloquently on her dead dream-husband. I'd gotten comfortable referring to Lenny as a dream, mostly because it made all of this easier to take in. When she spoke though, she became less like the Rose I knew. Her voice was young, but her cadence was of a different generation. It was hard for me not to think of her as an old woman telling her story.

"So, you read his book. What did you find?"

She took a deep breath and closed her eyes for a half-second too long. I couldn't decide whether this was the Rose I knew or the Dorothy she purported to be. Whatever she was didn't matter anymore. She had become alien to me.

"It was about me. Or rather, it was about a woman and her last days on earth. Her husband had died like mine. She spent the rest of her days milling about the house, touching his things, and then finally she also read the book he wrote."

"What was the title?"

"*Drowned Pigs.*"

"That's strange."

"Yes, I believe it was a biblical reference. It refers to a passage where Jesus performs an exorcism on a man and then puts the many demons inside him into pigs, who then are drowned in the sea. We were not religious, but Lenny was a librarian—he knew the bible well."

A memory dislodged within me, something from Sunday school. "I think I remember that. 'Call us Legion, for we are many' or something like that. What did the book within the book say?"

"All I remember is that the woman had nightmares—or rather, I had nightmares. I believe I was supposed to be the woman. I don't recall the specifics, but eventually the nightmares got her and she was taken in the night. The bed was empty and she was gone."

"Okay, and what happened to the woman who read the book inside the book?"

Rose looked past me, at the clock behind my head, as if she were counting its seconds. "It was terrible," she said, finally, but did not continue.

I sat there—staring at her—waiting for her to speak.

"She woke up," she said. "And she wasn't who she was anymore. Just like me." She wiped the tea from her lips.

She was reeling me in, I was starting to believe her. "I think it was just a bad dream. Or maybe you hit your head."

"No, I didn't hit my head. I died. I died after I read it."

"Okay then," I said. "Tell me how you died."

She cleared her throat, blinked tears away from her eyes. "After I read the book, I felt... un-alone. Do you understand that?"

"It comforted you."

"No, not like that. The opposite. It discomforted me. I felt like I should be alone, but I wasn't. I felt like I was being watched."

"Oh."

"After the woman woke, the book ended. I read it in one sitting and I felt this terrible sense of dread that what happened to her would happen to me too. It was silly, I knew I had just spooked myself, but still. In that basement, where the only light was the lamp, I swear I could see faces in the dark. I figured it was simple pareidolia—I knew about that because Lenny was obsessed with it. He talked all the time about how he saw patterns, faces in the mundane. That man could see anything in a cloud. But in the basement, night had fallen and the corners of the room were black. At eye level, in every corner, I thought I could make out—just barely—a corpse-like face. Greenish skin, cadaver smile, and black eyes that reflected the lamplight. I held my breath and blinked rapidly, like I was trying to wipe my vision clean. But that face remained."

"Lenny's."

"No, mine. Or rather, Rose's. My face now."

"A premonition."

"I turned away from it but it was no use. I saw it in the

wood grain on Lenny's desk. I saw it in different corners. I was so scared, my heart was beating in my ears. I hadn't moved an inch and I kept looking at the stairwell, trying to time my way toward it. If I ran, would it come out of the shadows? Would it grab me? I didn't know, so I closed my eyes and counted to ten, but even beneath my eyelids I saw my own dead face. At one, I dashed up the stairs, holding my breath the whole time. I climbed the stairs like a kid, skipping steps. I closed the door without looking back. I kept turning my head, trying so hard to look at nothing. If I looked at something too long, I was afraid I would see that same face. I turned on every light in the house and waited.

"But nothing happened. The house was my house and I felt alone again. I laid on the sofa and kept testing my eyes. Blinking, looking at different things, trying to see that face. But I couldn't. I almost laughed, because I was *sure* that I could make myself see it, if I tried. But as soon as I tried to see it, it wasn't there. I went to bed that night unsettled, sure that I was just a silly old woman. But then the nightmares came."

Something she said made me remember something, but I couldn't bring it to mind. "What did you dream?" I asked.

"In the dream, Lenny was with me. We were on the porch in the rocking chairs and he was smoking a cigar. He never did smoke cigars, not around me at least. He turned to me and said, 'I'm sorry. I'm sorry.' He kept going on about it and I kept trying to tell him it was okay. But it wasn't, not really, because I felt like I was being watched. He kept motioning to the woods when he talked and kept saying he was sorry. I squinted to see what he was talking about. It was twilight and the magic hour had passed. We were on the doorstep of night. I couldn't see what he was talking about, but I knew that it was there. 'I'm sorry, I'm sorry,' he said. 'I wish there was a way you could escape.' He smiled when he said that, like I was supposed to know.

"But then, I saw them. *People.* All with the deathly pallor of corpses. They stood like statues amidst the trees. 'Yep, here they are,' said Lenny. 'That's them. Blink and you'll miss 'em.'

"At this point, I ran. I ran through the house but I realized they were already in the house. They were everywhere. They stood blocking doorways and hallways, every avenue of escape.

"The only place they didn't block was the basement.

"Even in my dream, I didn't want to go back down there but when I turned around to go back outside, I saw Lenny was now standing, blocking the door. He had a corpse face now too. The doorway to the basement was a black gaping mouth, and I was sure it was going to eat me.

"So, I had no choice.

"Scared to death, I ran down the stairs into the blackness, to Lenny's old desk. I switched on the lamp and my head swiveled around the room." Rose stopped, catching her breath.

"What did you see?" I asked, something on the tip of my tongue.

Her eyes lit up. First in amazement, then in horror. "I saw you."

"We've been together for a long time. This was just a dream. Of course you saw me. It'd make sense that you dream about me. I'm a part of your life." I stared down at the placid surface of my coffee, cold and bitter, and saw my own face. In the reflection, my lips were pulled back, my teeth shaded yellow. I shook my head.

"You were there," she said, accusingly. "I thought I recognized you. You were *there.*" She thought about this for a moment. "I didn't realize that at the time though. I just thought it was a woman, I didn't make the connection. In my dream, I didn't remember dreaming about you, or living with you or whatever. You were just another random face."

"And?"

"You spoke to me. You said, 'He knows.'"

"I don't know why I said that." But then, I looked back into my coffee and I realized my face had changed. I looked different. My edges were sharper. "What happened next?"

"I talk in my sleep, you know?"

I did know that. We used to record her mumbles and listen to them in the morning, laughing.

"I didn't realize that at the time. But when I woke up, I guess I knew that."

I swallowed, relieved. "You think you talked about me in your sleep?"

"Now, yes. I remembered you when I woke up. My dream from when I was a girl. I wondered if Lenny heard me talk about it."

"And that's why all this happened?"

"Maybe."

"But how did you die?"

"Slowly."

I cleared my throat. The thought of Rose dying made me uncomfortable, but by now it had become familiar. I questioned myself. Why did I care? I didn't know Dorothy. Dorothy was a dream woman. A product of my fragile spouse's mind. But at the same time, the memories she shared became mine and I could almost remember sitting up with her at night, listening to her babble while rage filled me. *Snapshots.* Bitterness, jealousy, disgust. Wounded masculinity. I stared back into my coffee and swirled the cup to remove the reflection.

"*He* found me."

"Lenny? I thought he was dead."

"He was dead. But he also wasn't. The night after my dream, I sat on the deck and stared out into the trees. I drank from a shaking glass of wine. Twigs snapped and I jumped at every sharp break. I told myself it was a deer. We got lots of animals out there. But no, it wasn't a deer." Tears welled in her eyes and I felt a sense of hatred that I quickly swallowed.

She continued. "I didn't see him at first, because he was dressed in black. Or rather, I didn't see him because he wasn't him. Not the normal him. I could only see his face—his dead, white face. But then, I realized, I wasn't just looking at one of him. The whole forest was filled with him. They were everywhere."

"Are you sure you weren't dreaming? Maybe this was a dream."

She looked at me strangely. "No, no. In death, he was *many*."

A memory came back to me. *Wood panels, cigar smoke. Old men with yellow teeth and wretched thrushy tongues. They exchanged symbols—through speech, through handshakes, through imagery. I spoke to them, laughing, explaining. And they shook their heads when my voice got gruff, when I was no longer laughing. And they said, "We are but brothers from Gerasenes."*

"I ran from him, because of course I did. There was no other option. I ran into the house, but it was just like my dream. Everywhere I turned, he was there. His corpse-like face leered at me. I couldn't escape. Where he was not, he still was. I saw him emerge from patterns in the floorboards, in dust in the light. He came from moonlight. His voice formed from the house's creaks. Eventually—"

I watched her sob, unfeeling. I remembered the old men, how I asked them how it all goes down. "You gotta put your heart into something," they said. *Like, a book?* "Sure, a book."

"They were all around me."

How was I supposed to know that I already had her, some-where else?

"They closed in on me, all around. I saw his faces, a thou-sand of them, the same twisted smile—"

—that I saw reflected back in my coffee.

"Their fingernails dug into me, they tore me limb from limb. I screamed but no one came to save me. No one came to help!" She lowered her head and cried. "When everything went black, I woke up here."

I ground my teeth, I nodded. Then, I reached out and touched her hand. Rose was beautiful, especially when she cried. "It was just a dream," I said. "Just a horrible dream."

"It was a life!" she screamed.

I smiled. "No," I said. "It wasn't."

THE SORROW OF OUR INTERMINABLE STASIS

The riddle seemed obvious to me. *What has two hands, a face, and is your greatest enemy?*

"Time," I said.

Mom nodded, encouraging.

Kaylie looked back at me. She licked her lips in that kiddish way I hated. "What does that mean?"

"You know what time means."

"No, but what clue does that go to?"

I pointed to the padlock, "There. Four letters. Time."

Kaylie spun the dials so that the lock spelled T-I-M-E. I had to let her help so I watched her fumble with it. After a couple tugs, it came loose and the tackle box opened. There was a clue, of some sort. There's always a clue.

Seagulls cawed in the background, the surf roared in. I flexed my toes and felt the grainy, wet sand squish between them. I loved days like this. Staring out at the ocean made everything feel like forever.

"Make sure Sasha gets to look, Kaylie," said Mom. "It's her birthday."

Kaylie frowned and backed off. She should feel lucky that she got to help at all. I was being a good big sister. She never let me help with her treasure hunt. I was being nice even letting her be here.

In the tackle box was a folded piece of paper. Minutes before, it'd been buried in the cold ocean sand. Now, it was in my hands.

Dashes formed a winding trail down to an X. "X marks the spot," I said aloud. "Is that where it ends?"

Mom shrugged. "You'll just have to see, I guess."

"Okay, but how do I read it? There's no landmarks, just a line and an X."

"Was there anything else in the box?"

Kaylie nodded feverishly, her mouth closed tight. Finally, she said, "I saw it! I saw it!"

I looked again. Taped to the side of the metal box was a pair of matches. I smiled. Mom got me a book earlier this year about secret codes. She knew I'd like this.

"Just be careful," she said. "Don't burn the map. There's not another one."

"I'll be careful," I said.

I lit the match and held it close to the paper. Just enough to let the heat kiss the invisible ink—probably lemon juice. It browned before my eyes and excitement filled me with nervous energy. I was practically jumping up and down.

Kaylie was saying, "What's happening? What's happening?"

"Shh, just watch," I said.

Before our eyes, a whole other world opened up on the page. I saw a crudely drawn image of our home, our street. I saw quickly jotted numbers. And then I saw the X, marked on a square block.

"The map starts at our house," I said.

"Okay," said Mom. "We better head back then, huh?"

Kaylie couldn't stop smiling. Neither could Mom.

We walked back to the car and drove the five minutes to our house. I stared at the map the whole way, trying to make perfect sense of it.

When we got out of the car, Dad was already waiting for us on the porch. "Having fun, birthday girl?"

"Yes!" I squealed.

"You're being careful, right?"

I nodded very seriously. "Yes, sir."

"Good girl."

"Is Mom having fun?"

Mom smiled at Dad. "It's going very well so far. I think I've outdone myself this year."

That changed something in Dad—he couldn't look at me for a second—but he didn't stop smiling. "Alright then," he said. "I'm going back inside. Too cold for me here. I'll wait for you to come back."

In the middle of the yard, Mom crouched down with us, so that she was our height. "You can read the map, right?"

I nodded.

"You're going to take care of your sister, right?"

I looked at Kaylie, somewhat begrudgingly. "Yes," I said.

"Alright." Mom patted me on the head. "You two have fun."

I opened the map and turned toward the street. Kaylie followed behind.

She was already annoying me, but I just ignored her. "We need to go down the block and then stop at the stop sign," I said. "And remember to look both ways."

"I will," she said, still fidgeting.

At the stop sign, we turned. It was a residential beach town, full of seafood restaurants and boating tourism. Off in the distance, I heard the sea lions barking. They were angry animals, but I liked them. They weren't like the animals at the zoo who never did anything; they were always doing something.

The street was a normal street, the sort of street we've played on before, only it was the one that started to get closer to the downtown, where all the shops started.

"You gotta be careful here," I said to Kaylie. "We don't wanna get lost." I sounded like a kid and I hated it.

We crossed another street and I consulted our map. "Looks like we've got to go a ways, down there and then to the right. Then straight for a while."

I puzzled at Mom's map. I don't think we'd ever been this far away from home before.

"Just let me know when we're there," said Kaylie. She said it like she was trying to suppress a giggle.

I frowned. I loved my sister but hated when she acted like a baby.

Adults downtown all turned to look at us when we passed. "Are you girls doing okay?" asked one woman.

"Yes, ma'am," I said. "We're on a treasure hunt."

"Oh, okay. Just be careful, dears."

"We will," I said, wincing.

The map took us past downtown into an area filled with factories. Salt and mist hung in the air. We were near the docks, I knew that much, but I couldn't tell why Mom would ever want us to go over here. It wasn't near anything fun. Smoke billowed out of smokestacks and men wearing goggles cursed while cutting open fish in refrigerated warehouses behind open dock doors. The smells made me want to puke.

The street was broad and wet. Misty rain fell from the sky. I was used to the cold over here, I think we all were, but being alone just made it all the chillier. I shivered, but pressed on because my birthday only happens once a year. And Mom always goes through so much trouble.

When we neared the end of the industrial area, the map took us in a new direction. Down the docks, along where all the ships floated serenely. They all had women's names and I had to laugh, because Dad always told the story, that when I saw all the boats as a little girl, before Kaylie was born, that I cried all day. I'd just learned to read and I kept saying the boat's names out loud. When he finally asked me what was wrong, I looked up at him with terrified eyes and asked, "Daddy? Am I going to be a boat when I grow up?"

"No," he said. "No, no, no."

Even now, it still makes me laugh.

I thought it was funny how big the map was. It didn't look big but it took us much further than I ever could have imagined. I looked at the little pictures, the clues that were supposed to guide me. Mom had drawn a cartoon boat beside the dotted line. Mom was always really good at drawing. She was good at everything. I thought she could do anything, if she wanted to.

The map only had one more turn in it, a left hand turn from the docks that took us down a little street, where that big X was. I was getting excited, I think Kaylie was too. She said, "Are we close?"

"I think so," I said.

"Okay. Tell me when we're there."

The boats rocked beside us. Out across the harbor, I saw the thick gray clouds. This made me happy, because I always liked storms. Especially on my birthday.

We made our last turn, onto a sharp hill. By the time we reached the top, our lungs were burning. I consulted the map. I looked up and around. "I guess it's there," I said.

The only building here was an old brick one. It was thin,

two stories tall, standing on an abandoned lot. A fence had been erected by a construction company to keep trespassers out. I thought it looked rather like a disconnected townhouse —a sliver of a home cut from its kin.

Kaylie and I approached it. There was a gap in the fences that we could both barely fit through.

I stood in front of the structure, somewhat underwhelmed. "What do we do?"

Kaylie giggled. "You have *instructions*."

"Instructions?"

She reached into her pockets, giddy.

"You're in on this?"

She nodded. "I was sworn to secrecy." She unfolded a piece of paper and a key with a red string tied to it fell out. "This is for you," she said.

It looked like one of those old fashioned keys you only saw in movies. "Does this go to the front door?"

"Try it," she said.

I approached the front door. The key didn't fit. It was much too large. "It's a newer door," I said. "It doesn't work."

"Guess you'll have to look somewhere else."

I frowned. "Can I see the note?"

"Nope. Not yet."

"Why not?"

"Because I have *instructions*."

The mystery was such that I was beginning to think that Mom had outdone herself. I approached the door and turned the knob. "It's unlocked. Can we go inside?"

Kaylie shrugged. "It's not *my* birthday."

I stepped inside to the small townhouse and listened. Distantly, I could hear the ocean. Kaylie walked in behind me, I tried to watch where she looked for clues, but she just kept looking at me.

"So, I guess I should try all the doors."

She was trying hard not to give something away, I could tell.

"Fine, fine," I said. "I get it. You're not talking."

The townhouse had only two more doors on the ground floor and all of them were unlocked. One went outside, the other went to an empty closet.

"Upstairs we go," I said.

Upstairs, there were three doors, all of them closed. Each of them numbered.

I smiled. "Now we're on to something." I reached for the first door, examining the lock. It was older, black iron. It might fit.

"Wait," said Kaylie. "I have more instructions."

"Okay," I said.

"As you have probably noticed, this key can fit into all three of these doors. But, there is a problem. Please examine your key."

I held it up in front of my face. I saw it immediately. Mom had played this on us before. "The key has a crack in it. We can only use it to open one door."

Kaylie smiled, because even though she was a runt, she still looked up to me for some reason. She cleared her throat. This was her big moment. "I have a riddle for you," she said.

"I'm ready."

She pulled out her paper again. "What are we without time?"

I scrunched up my face. I surveyed my surroundings. "I'm not sure what that means," I said, thinking. I paced back and forth.

"If you knew, it wouldn't be fun."

Mom usually hid clues. The clues were what mattered.

With the clues it'd be obvious. The doors were numbered 1, 2, and 3. So, I knew I needed a number.

There was a small table, the kind you'd put a lamp on. I opened the drawers and found nothing.

"I don't see anything up here," I said. But as soon as I said it, I had it figured out. Nothing up *here*. I went back downstairs and I knew by the way Kaylie's smile made her cheeks fat and chubby that I was on the right track.

On the first floor, I looked for something out of place.

A broken wall, the dials on the stove, a bit of chalk writing left by a demolition crew. I didn't find anything though, until I looked to the front door, right beside it. And that's when I saw the clock and said, "But we left at two."

Clock. A dead one, an old one. The kind Mom would've found at a yard sale somewhere. Hands neatly positioned at exactly one o'clock. Then it all made sense.

I ran back upstairs. Kaylie waited, shifting her weight from foot to foot. "Did you figure it out?"

"Us without time. Two minus one," I said. "Door number one."

I slid the key into the door and turned it carefully. Mom always had these so perfect. I don't know how she did it. As soon as the lock clicked, the key snapped.

"Are you ready?"

"Let's go!" she squealed.

I pushed the door open and saw nothing but blackness.

"Is there a light?"

I fumbled for the switch. "Nothing," I said.

"Is it going to happen?" asked Kaylie.

"I don't know," I said. "Maybe."

"Can I go too?"

"It's not your birthday," I said.

She was pouting in the dark. I knew she was. But that's

how she was made, she was the baby of the family. She'd always be the baby.

As I traveled into the blackness, I felt myself grow, lengthen, fatten. My mind exploded with a thousand implanted memories.

I took a deep breath, filling my great lungs.

The air was cool and smelled like the ocean. I didn't care that it was cold. I would never care. Mom knew all of my favorite places. The blackness was not so black anymore, and when it dissolved completely, I was on a beach.

I swallowed, letting my hands run down the length of my body. I was tall now, like Mom. I wore a sundress and flip flops and I had money and a job and maybe a husband and maybe kids. Waves crashed, rolling in, their white churnings giving birth again and again.

I tried to keep every one of those seconds, to swallow them up and make them a part of me forever. I ran along the beach to fall in love with the length of my stride. I cherished my breasts and hips.

Children screamed somewhere down the beach. They played and thrashed in the sand.

I walked to them, it'd been a year since I last saw them. They were the same age, just like me. Two boys, both with brown hair and eyes, three and four.

"Mom?" said one.

The word sliced through me.

"I'm here," I said.

"Can you help us with this?"

I got on my knees, smiling. "What are we making?"

The younger one said, "A sandcastle." I loved how he said it, pausing at each syllable.

"You're both doing so good," I said.

We went to work, crafting the spires. I pulled bobby pins

from my hair to carve doorways and sawtooth battlements. In between, I drank in their determined expressions and clumsy hands.

I relished every second, while it lasted.

It's the best Mom could do—or would do.

As my hours waned, the darkness crawled back to me. It took me into its arms and made me feeble, child-like. It changed me again, it brought me back to something I knew all too well. Kaylie was waiting for me.

"Was it good?"

"Yes," I said. That was the only thing I could say. We stood in the dilapidated townhouse again.

I felt a deep sorrow, of some unarticulated miracle lost forever. A mysterious syllable gone from my memory, an incomplete word spinning within my mind.

We walked home in silence. It was always sad coming back.

At home, I learned to be twelve again.

Dad took me into his arms, begrudgingly. When I went to kiss him on the cheek, I thought I felt him recoil. But if he did, he immediately corrected himself. He stood still as a statue as I gave him my kiss. He took me in his arms and cleared his throat, "Happy birthday," he said.

Mom touched my hair. "You look good." She never once said, "You look older." Not in a million, billion years. Or however old she was.

They held hands and watched me as my old self snapped

back into place like a rubber band. Our little bodies were good at out-running our thoughts, our stolen futures. Precious hours, devoured like a slice of birthday cake.

Mom was so good at these though, so good at these treasure hunts. She was so good at everything. And I was so scared all of a sudden, because I didn't know what to do if I lost her. Kaylie and I would be so alone. We'd be nothing. We'd be us. We'd be nothing. Mom sat in the chair across from me watching Kaylie and I watch our favorite shows in our jammies. I suddenly started crying. I thought about never going on a treasure hunt again.

When Mom saw the tears roll down my cheeks, she stood up from her chair. She took me into her arms. I looked into her eyes and I felt so much better, because I knew she would never die.

"There, there," she said.

ALIVE AND LIVING (PILOT)

F ADE IN:

Swirling colors introduce us to the world of our main character, BRIAN PARKER (14). He smiles at the camera, a baseball bat resting on his shoulder. Then his grin slackens. A look of terror comes over his face; he runs out of frame.

His older brother, MATT PARKER (17), holds a whoopie cushion. His face is twisted in fraternal rage. Mid-screen, he stops. He looks at the audience and flashes shiny white teeth.

He too passes beyond the swirling background, then PRESTON PARKER and MEREDITH PARKER enter. The man wears a button up, he grins haplessly. The woman wears a dress and is holding a feather duster. They sigh with their entire bodies.

Through all of this, the credits roll—a dozen names none of us have ever heard, and never will again.

CUT TO:

. . .

INT. BRIAN'S ROOM. EVENING

Brian is sitting on his bed in the upstairs of his parents' two story house. His friend, ETHAN (14), sits at the small desk across from the bed.

> BRIAN
> You really think he's not gonna notice?

> ETHAN
> Let me tell you something, Bri. Parents are smart, but we're smarter.

> BRIAN
> You think?

> ETHAN
> Occasionally.

Pause for laughter.

> BRIAN
> So, how do you want to do it? I don't want to get in trouble.

> ETHAN
> You're not going to get in trouble. Besides, I have a plan.

> BRIAN
> It's not going to end like the Grand Cherry Bomb Fiasco of 1994, is it?

> ETHAN
> More like the Toilet Paper Revolution of '93.

BRIAN
You got caught for that too!

ETHAN
(Whimsically)
But I never broke.

Laughter.

BRIAN
I just don't know, man... Do you really think we can do it?

ETHAN
A guy like you can do anything.

CUT TO:
INT. PARKER FAMILY LIVING ROOM. EVENING
PRESTON and MEREDITH PARKER are sitting on the couch, downstairs, enjoying a glass of wine as they watch TV. It's a quiet night-in for the heads of the household.

MEREDITH
Is Brian up in his room?

PRESTON
He better be.

MEREDITH
This could be our chance... Say, when's the last time we got to be a little...romantic?

PRESTON
When was Ross Perot last in the news?

Laughter.

Preston extends his arm around his wife's shoulder. They lean in for a kiss.

MEREDITH
Maybe we can make some news of our own...

PRESTON
It's 5 o'clock some—

The front door opens and their eldest son, Matt, walks in.

MATT
(Oblivious to his parents' intimacy)
I can't believe Vicky dumped me!

Meredith and Preston look at each other and throw their heads back.

MEREDITH AND PRESTON
(In unison)
Oh no, Matt. Girl trouble?

Laughter.

MATT
How did you know?

MEREDITH
What happened with Vicky, honey?

Matt leaps over the couch and settles in between his parents, further ruining the mood.

MATT

Just the usual. I'm not cool enough, apparently.

PRESTON

Son, there's more to life than being *cool*.

MATT

(Sarcastic)

Yeah, right!

Laughter.

MEREDITH

Why aren't you cool enough for this girl?

MATT

She says it's because I'm not on the football team. She wants to
date a quarterback.

PRESTON

You don't have to be a quarterback to be cool, son. I'll have you
know that I was pretty cool back in the day myself. And I was
no quarterback.

MATT

Is that true, Mom?

MEREDITH

It's true, Matt. Your father was no quarterback.

Matt looks around the living room.

MATT

Where's Bri-guy?

PRESTON
Upstairs. Probably telling his delinquent friend what a horrible
father I am.

MEREDITH
Oh, stop it. He'll be fine. It was just a tiff.

MATT
What happened?

PRESTON
I told him that he couldn't go to Minneapolis with his buddies
and he got mad. He's acting like I'm a dictator just because I
won't let him go off to the big city with a car full of criminals
and no adult supervision!

MATT
Those teenagers, huh?

MEREDITH
Yeah, those teenagers.

They both stare at Matt.

MATT
You want me to talk to him, don't you?

They keep staring. Matt hangs his head down.

MATT
Fine. You got me. Older brother, to the rescue.

                              PRESTON
                             Thanks, son.

Matt goes upstairs.
Meredith leans in close to Preston.

                              MEREDITH
                         Now, where were we?

CUT TO:
INT. BRIAN'S ROOM. EVENING
Brian and Ethan are throwing a softball back and forth.
When Matt walks in, they stop.

                               BRIAN
                Weren't you supposed to be on a date?

                                MATT
                          Let's not talk about it.

                               ETHAN
                            Dumped? Again?

                                MATT
                              (To Brian)
           Your buddy here is just full of questions, isn't he?

                               BRIAN
                        He's the inquisitive type.

                                MATT
                        He's the inquisitor type.

The two boys share a conspiratorial glance.

ETHAN
You have *no* idea.

MATT
(Sitting down on his own bed)
So, Dad says you're bummed about him not letting you go into the big city?

BRIAN
Are you here to tell me that I need to forgive him? To remind me that he loves me, that he knows best, that he knows exactly what I'm going through and...

MATT
No, I don't care about any of that.

BRIAN
Then why did you come up here?

Matt lies back on the bed.

MATT
Uh, I live here.

BRIAN
Ignore him.

ETHAN
Easier said than done.

Riotous laughter.

                    BRIAN
          When should we do it though?

                    ETHAN
          Tonight, of course. When else?

                    BRIAN
              Will it work?

                    ETHAN
            Of course it'll work.

                    BRIAN
          How do we know it'll work?

                    ETHAN
      You've been over to my place a bunch, right?

                    BRIAN
              Yeah. So what?

                    ETHAN
      When's the last time you've seen my parents?

Brian thinks to himself, his eyes go wide.

                    BRIAN
              Oh my God.

                    ETHAN
      They prayed. But he had nothing to do with it.

Matt opens his eyes. He sits up on the bed, exasperated at

the two boys.

                    MATT
          I'm sensing a scheme here.

                    BRIAN
              Schemers? Us?

                    ETHAN
            We're not schemers.

                    MATT
   No? Then what's this little pow-wow about here? Something
                you wanna tell me?

                    BRIAN
   It's not a scheme. It's just... Ethan has a plan to deal with my
              Minneapolis troubles.

                    MATT
            Oh? And what is that?

                    ETHAN
        You ever made a problem disappear?

                    MATT
     Minneapolis is pretty big, Copperfield.

   In the blackened seats of the audience, someone SCREAMS,
HOWLS. Their laughter is agonizing.

                    BRIAN
   No, Matt. He doesn't mean the city. He means Mom and Dad.

Matt looks at his brother and his friend. He cocks his head.

MATT
Your friend's lost it, huh?

ETHAN
I haven't lost *anything*. It works. I did everything right and my parents are gone.

MATT
They must have gone out for smokes.

ETHAN
Trust me, they already tried that.

MATT
So, you're going to just make them disappear? How are you going to do that?

BRIAN
(to Ethan)
Tell the man!

ETHAN
(digging into his backpack)
This is called the Demodorum.

He pulls out <u>an old book, comically thick, bound in old worn leather with straps and buckles that close the cover.</u>

ETHAN
It's an old book.

BRIAN
No kidding.

ETHAN
They don't make 'em like this anymore!

MATT
I wonder why.

BRIAN
Keep an open mind. This is going to be cool.

Ethan opens the book, one buckle at a time. The wind
HOWLS outside, the windows FLY OPEN, lightning CRASHES,
and a DEEP, GURGLING ROAR sounds all around the three
young men in the suburban home. The pages flutter and
Ethan's eyes roll back into his head.
CLOSE UP ON ETHAN.

ETHAN
(In an unearthly tone made of icy consonants and bottomless
vowels)
Ka'thar! Qi psol'uta! Barati narku!

THUNDER ROARS again, LIGHTNING FLASHES.
Brian's mouth opens in shock.
Ethan shakes his head. He's coming out of it. He closes the
book.

ETHAN
Dude, sorry. I didn't mean to...

MATT

What do you mean...?

They both stare in horror at Matt, who's body is fading away in front of them. First they see his skin turn translucent. Then Matt looks down in <u>utter terror to see his rippling insides wither away to nothing</u>. When he tries to scream, he realizes he no longer has vocal cords. He VANISHES into thin air.

The two boys look at each other, their expressions commingling in awe and horror.

ETHAN
Told you it'd work.

FADE OUT TO COMMERCIAL.

INT. BRIAN'S ROOM. EVENING

The boys are right where we left them, they're staring at each other in awe. The hint of horror is gone. They're now clearly excited, their mouths agape.

BRIAN
We did it.

ETHAN
Sure, if we're not grading on accuracy.

Foul laughter from a degenerate congregation.

BRIAN
He's really gone.

ETHAN

Cut from the cloth of reality, just like that.

> BRIAN
> (beat)
> *Cool.*

> MEREDITH
> (Off screen)
> Dinner's ready!

> BRIAN
> Quick, start reading again.

> ETHAN
> She's not even in the room.

> BRIAN
> So?

> ETHAN
> C'mon, man. If we're going to make your parents disappear, we
> can at least look them in the eyes.

Meredith enters.

> MEREDITH
> Are you staying for dinner, Ethan?

> ETHAN
> Yes, ma'am. If it's not too much trouble, that is.

> MEREDITH
> No trouble at all... Where's Matt?

BRIAN
Date.

ETHAN
Bathroom.

BRIAN
He's on a date... in the bathroom. He's getting ready for the date.

MEREDITH
I thought he just got dumped?

Brian stands up, affecting sympathy. He pushes her toward the door.

BRIAN
Please, Mom. I thought you'd be more sensitive to this sort of thing. He's going through a lot right now. I think Matt deserves a chance to get back out there without our cruel jokes.

MEREDITH
But—

BRIAN
(Pushing her through the door)
No buts, Mom!

He closes the door behind her.

ETHAN
(Yelling to the closed door)
We'll be down in a second!

BRIAN
Phew, that was close!

ETHAN
Cool, calm, and collected... I think you've made it to the big
leagues.

BRIAN
Really?

ETHAN
Nope. But give it another hour.

Brian takes a deep breath and smiles. His friend hugs the
Demodorum tight to his chest.

FADE TO:
INT. DINING ROOM. RIGHT AFTER
Brian and Ethan are helping themselves to massive
amounts of mashed potatoes. There's a great heaping pile of
food on the table. Preston is slicing a slab of ham slathered in
ketchup. Meredith is sipping chardonnay. They eye the boys
suspiciously.

PRESTON
You know, boys, when we said we had plenty, it didn't mean
you had to have plenty.

MEREDITH
Is this a puberty thing?

Brian and Ethan share a glance.

BRIAN
Yep, Mom. Nailed it as usual. We're going through a lot of
puberty.

ETHAN
That's right, Mrs. Parker. My bones ache as we speak. And—
(He raises a hand to his face)
Ope! I think I just sprouted a mustache.

PRESTON
(Squinting)
I think that's gravy.

Laughter, cruel laughter.
Ethan wipes his mouth quickly.

ETHAN
Clean shaved and soft as a baby's bottom!
Meredith looks to Preston.

MEREDITH
Is there something wrong, boys?

BRIAN
Wrong, Mom? What's wrong? What could possibly be wrong
—why do you think something is—

Ethan slaps his hand across Brian's mouth.

ETHAN
Brian is having stomach issues.

BRIAN
Stomach issues?

ETHAN
Yeah, diarrhea. *Verbal* diarrhea.

PRESTON
Something's up. Where did you say Matt was again?

BRIAN
Matt? Who's Matt?

Ethan covers Brian's mouth again.

ETHAN
Matt's on a date.

PRESTON
(Nodding)
Right. A date.

BRIAN
Matt's just out there... dating away. Food's great, by the way.

MEREDITH
(Suspicious)
Thank you.

BRIAN
Hey, Mom. I was wondering if we could start a new tradition
tonight?

MEREDITH

Depends what you had in mind.

BRIAN
Well, Ethan here has this book.

Thunder.

BRIAN
(Continued)
Maybe we could let him read from it. Like dinner and a movie,
but a story.

PRESTON
Oh?

MEREDITH
A book? I didn't know Ethan read!

ETHAN
Oh, I'm a big reader.

Ethan pulls the Demodorum from under the table.

ETHAN
And this bad boy is my new favorite.

PRESTON
Looks older than dirt.

BRIAN
You know, Dad, that's surprisingly accurate.

Cold laughter filters in from the soundstage, because THEY REALLY DON'T KNOW.

<u>Ethan opens the book.</u> The THUNDER ROARS outside. Preston and Meredith turn their heads to see RAIN PELTING their windows. WIND HOWLS.

> ETHAN
>
> C'thyn har'kh c'ollata...Ka'thar! Qi psol'uta! Barati narku!

The boys look at each other and smile wickedly.

> MEREDITH
>
> I don't feel so good.

Preston rubs his chest.

> PRESTON
>
> Me neither. I feel... strange. Like... I'm—

> BRIAN
>
> Dying, Dad?

> ETHAN
>
> Erased?

> PRESTON
> (Standing up)
> Yes, actually.

Meredith turns to her husband, her eyes watering.

> MEREDITH
>
> What's happening? Boys, what did you do?

Brian gets up from his seat to stand apart from the table.
The wind SCREAMS outside. Preston and Meredith claw at
their own bodies as they begin to waste away.

BRIAN
Sorry, Mom. You're just collateral damage.
(To his father)
He was the one I wanted.

ETHAN
Yep, guess that'll teach 'em.

BRIAN
(High fiving Ethan)
Minneapolis, here we come!

MEREDITH
But—but—we love you.

Meredith begins to <u>bleed from her eyes</u>. She's holding on to
the table for support.

PRESTON
I just wanted you to be safe. That's all I wanted. I just wanted
you to be safe. Please, please, please. Stop it. I don't feel so
good. I'm dying, son. Do you understand what's happening?
(He looks at his hand, <u>dissolving into wispy black liquid</u>)
This is forever. I don't want to die. I don't want to be dead
forever.

ETHAN
Yeah, my parents didn't want to either. But they haven't
complained since.

Wicked, wicked laughter.

Preston and Meredith weep openly as their bodies dissolve. They reach out to each other, but they can no longer touch. On contact, their bodies dissolve further. When they touch each other, it's like sand hitting sand. They scream as they realize they will be no more. These are their last moments and they can't even touch each other. They look upon themselves and their son in pain and horror. And then, they are nothing. Gone. Forever.

                    BRIAN
                    (beat)
              Well, that's that.

                    ETHAN
            Yep. What's done is done.

                    BRIAN
            What do we do now?

                    ETHAN
            Whatever we want.

The house is silent. They look at the spot where Brian's parents used to stand and seem to consider what the rest of their teen years will look like. The silence is deafening. The STORM has stopped.

                    ETHAN
            To Minneapolis?

                    BRIAN
                    (smiling)

I call shotgun!

We freeze frame on the boys in their glee.

The audience rustles in their seats, they get up to leave and tell their loved ones about the pilot they saw that one afternoon. They misremember jokes and retell them at dinner. They lie about the actors. "This starred so-and-so" or "It was the kid from that thing." But they don't remember, not really. Decades later, they recall sitting in a dark room, wondering which parts were real and which parts they invented. They wonder how the parents dissolved live on the soundstage. And then, they shake their heads and think, *No, no, no. That's not what happened at all.* And sometimes, when they're especially brave, they'll wonder what *did* happen that day. Why it lingers like a bad dream. Why the pilot never made it to air. But they do know one thing: that for 22 minutes, they were entertained.

And that's something.

The credits roll. We realize we don't know anyone here. We don't know who these people are. We've never seen this show before. And yet it is here, right before us. It is alive and well and living. It exists. It exists. It exists.

BY THE GRACE OF SAINT PIERS, POOR AND DEAD

I sabeau did not speak Latin, not truly. Nor did her husband, Jehan. But still, they listened as the priests joined in a circle around the bishop and whispered.

It was night, which was strange. They'd never expected to be ushered in from their humble home, into the cold night, to the Great Cathedral—but for Isabeau, who held her beliefs deeply, there were few places she'd rather be. Jehan—of that old Germanic blood, a Norman only a father back—was not as keen to see priests at his door in the middle of the night. But still, they came. And in the flickering light of the many torches, they waited.

When the bishop ushered them forward, they felt small and insignificant. "Greetings," he said, in the vulgar tongue. His mouth was a grim line, deeply creased—a throbbing wound. "I'm sure you have some reasoning of why you're here, do you not?"

"We do not," said Jehan.

"No," said Isabeau, who adjusted her accent when she could not adjust her language.

The Bishop grimaced. "Do you know my name?"

"I do not," said Jehan.

But Isabeau touched his arm when he said this. "We know who you are," she said quickly. "You're the Most Reverend Garnier Alarie. It's an honor; *we* are honored."

Jehan gave a curt nod. "Of course, we're honored."

"And you have heard what I do?"

"Yes," said Isabeau. "You are the Wandering Bishop."

Alarie nodded brusquely. "Very good. You are God-fearing people?"

"Yes, we both are."

"And what of your son?"

Jehan said, "He's just a boy. He fears nothing now."

"No, he is a Christian. A good Christian. We bring him to church."

"Young, is he not?" asked Bishop Alarie.

"No more than three," said Jehan.

Bishop Alarie frowned. "And how long has he been missing now?"

Both of them, in their own way, sensed the inevitable. Jehan crossed his arms and shrank. Isabeau's voice lost its forced opulence.

"Two days," she said.

The bishop flexed his fingers. He stared down at the stone floor. He brushed his vestments as if all of these small actions would make it easier to continue forward. "Earlier tonight," he started, "we found your son." His eyes watered, catching torches that made his pupils burn with light. "We found him hours ago, outside the church, on its very doorstep. He is dead, I'm afraid."

Isabeau crumpled to her knees, her voice strained. "No, no, no!" she cried.

Jehan went down to help his wife. "How did it happen?" he asked. "How could this have happened?"

Above him, Alarie's voice seemed the voice of God himself. "It cannot be known why he died." A brief pause. "But that is why I am here. That is why I have traveled. We have witnessed a miracle."

"A miracle?" Isabeau spoke in the voice of a child.

"Yes," said Alarie. "A miracle."

"The death of my son is no miracle."

But Isabeau's grief had already been transformed. Jehan saw this with his own eyes. She stood up, straighter than before, and while her eyes were red and wet and her syllables quaked, she was *listening*.

"I have deemed his demise a miraculous event," Alarie said evenly. "A tribute to the Church."

Isabeau wiped her eyes. "Oh, he did love church. Oh, he did love God!"

"He was a boy," Jehan said thickly. "Where is the body? I want to see my son."

"You will see him when I say you can see him," said Alarie.

Jehan balled his fists. But before his violence fruited from thought to action, the bishop continued.

"I'm petitioning Piers as a candidate for sainthood."

Jehan's fists loosened. "Our boy? Piers?"

Isabeau's eyes went wide. "A saint!"

"Yes, a saint," said Alarie. "Over the next three days, however, we will need assistance from the both of you. The process is tricky, and for such a young boy it will indeed require the help of his loved ones. Do you find this agreeable?"

Isabeau stood with Jehan, the two stared into each other's eyes, searching for an answer, a course to continue on. Isabeau spoke first, "We'll be here for whatever you need."

"And you, Jehan?"

"Yes, me too. I'll be here, for my son."

Alarie clapped his hands. His smile as warm as heaven itself. "Join me in a prayer," he said. "For Piers."

Jehan was working in the field when a trio of priests appeared. He sang to himself, as he always did when he worked. His muscles and soul ached in synchronicity, but children—his very own—had died before. And while he grieved each deeply, there was still work to do. When he turned around and saw the priests, his shovel dropped from his hands. They stood at the edge of his field, watching. *Surely*, he thought, *they had seen a man sing before. It was not uncommon for a man to sing while working. An old ballad or a bawdy drinking song—these things were to be expected, were they not?*

Jehan approached the priests with a sense of shame he did not understand. Isabeau came out from their home, wearing her nicest clothes. She bowed before the priests whose faces were stern and unimpressed.

"You are needed at the church," said one of the priests. "We will come for you each day of the canonization process. You will be ready at this time. Understood?"

Jehan made his way to his wife, holding her hand. "Are we to go now?"

"Yes, please hurry. We're already behind."

In the daylight, the church glowed. Its stained glass windows shimmered with ruby light. Depictions of Jesus on the cross loomed large and brilliant above them as they walked into the Cathedral. Isabeau and Jehan, the both of them, realized at the same time that Piers would join this grand tradition. He would be immortalized, another saint put to glass, alive in the church much longer than he was alive on earth.

Jehan tried to put this into words, this feeling of immortality, but all he could say was, "He was just a boy."

"I know, I know," said his wife. "A good boy. A God-fearing boy."

Alarie came to them at once, and as he did, the priests that brought them disappeared into the corners of the church. "We shall start at once," he said simply.

The two of them followed Alarie, his clicking boots echoing across the Cathedral. Isabeau's eyes went wide as he took her deeper into the church than she'd ever been. Past the pulpit, back to where the scribes worked, and then further still.

"You understand this is an honor, yes? That it is a privilege to be where you are now?"

"Yes, oh Lord yes!" cried Isabeau.

"We are honored, Bishop."

Alarie looked at the both of them, up and down, as if to judge whether they meant this. When he deemed their answers satisfactory, he said, "Very well. We go deeper still."

The Cathedral was a labyrinth. Its corridors twisted and turned and intersected. There was more to it than Jehan and Isabeau could have ever imagined. To them, it was a single room, because that's all they had ever seen of it. But now, it was as if it were expanding before their very eyes.

Eventually, after following Alarie through the church's maze, they found themselves at a descending staircase of white stone that spiraled into darkness. "Go on, go on," he said. "We must hurry. This is where we will meet from now on."

Jehan and Isabeau gripped the stone walls as they went spinning into the purest black they'd ever seen. The whole time, they felt Alarie's voice in their ears. "Yes, just like that. Keep going, keep going." And eventually, they felt the earth level out before them and they realized that after what seemed like an impossibly long descent, they were now in an underground clearing.

"Please, kneel. Pray for your son."

Jehan and Isabeau both brought themselves to the floor, where they felt bare earth move under their weight. The darkness was thick and inhospitable, and in these catacombs they smelled death.

Alarie's voice found them in the dark. "Piers has found beatification under my leadership. You can be assured that he is in heaven now. But to continue this process, we must find miracles—acts of the supernatural that occurred before and after his death. Do you understand?"

"Piers is in heaven?"

Jehan reached out to touch his wife, who was no longer beside him. Somehow, she'd drifted away. They were both lost in some eternal blackness.

Alarie sounded annoyed. "Yes, your son is in heaven. Do you understand miracles? The word? The nature of them?"

"Yes, yes, of course. We understand miracles. They are magic made of God."

"That's right. God's magic—the only pure magic. The only right magic. So, let us talk here, where it is safe to talk about such things. Think back to the day before your boy Piers fell dead—a miracle in itself—what do you remember?"

Isabeau sounded as if she were miles away. Jehan wondered if he was hearing her at all, or just an echo of her. "There was one miracle," she said.

"A miracle? What? When?" Jehan asked, confused. Piers was just a boy. He played as well as he could on his little feet. He ran around their small property with small crops and laughed and giggled and sometimes cried, but to his father's knowledge, there was nothing miraculous about the child.

Isabeau's voice was dreamy in the dark. "It was the morning before," she said, her tone undulating unnaturally, shifting from very near, whispering in his ears so he could hear the crackle of her spit, then: very far away, so far away that she sounded more like a wailing ghost than the wife he knew so well. "It was in the morning and there was a deer. Dead, killed, skinned."

"Who dressed this animal?"

"Jehan did."

Jehan remembered. "Yes, I went hunting in the early morning. It was a young buck. It took only a single arrow."

Isabeau continued. "The animal was outside, his flesh had been flayed and I was washing its hide. Piers was beside me and he kept poking at the deer and his hand was bright red. He kept touching its muscles and when he did, the animal twitched. He kept looking up to me and laughing as he did this. He said, 'Maman, look!' and then he would touch it again and another part of the animal would move. I told him to stop, of course. 'Stop,' I said. But he ran to the other side of the animal and I couldn't catch him and then he put his hand on the white of the animal's skull. It was so sudden, I barely understood what had happened. I had heard about such acts, but had never witnessed them—but also, I had not slept well the night before and thought that perhaps I had fallen asleep and was dreaming. The buck stood up and galloped off the dressing table. He struck his hooves against the ground. I swear I could see his muscles flexing as he moved about our property, in one wide circle, as if he never died. Then, as soon as it happened, the beast fell down once more, exactly where he'd been, and was still."

Jehan stood, silent, in disbelief. Could his wife have really seen such a thing? Would she not have mentioned it before?

"This is indeed a miracle." Alarie's voice came from all

around them. "You two are very lucky to be the parents of such an important child. Tomorrow. Come back tomorrow."

A torch appeared, distantly, and Isabeau and Jehan found each other in the dark, and began to climb the staircase back to the world above.

* * *

There was a small private vigil at their home, where neighbors came after the day's work was done to offer food and well wishes. Men came with strong handshakes and meager portions of wine, women came with bread or dried meat. They ate and drank and cried together, some of them remembering their own lost children, some of them anticipating losing the ones they had.

Isabeau took their well-wishes with wet eyes and demure humility. Jehan drank and yelled and sang, as if the death of a child unleashed something feral within him. Each of them, in their sorrow, surrounded by their community, let slip what had happened in the church. Jehan, after a boisterous bout of singing, hugged one of his friends close and said, "Piers will live longer than the lot of us." His cheeks were rosy and a smile crossed his lips, partially hidden by his beard. "It's true," he said. "My son is a saint. A miracle worker. He died to be closer to God." And when he said that, there was a hushed silence, then questioning eyes, then a great and solemn reverence. Each man in turn placed a hand on Jehan and suddenly his grief was no longer so acute.

Meanwhile, in their home, Isabeau detailed the entire experience to the other women. "Tomorrow we'll be back," she said. "Bishop Alarie explained everything."

"Aye, I've heard of this Alarie. He's made many saints. When did he come?"

"I don't know," she said. "But he was here."

"These circumstances are very strange. Is it not odd for a child to be named a saint so soon?"

"It's his miracles," she pleaded. "The buck! The buck rose from the dead just like Jesus Christ!"

"Yes," said another. "I suppose."

"We're going back tomorrow. In the morning, to continue the process." She felt herself wilting under their disbelieving stares. "Perhaps, as his mother, I could pray to him, my son, to bless you and your livelihoods? He was a good boy, you said so yourself. Our town has never had a saint before, has it?"

Slowly, the women nodded. "I would like us to have a saint," said one.

"I do not see how this could happen, but if it did, it would be an agreeable turn of events, yes."

And soon too, the women had gathered around Isabeau and were now revealing their innermost troubles, their innermost hopes. They talked of sewing needles and milking cows and spices while the men outside talked of plentiful hunting, strong plows, and kind nobles.

To the stars, they each raised a mug. "To Saint Piers," they cried. "To Saint Piers!"

* * *

The next day, they arrived on time—early even—to find Alarie waiting for them on the stone steps outside the church where Piers had perished.

"Do you remember how to descend into God's Grotto?"

"Yes," said Jehan. "I have a perfect memory for such things."

"My husband has a keen mind for tracking," she said. "We will find it, yes."

Alarie's eyes gleamed under his heavy brow. "Is that so? If it is, I will have you lead the way, since you seem to know the church better than any other."

"Bishop, no!" said Isabeau. "We don't claim—"

"It was only, you asked—" explained Jehan.

Alarie lifted his hand and pointed toward the pedestal where the priest's Latin rang out in sing-song. "Go then, show me. I will follow."

Jehan and Isabeau stood rigid for a moment, unsure under the Bishop's gaze. Eventually, it was Jehan whose eyes went downcast and turned toward the pulpit. Isabeau followed just steps behind him, and Alarie just behind her, his boots clicking loudly, snapping at her heels like a rabid dog.

It was true, Jehan realized with a sense of wrongdoing. He had navigated the church well. He had followed its labyrinthine corridors and somehow found the spiral staircase that led to what Alarie called the God's Grotto.

Alarie took his place at the front of them, rushing past the bereaved parents. They stared at his back, his vestments swaying from some impossible breeze. "Of course you did," he said, his voice low.

When he turned around, they saw the hints of a smile on his lips. "Another miracle. A minor miracle, of course. But another from our future saint."

Isabeau cried out in relief. Jehan held his head in his hands. "Of course it was," he said. "Oh, Piers, praise be to you!"

Jehan had never been as devout as Isabeau. Where she found comfort and the sublime in the halls of a cathedral, Jehan found it in the multitude of sounds in the forest. He often thought that he'd prefer to live as a beast—out in the woods where he would never have to grow food for nobles, where his meager earnings would not be taxed. Where neighbors and clergy would not look at him as if he were a fool for simply existing. But here, for the first time, he felt what Isabeau felt. Inside him, some great chasm cracked open and just as it split and showed its enormity, it too was filled. *Is this God?* he thought. Suddenly, he felt the loss of his son more than ever, more than any other son, because he realized this son was more important than any crib death in history. This child was a Saint. This child demanded love. And so Jehan responded in kind, opening his soul in ways he never thought possible.

Together, they descended. Isabeau beamed in the blackness, holding on to her husband. She too felt this spiritual revolution within him while her own devoutness only intensified with each step further into the blackness. They were so united they may as well have been one.

Downstairs, in the blackness, Alarie's voice surrounded them, inhabited them. "We must continue on with our work. You must open your mind down here and begin the real labor. Listen, closely."

Isabeau focused, shutting her eyes tight. Faint, but she could hear it. A voice. Ghostly and low and impossibly far away.

"Piers!"

"My son!"

"Yes! Listen! He is here with us!"

Jehan's voice went an octave higher, cracking in his own delight. "I'm coming for you," he called. "I will find you!"

Alarie, an inch from his ear: "You cannot find him, Jehan. He is everywhere."

Isabeau laid flat to the earth, face down, listening. "I hear him," she said softly, her words choking in her throat. "I hear him!"

"Can you repeat to me what he is saying? I will have to write it for the church, to submit to its leaders. This will make what we already know official, that your son, in his inexplicable death, is a symbol of our Lord."

Now, Jehan too was laying on the earth of the Lord's Grotto, listening intently. They might have been miles apart, him and Isabeau, but that didn't matter anymore because they were one. Sibilant whispers hissed through the eternal blackness, slithering in and around their ears. They concentrated, trying to find the words that the air spoke to them.

"*Cold cold cold love love help love hello buck great home.*"

Isabeau mouthed the words, or the words she thought she heard in the darkness. "They don't make sense," she said. "He isn't making sense."

Both of them waited in the blackness, because they knew Alarie would have something to say about this. He would have an answer. The Bishop was able to keenly answer any question that came to him. And just as they suspected, this too was further proof of the boy's place next to God.

"That would be sensible, would it not?" he began. "That the boy would say nothing of import? His soul is but a child's. He was not literate and only knew some words, correct?"

Why hadn't he thought of it before? Jehan rolled onto his back, his arms fully out. This was a love he knew. Close to the earth, fully submitted to the infinite. Isabeau must have felt it too.

"You heard him?" he asked.

"Yes!"

"It was his voice?"

"Yes!"

They screamed in God's Grotto, back and forth, where their voices carried on forever, until Alarie gently touched them where they lay, as whispered syllables babbled in the darkness.

When they went home, they could hardly focus on their work. Work had become pedestrian, dull.

Jehan could not plow, he was too distracted. Isabeau could not sew or milk or cook, so instead they sat and talked alone. They excitedly considered their futures, as the mother and father of a saint. They tried praying, each in turn, to reach their son. When no answer came, they decided that he must be very busy now, very busy indeed.

In an hour, there was a knock on the door.

A man had come to bring meat. He wished them well in their grief. "Keep me in your prayers," he said.

Jehan hugged the man tightly. "Saint Piers is the saint of the worker! The protector of the poor!" he exclaimed. "He will keep us all in his sights!"

Then, a woman came. "Please accept this. These are spices, my dear. My husband—dead, now, I'm afraid—brought these back from his servitude in war. Do not let anyone know you have them and keep me in your prayers."

Isabeau came to the door this time too. "Of course, of course, dear. Saint Piers will bring you prosperity."

There were more that came, more believers. Word had spread as quick as plague. One after the other came to the former home of Saint Piers, bringing food, ale, candles, spices, blankets and whatever other secret wealths were hidden in their peasant homes. By the end of the night, both Jehan and Isabeau had a veritable feast. They drank and danced and ate till their stomachs threatened to pop and spill their guts to the ground. They kept their fire going all night and made love, for the first time in a long while. Each of them, united in thought, realized the power their bodies had. As the act progressed, they wondered if they could do it again. If they could make another saint.

* * *

Isabeau and Jehan came to the church earlier still the next day, their bellies full and bodies sated. More would come to their home today, there would be more gifts, more expectations of blessings. They talked briefly about charging a small donation fee, if only for their time. After all, they would need to get back to their crops, eventually. But, with Piers dead and soon to be canonized, they decided to enjoy the moment. People waved to them on the street, they wished them well. They quite openly wanted to be them, the parents of such a spiritually adept dead boy.

Alarie came to them smiling. "You know the way, correct?"

"Piers will guide us," said Jehan. He never thought he'd say such a thing, but the words felt true on his tongue.

Isabeau closed her eyes and bent her head down, the image of the Mother. "We trust in the Lord and His wisdom."

Alarie threw his hand out, as if to tell them to lead the way. He followed behind them leisurely. His demeanor was so much more relaxed; he was smiling, chuckling. "You know," he said, "this is the final day of our process. I've gotten the word that, if all goes well, Piers will indeed become a saint this very day."

"We never had a doubt," said Jehan proudly. "Our boy was always God-fearing."

"I witnessed his miracles firsthand! I was there!" said Isabeau.

"Of course, for you both, I'm sure this was of no surprise." There was something in his voice, an ironic edge that sliced through the air. "But, we must still take today seriously, even if it is only a formality. This will be our most difficult session."

"Oh yes?"

"Yes, very much so. You'll need to traverse the Grotto alone. It is something you, and only you, must do."

They reached the staircase, again by intuition, and Alarie praised them. "The Saint's influence is so strong! To find your way through this stone maze! It is no wonder the church is moving so swiftly to bring Piers close to God."

"It is our humble burden to serve the Lord."

"We are servants to the divine."

Alarie pointed to the staircase that led to the impenetrable black. "Your son, his corporeal form, is down there. He is in God's Grotto. When we found him, it was necessary to take him there as it is a sort of conduit, a place most Holy. It was a place where we knew God would see Piers and make his decision."

"Yes, of course," said Jehan.

"The only right place for Piers is to be at God's right hand," said Isabeau.

Alarie placed a hand on both of them. "Go now," he said. "Retrieve his body and he will be given the burial he deserves."

And with that, they left Alarie's toothy grin behind them, and descended into the void.

Isabeau and Jehan, because they were so united now, both affected the same gravity as they made their way into the blackness. They did not speak of anything trivial. They did not think of the gifts they were sure to receive or the relative ease through which they would live the rest of their lives. They kept sober faces, even in the Grotto, where no one could see them.

"We should hold hands," said Isabeau, "so that we don't get lost."

Jehan agreed, so they locked hands and wandered far into the darkness, repeating their son's name until it lost all meaning.

The black was cold. It bit at their extremities. Every once in a while they stopped and hugged each other for warmth. At certain points, they wondered if they could see at all, or if they would ever see again. There were no walls in the Grotto, there was nothing but infinite blackness. Isabeau tried not to think of this, because the God in her mind was warm, like a sunny day. She decided quickly, that if this place did indeed represent God, it was only incidentally cold and black and lonely. That God was here for some other reason, because it was beneath the cathedral, perhaps. And when she came to that conclusion, she thought nothing more of it.

Jehan, though, considered this as good a place as any for a God to reside. He had some amount of wonder fueled by this strange and infinite cave. It was closer to his vision of the sublime than any stained glass. He could learn to worship the Grotto, as it was the nothing that surrounded everything—the trees, the earth, the seasons, and life itself. If this had been God all along, he felt a fool for not giving himself so fully to it in the first place. This was a God he recognized.

They had gone for hours before they heard the first call. It was barely more than a whisper, but they heard it all the same. They cupped their ears and listened intently, hoping to find the source.

"Piers!" Isabeau screamed. "Lead us!"

"We could've passed him by now," said Jehan. "This place is too large. We could've walked past the poor thing's body within ten paces and not known it."

"We would have known it, he would have revealed himself—"

Then, clearly:

"*Maman! Papa!*"

"Oh God, our God! He's here! He's guiding us!" cried Isabeau. "Piers, show us! Where are you?"

"*Maman! Papa!*" the voice whistled again. It sounded like a cold wind, blowing underwater; distorted, from another world entirely.

"By the Grace of God, he is our guide!" screamed Jehan,

into God itself. "Show us where your body has been taken, boy! We will give you the Christian burial you've earned!"

"Please, Piers, please show us the way!"

But in the distance they heard the voice again. "*Maman? Papa?*" Only now, it was closer.

They ran forward hand in hand, so as not to lose each other. They screamed out toward their son as the voice grew louder and louder still. The child's cries for his parents broke their hearts and began their grieving anew. Their legs were tired, their limbs were frostbitten from the void that was as chilled as a winter morning. Eventually, they stopped, heaving, unsure of how far they'd gotten, how long they'd been down there.

But then:

"Maman! Papa!"

The voice was coming from right in front of them. They could not see its source but it was there.

"Piers!"

"My boy."

And then Isabeau and Jehan, together, went down to scoop up his dead body, and stopped.

The boy was standing.

Jehan wrapped his arms around him, in the dark. He felt his chest move in and out.

The boy was breathing.

His tiny arms wrapped around his parents who stood, dumb-founded.

The boy was alive.

Together, as one, they realized the boy had been down here for three days. He was cold, tired. He had not had food or drink and had been calling for them, in need.

"You're okay?" asked Jehan. "Are you alive?"

The boy's voice went high, trying to explain, and the rapid

syllables that came from his mouth tripped over each other. Jehan could never understand the boy when he got like this and even now, in God's Grotto, he felt the urge to strike him.

Isabeau cried, but she released her son. She did not want to touch him. "You're alive," she said, defeated. "You're alive."

They winced at the thought of bringing the so-called boy saint, trembling and scared, a pathetic animal, back up to the church, back into their homes where he would ask about the presents, the meats, the blankets, the spices—and then proceed to eat and use them like they were his own.

"You were supposed to be a saint," she said.

Jehan wiped tears from his eyes, tears only he knew were there. "We can't come back with you in this state."

He reached a hand out, to make sure Piers was still there.

The boy started to talk again, his incessant verbal rambling.

"Stop! Shut up, boy!"

Isabeau hugged her husband, and then placed a hand on the boy too. Together, as one, they came to the decision.

"Can we go home now?"

"We can," said Jehan.

Isabeau kneeled down to the boy, who now seemed to know something was very, very wrong. "Close your eyes, Saint Piers," she said. "You're going to meet God."

WHAT WE WILL BECOME

A EULOGY FOR THE FIFTH WORLD

Trudy stared at her phone. "Kay hasn't called."

"No," said George, his voice cracking. "She hasn't."

She reached for his hand and wrapped her fingers over his own. They both looked out the window. "We knew that would happen though," she said. "I guess that's that."

"The kids," he said absently.

"I know." She placed her hand on his shoulder now. "It isn't fair."

Both of them leaned into each other, but they did not cry. There were too many funerals and only so many tears. They weathered everything else up to this point, there was no use stopping now.

"They're gone," said George.

"Yes," said Trudy. "God help them."

"I can't believe it."

"We will be too," she said.

He rested his head on her shoulder. "How long?"

"An hour. Two, maybe?"

"Have you watched the news?"

"No, I've been avoiding it. What does it look like?"

"No one's filming it. No one's working today." He choked out a laugh, despite himself.

She laid back on the bed, looking up at the cross that hung above their pillows. "I don't know why I keep that up."

"Wanna chuck it? You can. You have time."

"What's the point?"

"I don't know."

George laid down beside her, wrapped her in his arms.

"Kay's dead," she said. "And the kids. That's everyone we know now."

"Everyone."

She looked out to the window, narrowing her eyes as if she were hoping to see something on the horizon. "What should we do?"

"We can't do much, I guess. Get drunk? Scream? Play our music too loud? Fuck?"

"We could do all of that, I guess. We have time."

"You want to?"

"If it's our last chance, we might as well."

"How long has it been?"

"Too long. Or maybe long enough."

"We used to do it a lot."

"When we were kids."

"When we were kids." She thought about that, the way George pinned her arms up above her head, kissing her hungrily. They'd been together for thirty-nine years. "We had good times, didn't we?"

George shook his head and smiled a wolfish grin. "I was insatiable." He looked at Trudy and leaned over to her ear and whispered, "Maybe I still am."

She laughed. "Maybe I am too."

"Two hours?"

"Maybe."

"Should I pour some wine? The good stuff?"

"Yes, please. Let's have some. Let's have lots." She slotted her fingers together and marveled at their age. "This is good. This is what young people would do, right? I mean, this is what we would do if we were still young. We'd ring in the end times while making love. That's the type of thing I could see us saying, back then."

George called from the next room. "What was that?"

"Nothing, nothing."

When George came in, he had two glasses, a bottle of malbec, and a corkscrew.

"You want to drink it here?" she asked.

"I just thought, because the bed."

Trudy stood up from the bed. "No, this is the last time, ever. We can do it anywhere we want, within reason."

"The bed is comfortable."

"It's not exciting though. We can always come back."

"Where do you wanna go?"

She thought for a moment. "Let's go outside, on the veranda. One last drink, outside in the afternoon."

He motioned upward. "The whole sun thing doesn't turn you off?"

"It's beautiful still, I think. Doesn't it symbolize rebirth anyways?"

"That's what they say."

"That deserves a toast then. Can we toast to rebirth?"

"Not ours," he said with a dry laugh.

She sighed. Shook her head. Stood on unsteady feet. "We better get going."

"Right."

She walked out ahead of him, her husband trailing steps

behind. She climbed down the stairs and waited patiently for him as he slowly caught up. She closed her eyes tight as she opened the door. She thought, for a moment, she might see something. But when she opened her eyes, it was all the same. The same world she'd always known, the same sun above.

"I'm coming, I'm coming," said George. "Right behind you."

He set the wine bottle down on the table, along with the glasses and corkscrew, and eased into his chair. Trudy looked up at the sun.

"No reason not to kick the bottle today."

"Nope, let's try to empty it," she said.

He raised a glass. "To rebirth?"

She turned to him and offered a limp smile. "To the sixth world."

"May they be better off than us."

The wine filled her mouth, a hint of bitter and dark fruit. She drank longer and deeper than she had for years. Across from her, George took a comparatively short sip.

"You know," he said, "I thought this would be worse."

"The wine?"

"No."

She shifted in her seat. "It's still pretty bad. Kay, the grand-kids, all of our friends..."

"Yes, but that's just time zones. In another one, two hours, we'll be with them again."

"It is sad though."

"It is," he agreed. "I guess I shouldn't have made it seem like it wasn't."

"No, no. I know what you meant." It was so quiet out. "It's serene. I wasn't expecting it to be serene."

They drank from their glasses, savoring their wine. The sun

licked at their skin with a warm, dry tongue. Their posture was loose, uninhibited.

Trudy said, "If this is the fifth world, what do you think the others were like?"

"I'm not sure," said George. "I'm not sure I even want to think about it."

"Oh, don't be like that. Let's talk about it. If this is the fifth world, what were the others like? It's a game. A thought experiment."

He thought for a long moment. "Do you think each world improves upon the last in some way?"

"I don't know. I think it may be like that, but I don't know what that would look like. Who knows what is so good about this world that was so bad about the last."

"Well, let's start at the first world," he said, reaching out to caress her hand. "What sort of world do you think that was?"

"A quiet one," she said, returning the touch.

"Too quiet?"

"Yes. It was too quiet. Nothing happened at all. It was very boring."

"But who lived there? There's only a new sun if someone dies, right? That's what they say, anyways. Someone had to live there and someone had to kill them."

She rolled her head back, feeling the sun on her face. George's touch crept up her arm, massaging her shoulders, working his way back down to her wrists. Wine sloshed in her stomach.

"I think there was one quiet girl, a child, and she must have lived in a small village—the first village. This was back a long time ago, where there was no one else. The whole world was one tribe. It was a quiet world. She ran out into the jungle and tripped and fell, breaking her leg. She could not scream for help, not effectively, because she was so quiet. No one at the village knew where she was. No one. Until her father went looking for this quiet girl and found her. She was shivering, bone-thin, and her ankle was twisted around. The poor thing was just so scared. Her father knew she wouldn't make it, but he did not want to live in a world where that was true. So, he killed her, and so ended the first world."

He lifted her hand to his lips. "Sad," he said.

"I know. But all stories about the end of the world are sad. Tell me about the second world."

George let go of her hand and stretched. He poured more wine. "The second world..." He thought for a moment. "The second world was larger than the first. There were more people. They were a very advanced people. We mirror them in some ways. They valued the same things we do. They looked like us. They fought like us. They lived in large cities."

Trudy unbuttoned the top of his shirt. "They can't be exactly like us, can they?"

He smiled. "No, of course not. The one thing that was different was that they could... fly. Yes, fly. They were all buzzing around the sky and eventually, over many thousands of years, they realized they could just keep going." He motioned to the sky, as Trudy pressed her lips against his neck. "Up there. They could go on forever, if they wanted. And so, as the world became more populated, more people began to fly away. They left earth until there was just one man. A father who loved his sons. And because there was no one left, he was so lonely that he felt like someone should do something. That no one should be so lonely. So, he did what he had to do to bring everyone back. Alone, on earth, he killed himself, so that a new sun would rise." He swallowed and Trudy pulled her head back from his neck. She rubbed at the mark.

"Think anyone will notice?"

George laughed at that, he drank more of his wine. She

drank more of hers. They kissed outside, under their current sun.

"And now?" he whispered into her ear. "What about the third world? We're over the hill now. We're almost to the present day.

His voice sent chills down her spine. Her cheeks flushed.

George stood up from his chair, and kneeled in front of her. His hands nimbly undoing her shirt buttons, from the top down.

"The third world was very bad," she said, giggling. "There was a return to normalcy, a return to order. No more flying people." George's lips found their way to her navel. She gasped. "The third world was a world of hiding. People hid from each other constantly, because there was so little... oh, George...trust."

George stared up at her, smiling. He tugged at the clasp of her waistband. "Go on."

"No one trusted each other, so they would often do horrible things. Really bad things. Really, really, really..."

George's tongue teased at the elastic band of her underwear, with his hands, he reached up and eased her pants down, sliding them off easily.

"People would steal, they would kill. They would fight. Oh God! How they would fight. Whenever one would get near another, some horrible thing would happen. That's why they would hide."

He reached behind her, working his fingers in the band of her underwear, pulling them off her. George kissed gently at the soft flesh between her thighs. "What happened next?" he asked.

"One day, a great monster appeared. A very large, very scary monster. And it began reaching its hands into the earth and pulling out the hiding people."

George looked up from between his wife's legs. "They were living underground? Like moles?"

"Yes," she said with a laugh. "They were like mole people. All in separate little holes. Growing like carrots. And the monster came through and picked them, one by one, and chomped them to bits."

George's tongue lapped gently at her clitoris, darting back and forth, as she let out a long shivering moan.

"George, really. That's..."

"You have a story to finish," he said.

The sun felt good on her face. "Well, these mole people dug a hole. A tunnel, so that they could put aside their differences long enough to defeat this monster. Jesus, George! They—they spoke for many nights, back and forth. They held councils. Yes! Councils. But at the end, they were at an impasse. They were tired of being plucked from the ground and eaten. But they also knew that they could not stand to be in a tunnel with each other much longer. They had no choice. Oh—oh—oh. They decided that they would all climb out of their holes, together."

George's mouth glistened. "Poor bastards." He buried his face into her.

Her mouth opened, her legs kicked out. "Oh no," she said. "No, not yet." She ran her hands through his hair and pushed his head back. "You've got to tell me about the fourth world now. The one before this one."

She got out of the chair and pushed George onto his back. She removed the rest of her clothing, the sun catching every crevice her age lent her. Trudy felt free, pure. Exposed to no one but the sky. She ran a hand across his groin, feeling him grow beneath her. "Hasn't changed a bit," she said.

George shook his head. "I took a pill," he admitted.

"You did?"

"I never told you."

"You could've," she said, rubbing it back and forth. "We're old, after all."

"Well, you know how it is..."

"I don't mind."

"...with us guys."

"Shh," she said, unzipping him. "Tell me about the fourth world."

"After all the mole people were eaten, their sacrifice gave birth to a new sun."

"Mmhmm."

"So, now the new sun rose over the horizon and a new world began. In the wake of the corpses that littered the earth, plants grew. Tall trees, and, and, and—"

Trudy sucked on him, slowly, using her tongue to draw lines across his heavy veins.

"The earth was green again, and it was so beautiful. The corpses disappeared with time, dissolving into rich soil. The new people of this world were not like the last world at all. They were very kind. They loved each other so much. They loved each other more than anyone could imagine." He closed his eyes and groaned as Trudy continued to work him up and down. "And they had children that they loved. They had children that they loved more than anything in the world. But as time went on, and age crept upon them... As they aged, and they saw the people they loved die, they became more bitter. But they never stopped loving each other. Not even for one second. They could never do that. Not ever. What happens next is—"

"Oh, does that feel nice?"

"I feel like a teenager."

"Enjoy it while it lasts."

"I am," he said. "I am."

"Are you going to finish?"

"Keep going and find out."

"The story," she said, as she stuck her tongue out, licking his length.

He leaned back. "God. If you insist." He cleared his throat. "These people loved each other too much. They felt everything too much. When one died, it was as if a part of them was torn out. Stomped on. And they got tired of it eventually, they realized life hurt too much. It just did. There was nothing they could do about it."

"What did they do?"

"They realized that their pain had limits, and that to end suffering, they would need to transcend beyond it. So they chose a mother, a lover like themselves, and asked her to do the unthinkable. She did not want to do it, but until she did, the sun would keep rising and setting on the same world, and it was not a world they wanted to live in. In the shadows of a great overgrown forest, in the silence, she resolved to never let her children know the same sorrow, and when the sun set, it was the last time."

Trudy climbed on top of him, kissing him. Tears touched the corners of her eyes. "You're a big softie."

"Not right now," he said.

She eased him inside of her, rocking gently back and forth. "No," she cooed. "Not right now."

Trudy looked at the man beneath her, her hands rested on his chest for support as she moved her hips. His eyes were half closed, but every once in a while, even in the wake of pleasure, he'd open them and squint into the sky. She did too. The sun felt warm on her back but it wasn't as warm as it was minutes ago. It would get colder still.

George reached up toward her breasts, caressing her nipples, as she rode him. After a moment, he rolled over, taking her beneath him. Trudy gasped as he held her arms above her head, kissing her deeply. She bit into his shoulder as he pumped into her.

"Now, tell me," he said, panting. "Tell me the story of the fifth world—our world."

She moaned. "Oh, George. No. No. I don't think I can."

"Let's do it together."

"It was a good world," she started. "Sometimes."

"It was decent," he said, his lips next to her ears.

"There was beauty in it."

"Yes."

"There was so much of everything!"

"Yes!"

"And yet... oh, keep going. Please, George, please."

He said, "But there was sadness too. Great... sadness. War. But also children. Lovers, there were still lovers."

"Yes," she said, clawing into his back. "There were lovers and they had a child."

"A beautiful girl."

"And she grew up into a beautiful woman."

"Headstrong, smart. Successful."

"And she got married to a nice man."

He thrust deeper into her.

"They had children. Great children."

"They were happy, I think. I hope. I think they were happier than most. But what about her parents?"

He stopped and they both stared into each other's eyes. The sky was pink. Trudy reached out to touch his cheek. "On the eve of their last sunset, they loved each other."

They kissed. "Yes," he said. "They did."

When they finished, they stared at the sky, the pink and orange hues of a drowning sun.

"But why did it have to end?" he asked.

"I don't know," she said. "I wish I knew."

"That's all it takes, I guess. One person."

"Or many."

"Or many."

They reached out to each other, breathing softly, and softer and softer still. Cool air kissed their faces as the fifth world came and went.

THE CHILDREN OF THE EVENT

The first *person* to see the wave was a fisherman. Like most of his kind, he was strong, fond of water, and a heavy drinker; he wore rubber boots and a yellow coat slicked with salmon guts. It's important to stress that there was nothing heroic about this fisherman. He was a normal man. He had friends and family. One bar server remembered that he used to show off on Friday nights, after the day's catch, impressing local women with his trick shots.[*] There was nothing that made him more special than all the other men and women who died early that morning, but because he reached for a radio, we know that his name was Jaycee Washington.

To this day, his body remains undiscovered. But it's his voice, his gasping SOS, that became the soundbyte that defined a catastrophe:

"Hello? Hello? This is, uh, Jaycee."

"Jaycee, this is the coast guard. What's going on? Over."

---

[*] Anonymous interview.

"Something's in the water. Something's... [*inaudible*]"*

The water crashes against the deck and Jaycee is presumably thrown overboard. That alone is enough for a tragedy. A man is dead, lungs filling with icy salt water. But as we know, fate is not so kind. Because after *Carbon Angela* goes down, the water stills. Then, after an hour, it breaks.

* * *

It's hard to talk about what happened next, because it's absurdity incarnate. Karin Delle of the Northwest Linguistic Institute posits that's why we collectively decided to call the creature the Event.

The name stuck. The being, or whatever it was, crawled out of the ocean. Scaly, with black skin and red markings. A crown of curved horns. A maw of dripping fangs. A large distended stomach. Observers calculated it as standing roughly seven hundred feet on its hind legs, and half that on all fours. Its tail was as long as its body and then some. It came to the coast first, scuttling ships and killing men like Jaycee Washington, before climbing onto shore. Most people heard the Event before they saw it. Its deep resonating roar rumbled through the earth, announcing its arrival.

Just as its weight crushed through the docks, sending shards of splintered wood careening through the air, two Coast Guardsmen made the decision to sound the alarm, eleven full minutes after Washington fired off his warning.†

The broadcast was hastily put together. Press releases were

---

* For myself and others, this was history. I remember repeating, "Something's in the water, something's in the water," while watching the news, doing the dishes. These words became a part of us.

† In the aftermath, this prompted a public debate. Some commentators praised the Guard for their reaction time. Others dismissed it as too little, too late.

rushed; news anchors and radio personalities were interrupted mid-sentence with breaking news.

Brian Seneca of WDFQ said, "It was like nothing I'd seen. We'd done emergency announcements before, of course we did. We're the news. But this carried with it a certain gravity. I could tell it was serious when the information hit us and the producers just looked at each other in disbelief. One of them, Randy, came up to me, dead serious, and said, 'Read the prompter. It's not a joke.' And that was that. I did it. Soon after, we were evacuated."*

The Event destroyed fifteen blocks of newly renovated waterfront property, burying restaurant-goers and the workers that served them in crumbling rubble. It continued its march of destruction for two hours, tearing through commercial and residential neighborhoods alike. Thousands perished during the Event's initial landfall. Whether by accident or design, however, is an entirely different matter.

One woman, one of several dozen to live in the city center and survive its destruction, said, "…[I]t wasn't doing much but walking, really. I was shaking. I'm still shaking thinking about it. We were all huddled up under a fallen support beam. I could still see out to the street though. Its claws were yellowish, as big as me, if not bigger. And I couldn't see much, all I had was a triangle between two slabs of drywall, but I could tell that it was bending over, like it was about to do something. Which terrified me, you know? Because until that moment, I didn't realize that it had thoughts. It was *doing* something. I didn't like that, I didn't like that at all."

---

* Seneca went on to mention that the evacuation itself was a surreal affair. "We were hustled out of the building, into a news helicopter, and flown 15 miles up north. We were terrified. The helicopter could only fit so many personnel. They took us first, 'the talent.' I never felt so guilty in my life. When we were safe, I watched it fly away. I didn't realize it was never going to come back."

What the Event was doing in that moment, is an example of dramatic irony on a cosmic scale. The woman, who wished to remain anonymous, was a partial witness to a paradigm shift.* Many of us, this author included, did not know what the monster was doing in the city. We evacuated early, or lived in the suburbs and quietly quaked, glued to the news. Those who lived in the city had front-row seats to what the rest of us could only imagine.

Helicopter footage showed us what happened in those two fateful hours. The Event crashed through buildings, first knocking them gently with its snout; then, when the tenants in waiting fled, it flattened them completely. This routine was repeated many times. But when the people ran into the streets —and there were a good many—the great beast unhinged its jaw and leaned over them. It becomes obvious, through the footage, that the Event was *sucking* people whole into its maw. Hundreds of them.

There is one short clip of footage from a supermarket, where the camera is so shaky you can barely see anything but white walls and glass doors. What you can hear, briefly, is one man screaming, "Jesus Christ! It's eating them!"

Street after street, this continued.

For observers, the horror seemed to last an eternity—and for many of us, the image of the great behemoth, crushing our structures, and vacuuming up our friends and family, would come to define that morning. We sat together in our homes or evacuation sites, hugging each other close. We knew that our lives, or rather, our reality, had changed forever.

At noon, sitting in my one-bedroom apartment, twenty-

---

* Many of those interviewed for this piece wished to remain anonymous, for reasons that will be obvious later.

five minutes east of the city, I heard one of my neighbors in the hallway yell, "It's gone! It's gone! The monster left!"

I, and others like myself, wiped the sweat from our brows and gave into our own nervous energy. We left our apartments and walked outside, watching the plumes of smoke rise up into the sky.

An hour later, someone's teenage daughter pointed at her phone: "Look at this," she said. Soon, a group of adults gathered around her, to see the video. So many people crowded around her that others were left to ask, "What's it called? What are we looking at?" and then they too pulled it up on their phones.

We were all watching the same helicopter footage. There it was, the Event, stretched out in the remnants of our city, its posture reminiscent of a cat voiding a hairball. Its back arched, jaws parallel to the earth. It retched. We all watched the video hundreds of times, over and over again.

The Event hacked and hacked and then, a mass of twisted limbs came out of its stomach. We couldn't make it out clearly from the footage until it zoomed in.* At the end of the video, you can see a large hill of wet humans squirming, separating from each other. The video cuts, a short time jump, and we're left with a lingering shot. The monster is gone, the Event is over, and on top of the rubble, an army of glowing survivors survey their surroundings.†

---

* An entire article could be written just on how we, humans as a collective, experience trauma on a mass scale through second-hand reporting. Many of us, myself included, never saw the Event, nor felt its presence until hours after it had left. And yet, we still have in us a deep throbbing sense of despair, of loss and terror.

† This went on to become an iconic image. The videographer who captured it refuses to be named and has donated the image to the public domain.

* * *

It was obvious that the people had changed in some way. We'd seen them on the news, listened to them talk. They described being in the monster's stomach as something akin to a womb, although they said it smelled of rot and sulfur. By all accounts it was dark, hot, and humid. They floated in a pool of thick saliva and stomach acids, gasping for air. Of the 376 that were swallowed, every one of them claimed that a warm calmness washed over them. When they came out (or were born, as some commenters put it), they glowed a peculiar green. In news segments, I watched them curiously as they struggled to articulate their feelings, as if they were newborn fawns taking their first steps with the English language.

The bias arrived immediately.* One man, a first responder who attended to the newly born, said, "I had an immediate reaction to them. I couldn't put my finger on it, but something wasn't right. They were normal, they looked like us, I thought. But, something inside me felt repelled by them."

This man, who wished to remain anonymous, captures the popular sentiment against the Children of the Event (who would go on to colloquially be called the Children). Although by all accounts they presented themselves as earnest, eager to help, and curiously humanitarian, their alien gestalt was almost universally off-putting.

The Children reintegrated as best they could. They went back to their families, hugged their loved ones (even when those loved ones cringed at their touch), and the rest of society began discussing the Event with a feverish intensity.

The first matter, of course, was where did the monster

---

* I myself admit to this, although I'm not proud of it. The first time I saw one on television, I recoiled.

come from? The answer was: we did not know. This ambiguity created an ugly back and forth as officials theorized loudly on television. The Event was from the ocean, it was a lost creation from prehistory. Or, it was a product of our invention—a byproduct of environmental waste. Religious officials held an uncomfortable notion that it was the biblical Leviathan. Fringe metaphysicians maintained that it was a God, a spiritual reckoning given shape and form to punish us.

We never received a definite answer. So, naturally, the question "Where did it come from?" became "Where did it go?"

That, too, proved to be unanswerable.* Observably, the Event came from the ocean and returned to it. Nations gathered to sweep the depths, but the Event was never found. It was as if it came to life, then dissolved into unlife. And all it left of itself was tragedy. And, of course, the Children.

* * *

My first interaction with one of the Children was at a volunteer event.† We gathered to begin the rebuilding process. There was also the hope of rescuing survivors, despite the utter devastation surrounding us.

We were brought together by the destruction of the city and we were determined to do something about it. That's all anyone could say at their television, for a while. "Somebody

---

* Ambiguity tolerance is a part of a country's cultural makeup and reveals how a culture deals with uncertainty. Ambiguity theorists such as Rosha Hundvirst believe that, while the United States typically is identified as being an ambiguity-tolerant culture, the Event challenged this norm in some way, and since then, neuroticism has become more acute and pervasive. This represents one of the few great cultural shifts we've seen happen in real time.

† I did this, in a way, to challenge my own biases.

has gotta do something!" Collectively, we came to the agreement that this is what somebody ought to do—show up and sift through the wreckage.

It became apparent very early on that there were Children among us. The eerie glow that emanated from them unsettled me deeply. I tried my best not to show my discomfort, because we were there to do a job. We were there to do something.

I was tasked by one of the Children, who was wearing an orange vest and a hard hat, to go with another of his glowing fellows, a man named Carlos.

Carlos was kind and friendly, often giving me advice on how to traverse difficult terrain. He smiled at me gently, helped me when he could.*

"Over there," he said. "There's more over there."

Carlos led me to the hollowed-out foundation of an apartment building that he seemed to know intimately, or rather, innately. We dug through rubble. I didn't talk much, because I didn't have anything to say, and also I was afraid of maybe saying the wrong thing. As if I would open my mouth too long and I'd have no choice but to ask about what it was like inside of the Event.

Carlos, it seemed, knew the question on my mind. But when he would look up at me, a smile spread thinly on his lips, a twinkle in his emerald eyes, it was like he was daring me to ask. That day, Carlos found twelve corpses amongst the rubble. I found none. When we reported to the organizer though, Carlos made sure to say *we* found them—a fine gesture, to be sure.

* * *

---

* On the day of, it was impossible to read this as anything but pointed condescension.

Everyone said it would take years to rebuild the city. We had all started to buckle down, ready for the long haul, while living in fear of the Event returning. It never did, thankfully. But some of us felt like it should.

In actuality, most of the destruction was cleared in weeks thanks to the hard labor of a group of efficient community-minded teams. It came as no surprise to us that they were made entirely of the Children. At bars and at restaurants, in conspiratorial whispers, we told ourselves that it was okay. *Of course they're taking the initiative, no one knows the Event better than them.* But even that thought left a cold clump of icy dread sitting in our stomachs.

I made an appointment with Marshall Wallace, the Senior Director of ReBuild—a non-profit organization dedicated to funding the re-development of the city. Wallace was a barrel-chested man who seemed ill-suited for his button-up shirt and slacks. He looked like the sort that found more joy in the solitude of nature, or as a calloused-hand in the trades. Wallace confirmed as much shortly after we met. When he shook my hand, I tried not to recoil, lest his glow penetrate me.

He pointed out a group of construction workers. "I used to do what they're doing," he said. "But not anymore."[*]

We sat under a tent, a sort of makeshift lunch space. Wallace was gracious and intelligent and looked me in the eyes.

"How do you feel about what people call you?" I asked.

Wallace sighed. "It's just a name, I guess. I don't think about it much. Except in the dark."

"Because of the glow?"

---

[*] While upward mobility is often a theme in whispered tales of the Children, it's important to note it's not always so. Most of the Children haven't reported a significant change in salary.

"Right."

"Have they figured out why that happens?"

Wallace shook his head. "Your guess is as good as mine, bud."*

"Some people have said that the Children have changed in some way. Do you agree with that?"

"I don't know shit about that, bud. I think we all changed. That's what happens when something like this happens, right? Being in the belly of the beast, so to speak, it gives you perspective. I'd say we're just like you, doing our best in a difficult time."

It was because of men and women like Wallace that the rebuilding began at all. While some of us held vigils and made talking points of the catastrophe, the Children acted. And not to be outdone, we followed.

There was pushback, of course. There was a sense that in the wake of the catastrophe, we were moving too fast. That we were not grieving adequately. This grief was for change. Because things *were* changing.

* * *

I first noticed the "Seawatchers" gathered in a long line along the boardwalk. I was on my way to interview a woman who worked in the rebuilding effort. They leaned over the railing, carefully eyeing the soft curvature of the horizon. Some of them locked arms; some of them wept. It was as if they were both mourning and pleading, all at the same time. These Seawatchers were urged internally by a sense of melancholy

---

* Currently, we have no credible scientific discovery regarding the Children's glow.

longing to be swallowed by the Event, to rest in its stomach acids, suspended in bile with their new brothers and sisters.

They could be seen from blocks away, many of them wearing glow stick arrangements to emanate a chemical shade of emerald—a weak substitute for the Children's natural glow. But, like the Children, they were resented and reviled. "It's disgusting," said one anonymous source. "Foul. Just look at them, the way they—I don't know—grovel."

I approached the Seawatchers with curious empathy. I too watched the same footage they had; I too felt a deep emotional reaction. We all did. Every one of us lived under the weight of the Event. The Seawatchers though, transubstantiated an invisible slice of the zeitgeist into something concrete—a movement.

They stood there in shifts, at every time of the day. Even in the dark hours of the night, they glowed—albeit artificially. They held each other and looked out to the sea and wished for one more chance to be something special.

It's funny how even in times of disaster those pesky human needs still roil under the surface. Death screams and rubble can only suppress our desires to be loved and recognized; however, they cannot annihilate them. Standing in the cool breeze, smelling the ocean, I felt what they felt, for a time— that everything we loved was gone, and soon everything would march forward, with or without us.

The Seawatchers, all in all, were a harmless sect. They watched the sea with pensive despair but did little more than loiter. The Children commented on them only when pushed. When it came time to renovate the waterfront and undo the damage from the Event, the Children paused construction. They created a plan to respect the mourning of the Seawatchers and convened with their representatives to find a workaround. The Seawatcher representatives could not hide their glee at shaking hands with the Children. Some wondered if this was the plan all along, to force their attention.

The Seawatchers continued on, as the new waterfront was built under a new architectural vision. They stood in their false glow, totally unaware that a new event was upon them.

* * *

I did not consider myself a Seawatcher, but I did spend time with them. They were the only ones who were willing to wear their hearts so plainly on their sleeves. It was exhilarating, in a nihilistic way. The desire to wish the Event back to shore, after so much devastation, was akin to an intrusive thought. It was driving into traffic, jumping off a bridge, playing Russian roulette—pure catharsis.

It was on a cold day in November when tensions reached a fever pitch. At first it was a minor bit of counter protesting. Four people, sans glow, holding picketing signs across the street. One read, "Green Unclean," while another urged Seawatchers to "Run toward the light." They laughed and jeered and did little more than tease. But then, slowly, more joined.

It wasn't until that day in November, six months after the Event, that I felt a more acute friction.

There was no name for the protesters. We just called them people. They were not the Children, they were not Seawatchers. They were just people, like myself. Ostensibly, they had no loyalty or connection to each other, besides the fact that they did not glow and did not want to glow. They came from all walks of life, and many of them brought weapons.

The tide was higher than usual that morning which caused some new chatter. The Seawatchers were prone to assigning value to randomness. They talked amongst themselves. "It's here," they said. "There's something in the water."*

For some reason, they were more elated than usual. The week before, a whale carcass washed ashore, but there was only a murmur of excitement. But on that fateful day, the crowd erupted. Speaking to one expert on crowd dynamics, Dr. Linda Wolk, this explosion in activity could've been building for a long time, and it was likely *because* it had been building, and nothing else. "When people get together in groups, especially for a cause, they want to see results. Eventually, through either fact or fiction, they'll find them."

As the tide rolled in, large waves foaming and frothing in collapsing crescents, the Seawatchers cheered. They jumped up and down, screaming. "Yes, thank you! Yes! It's coming! Take us!"

I watched it come in, bemused, but also energized. I bounced too, throwing my body against them, back and forth, screaming nonsense.

Later, I was told that the people—the regular, plain people —were pacing, agitated. I didn't see them at all, I couldn't. I was with the Seawatchers, bellowing my lungs out in the glow of filtered light.

Somewhere down the waterfront, a bullet found its target. We did not hear the gunshot. They found the body and then slowly hushed those around them, craning their necks like meerkats as the unseen rifle kicked and sent another Seawatcher sprawling to the ground, blood rushing from their neck.

Silence overtook us in a wave, spreading whisper to whisper, until it reached myself and beyond. I did not know what had happened; I only knew to be quiet. Many of us, for a

---

* This was a rallying cry of sorts for the Seawatchers.

moment, thought that the Event had returned, so we turned back toward the ocean to look for a great shape rising from the water.

As another volley of shots arrived, another handful of Seawatchers fell to the ground, dead. Pandemonium struck soon after.

The Seawatchers, once docile and melancholy, turned toward the protesters in rage. The protesters, in turn, ground their teeth and reloaded. They didn't wait to fire, they kept killing until the rush of the crowd overtook them, until their bodies were trampled under the false glow of angry boots.

I ran, dodging people and bullets, ducking behind outhouses and construction equipment. The city's pressure cooker of rage exploded all around me, and I ran into a dig site, through the skeletal beginnings of a building I could not recognize. I went up a flight of iron stairs that looped about like the curves in a roller coaster.

At the top, I collapsed, hot breath steaming into my palms. I stared down at the wreckage below me, the violence that overtook the streets.

People were being pounded into paste. It was a squirming mass of wriggling bodies, tearing each other apart. Those who ran stomped away in splashes of blood.

Police cars and ambulances arrived soon after. Men and women exited the vehicles with riot gear and an emerald aura. They used minimal force, I realized. As I watched from my perch, I saw the crowd disperse, the violence mute itself. Once enraged murderers were taken calmly into the backseats of police cars. Green EMTs mended wounds for both people and Seawatchers.

I watched this for hours, a sickness growing inside me.

By the time I left my hiding spot, the streets were clean and quiet.

* * *

There was no great violence after, no more events—capital or lowercase. Time marched forward and so did we, as best we could, with the knowledge that our home was not our own. The new world will belong to the Children and their children.

And yes, there were births. The Children reproduced, but only with each other. They bear illuminated children that don't cry much and hit milestones early; they're a friendly, insightful bunch. Now, in the city, I can't help but think the only people I see anymore glow a vivid emerald. They're eating sandwiches, talking about the news, pushing their brood in new baby carriages. Sometimes, they open the door for me and smile as if they're holding bile in their cheeks.

There is no more blood in the streets though. There is no more rubble. They don't live with the memories of before and after.

The city is different. The towers are taller, thinner—like needle points reaching to sew a seam in the sky. They have no windows. Some of them are short and squat, round and metallic. Others curve and loop, serpentine, around the older buildings, threatening to constrict them with their new construction.*

But now that the Event is long gone, unable to be located the world over, and the city is rebuilt, it seems that that just isn't enough. The old buildings that survived are now being demolished. Glowing men set the charges and stare solemnly as they crumble. The city is almost done, I hear, but that's a

---

* We didn't think about how strange these were when they were built. We accepted them. We didn't even consider that the world that we were building, under the direction of the Children, was a new one.

funny thing to think about. The word "done." When is a city done?*

<hr />

* We'll know when they tell us.

THE MUSHROOM MEN

I t was because of my trauma that I was invited; sitting in the backseat, listening to the symbolic jabber of old friends. Paulie brought a thermos of tea. He asked about my job—how everything was going. Grant talked about the housing market. The city gave way to the country and we headed toward the mountains.

It was eight months ago that my daughter Vera died with a belly full of deadly nightshade. I still see her thick black pupils shining watery in my dreams. With the daughter, went the wife. Now: three old college buddies, a road trip—just like the old days. The destination: a cabin in the woods. The reason: *morels.*

We are hobbyists, mycological enthusiasts—we belong to a club. For us, morels are something of a delicacy; rare and expensive, gourmand and mythic. They appear in the wake of fire. Maybe that's why I agreed to come—hoping, sadly, that I too would come rising from burnt remains.

This is why we were traveling, why Paulie chanced a working relationship with a shut-in anarchist. And in the same way that he didn't speak about Vera and Sam, but kept looking at me like he wanted to, I wondered if he made the same connection between morels and myself as I had.

"We're real close, boys," he said from the driver's seat.

We turned up a dirt road flanked by an infinite wilderness of sky-tall pines. My eyes jumped from trunk to trunk, further and further out until dead space gave way to more trees and foliage.

"Pretty green for a burn," I said, my conversation pointedly neutral.

"The man in the tinfoil hat said it was a *controlled* burn."

The road went upward, a snake coiling through the elevation. No mailboxes on the side of the road, just us, bouncing over rocks at fifteen miles an hour. A three-hour road trip became four, as dawn dissipated, and we were left with the cold sun high in the air. As we came over a hill, I found myself blinking rapidly, trying to shake off the illusion that made my innards tremble within me. The three of us on a road trip; hobbyists; morels; and the cabin, hovering over a sea of black charcoal.

My eyes adjusted. A softly rolling hill had been burned clear of all life. The cabin stood in front of it, framed by the blackness—pristine and illogically intact. I couldn't shake the trick of perspective. It looked as if it were floating against eternity.

My fingers drummed against the seat as the details came into focus. Grant and Paulie whooped and hollered in the front seat. "Jesus," said Grant.

"Fucking told ya," said Paulie.

Indeed, the burnt-black earth was riddled with tumorous splotches of brown. From the ever-decreasing distance, it reminded me sickly of news footage I watched as a child—the mounds of morels grotesquely associating in my mind with a smallpox outbreak in Africa, all those tiny fluid-filled bumps grouped so close to each other, irrevocably changing the topography of a child's flesh into something vile and abhorrent. This thought, inevitably, led me back to Vera in the grass. My daughter, dead.

"I've never seen this many."

"It's the fire," said Paulie, voice drugged with wonder. He parked the car and the two stumbled out, cloth bags dangling by the drawstring from their wrists. I followed a couple steps behind them.

"Just a couple pounds each?"

Paulie turned and looked at me. He smiled.

"Apparently, rules aren't applicable," said Grant, " No mailbox, no house number—what do you wanna bet this is public land?"

He was right. It was a house scrubbed of fingerprints. "No power lines out here either; I'm going to guess no plumbing."

"He's a character, all right—total live-off-the-land, don't-tread-on-me type."

"Off the grid," said Grant.

I silently mouthed the words and considered their possibilities.

"He's not like some sort of militant, is he?" asked Grant.

Paulie shook his head. "No, just eccentric, I think. More of a demonstrator than a Unabomber."

"Well, gee," I said. "Sounds pretty above board."

He knocked on the door. Silence.

Three more hard knocks.

"Nobody home?" he said with a nervous laugh.

"Does he have a car? Some old beater with a Fuck the Police bumper sticker, maybe? Because there's no car here."

"No, he doesn't have a car, not that I know of. No car, no phone, no plumbing, no electricity."

I looked through the window to try and see a sign of life. Absently, I asked, "How did he contact you then?"

"Huh?"

"No phone, right?"

"Oh yeah, we correspond via snail mail," said Paulie. "Pen pals, you'd say. I got his last letter yesterday, he said come up whenever."

I nodded slowly.

"Maybe he's out foraging," said Grant, "that's within the realm of an anarchist's day-to-day, right?"

Paulie shrugged, squinting into the endless expanse of black—as if he were trying to remember something. "Yeah," he said. "Maybe."

We all stood in silence, wondering whether this meant the end of the trip or not. The ache inside of me had already decided I should've stayed home and looked at old pictures, smelled old clothes.

"He's probably out in the woods, doing weird-guy shit," said Paulie, after a pause. "He said we could take what we want, we best not let him down." He waved us forward. "Let's get what we came for."

We did as he suggested, following in a reluctant single-file line until Grant, perhaps exhausted by my visible grief, jogged up to Paulie and walked beside him, leaving me as the distant peak of a floating triangle. The black earth crunched beneath my feet and I had a brief vision of burnt bones and black, wet eyes. I shook my head and jogged ahead to catch up with the two others, doing my best impression of *just tired.*

Paulie tossed me one of his bags and said something distinctly false and cavalier like, "Go get 'em, my man." We were surrounded by them. I crushed them under my feet with each tentative step. They stared back at me, they were perfect. Tan stalks grew into grotesque looking folds, like a melted honeycomb, a deformed brain, a fleshy vulva. Meaty, succulent, coveted. I was a mycophile, and this was a dream. You ask any enthusiast what they're looking for, they'll rattle off a bunch of Latin, but morels, morels are always coveted.

And there were so many.

The black of the charred earth became brown with distance, as the morels clustered and overtook the burn.

Paulie smiled, as if to say, *I know*. I was thankful. The hurt, as far as I could tell, would continue forever, but now, I was distracted.

"You guys wanna get a little weird?"

Grant cocked an eyebrow as Paulie dug into his pocket.

"Just enough to take the edge off."

I could name it by sight: *Psilocybe azurescens*. Long stalk, an almost cartoonishly perfect cap with closely grouped gills. Caramel colored, except for the bruising, a fact about *psilocybes* that always unnerved me. They bruise blue, just like us.

Street name: blue runners.

Paulie grinned and then, as if to convince us they were okay, he popped a cap in his mouth.

Grant took one too. "So we're taking flying saucers and picking morels today? That's what we're doing?"

Paulie nodded. "Only if you want, I'm not one for peer pressure."

"Bullshit," I said as he handed me one. I smiled gamely until they turned. The blue bruising bothered me, made me think too much of—

I shoved it in my pocket. Maybe later.

We exchanged words of wonder and cordial joking and gathered our morels as we wandered further into the blackness.

* * *

Now, everything was different.

I don't know what happened, but the unspoken had shifted and suddenly, we were not following Paulie. Grant was standing in front of us, and being deferred to. I don't remember what happened. We were just walking, then everything melted like candle wax and reformed before my eyes.

"Do you see it?" he asked.

I didn't at first, but then I took another minute and let my eyes focus. I lapped my tongue around my mouth, tasting my teeth, searching for fleshy strands stuck to my gums. I felt my pocket, patting it in the *keys-phone-wallet* motion of a perpetual mover. I felt for the cap in my pocket. It was gone.

"This was for you, man, you know?"

I turned to Paulie. His face was serious. He repeated what he said. "This is for you, okay? Jim?"

I shook my head and scrambled for whatever happened last. *Phone call. Car ride. Cabin. Burn. Morels.* And then it all just started repeating, like a wheel spinning time itself. I jerked around and looked at the earth and the burn went further than I could imagine.

Nothing was right.

"This is Grant's area, you know. I'm the mushroom man, after all."

"Do you see it yet?"

My mouth was dry, my pupils felt like they were straining against the edges of my iris. "What's going on?" I asked. And then—I saw it.

Grant put a hand on my shoulder. "Yeah?"

"Yeah," I said. My breath was icy and hung in the air.

We were in the middle of the field. We had backtracked, but the blackness of burnt earth stretched far beyond the acre it had originally taken.

"Just look at it, Jim. Look at it."

On the ground, stretched out in a deathly yawn, was the body of *something*. A mammal, maybe, but it was hard to tell because of the vivisection. It was large, it could've been a man with horns or an elk with a face pushed inward, or maybe a mangy bear with tusks and a face licked clean by predators. It had been torn apart days ago, and its flesh was pulled outward in taut sheets. I felt vomit rising, not sure whether it was the violence inherent in its form or the undetermined nature of its biology. But they kept saying, over and over: *you can see it, right?*

"It was here earlier, too," said Paulie sheepishly. "Just so you know."

"What?"

"A week ago," said Grant. "It was here a week ago. This is Paulie's cabin, Jim."

Paulie shook his head. "No, that's not true. The anarchist was real. You're getting mixed up. And it wasn't a week—closer to a month."

"You dosed me, I'm fucking high. I'm hallucinating, you brought me up here to get me high." My cheeks flushed, I wanted to sound angry but instead I sounded desperate, rattled.

They just stared down at their boots.

"Again, dude, this is Grant's department."

I looked at Grant. Neurotypical, empathetic, rock solid, quick with a joke. Closer to Paulie than myself. But here he was, standing over the dead thing like the cat with the canary. "Touch your hands together for me, real quick," he said. "Go ahead."

I hesitated, but buckled under their insistent eyes. I slapped my palms together as my stomach felt weighted with dread.

"Great. Now, look at the thing. Just tell me what you see."

"Some sort of... dead animal."

"Do you recognize the animal?"

"No."

"Perfect, we're on the same page. So, think about what you felt when you clapped your hands together. Did you feel warmth? Cold? Are your hands rough, soft? What about a sound, did they make a clapping sound, or did they just kinda touch each other? How do you know any of this?"

I stammered, confused, with an uneasy stomach. The black stretched endlessly.

"It's your brain. Your brain interprets the world around you, and that is how you *know* anything. Like, who knows if you were to have my brain, or a broken brain, or a malfunctioning brain, how you'd interact with the world."

Grant was a doctor. He was using his doctor voice. Very calm, almost soothing.

"You did dose me. I'm high. Wait, it was the tea wasn't it?"

"Just listen," said Paulie.

"We don't know what's happening, not totally. Not at all, really, but we know there is more than one—more than one interpretation of the world. I don't want to say it's a different, separate, or new reality, or whether it's connected, or not, to our own. We'll just call it a reinterpretation and leave it at that. Look at the body, do you see what else is there?"

I looked closer and I saw the spores, long gnarled stalks bruised blue with pale white caps. They grew in clusters on the thing's innards. *Psilocybe azurescens*. I patted my pocket. There was no cap.

I looked to each of them, questions in my eyes, pupils dilated with fear and psilocybin, except I didn't feel high, I didn't feel anything but a deep, nervous confusion.

My fingers dabbed at my temple, to feel my pulse. I started

counting my fingers. Nothing. The burnt black earth went on forever.

"I have a theory, though," said Paulie. "And that's why we brought you, so you gotta stay with me. We don't know how the reinterpretation works, only that it works through some kind of combination of this place and the, uh, reconfiguring of senses and memory. We know that the world changes and it has the potential to stay, to cement itself." Paulie fished in his pocket, pulled out the mushroom, what I thought was a blue runner, "We plucked this here, and brought it back to the original interpretation, our world. Do you understand?"

"I didn't take mine though, I just put it in my pocket, I shouldn't be seeing any of this."

It was their turn to look at each other.

"It doesn't matter if you did or not. A version of you did, and here is where worlds merge."

* * *

They told me their story, but none of it made any sense. Grant and Paulie bickered over the details like an old married couple. The anarchist was real and not real. He had a cell phone in one version, he mailed letters in another. The cabin belonged to Paulie or Grant and sometimes it belonged to no one. The flying saucers started the strangeness and sometimes were totally absent.

The one thing Grant and Paulie could agree on was this: that after their first visit to the cabin, nothing was the same.

"Come here, let me show you something," said Grant. He led me out of the cabin, out to the black earth and morels. "Just watch this."

We were a triangle. But out, ahead of us, was another triangle: *us*. Paulie, Grant, and myself walked in a loop, vanishing from point B and reappearing at point A. I turned to the others, confused. "What is this?" I was struggling, I was falling. Teetering over the edge. *Impossible*, I thought, *this isn't real.* But they were there, and there I was too, as morose as ever.

"I don't know," said Grant. "It just is."

"You dosed me."

"We *might* have dosed you."

I shook my head. I could remember the taste of the mushroom. I thought about the tea. But then, it slipped from me, like a forgotten word falling back from the tip of my tongue, tumbling back deep inside of me, into an eternal blackness. "I'm forgetting things," I said.

"So are we," said Grant, a hand on my shoulder. "But let me ask you this: do you even know if we were friends before this?"

I stared, blankly. Confused.

He continued. Grant, the doctor; the explainer. "What if this was a chance meeting between three men who knew nothing of each other? What if Sam and Vera never existed but we all collectively decided that these two people are part of our shared histories and from that conversation, they have multiplied into distinct memories."

"Fuck *you*," I said, teeth clenched. "I remember them."

Grant shrugged. "I remember them too. But, if we're forgetting things, if new ideas are cementing themselves into our reality, we could have easily already been through all of this. This could've been the eighth time we've taken you to this cabin, or the first. We could've known you forever or known you for three hours. The end result is the same. The reality we have has been built, and currently, you are miserable."

Paulie smiled, he could tell I was having trouble. "We don't want to scare you. This is a good thing. For you. It could be a good thing for you."

I shook my head. "This doesn't feel good."

"We're fairly sure on some things, the broad strokes at least. There's always one thing that stays the same though."

"What's that?" I asked.

"The animal," said Paulie.

Grant nodded. "The animal is always here, always blooming with mushrooms."

I turned to the window and looked out. There it was, dead and permanent.

"It happened again," said Grant, a smile on his lips. "Did you catch it?"

"What?"

Paulie nodded. "We were watching ourselves a moment ago, outside. Where are we now?"

I blinked. He was right. "Inside," I said.

I recoiled. I thrashed around, clawing at myself as if I were covered in crawling insects. *We were outside, and then suddenly, we were not.*

"You must have been thinking about it, it must have felt right. Or maybe one of us thought of it. Or maybe all three of us decided on it subconsciously and everything fell into place. I don't know. But where are we now?"

"The cabin," answered Paulie. "Back in the cabin. It's just like lucid dreaming—I think I took a class on that once. Grant and I have gotten better at keeping track of the small things, where we are, what we're talking about. Anchors."

"You'll learn it too."

I looked out the window, desperately trying to make it a part of my life, my world. *I am inside and I will stay inside,* I thought.

"It's scary," said Paulie. "Really scary. But it's cool, right?"

"Yeah," said Grant. "Think of the possibilities."

I looked back to them, keeping careful track of the floor and the ceiling. "What possibilities?"

Paulie sighed. "Vera," he said.

In the grass.

And then the cabin didn't matter at all. The glass in the window stopped reflecting my sad, tired face and there she was, on all fours, beside the animal. She was playing horsie. Her mouth was black, she kept eating the charcoal as if it were grass. I felt renewed, reenergized. A deep pain in my chest melted away and I started chuckling whilst shaking my head.

"Don't eat that, honey."

She looked up and smiled. I took a step toward her, my feet crunching through the lumps of coal. "That's not good for you," I said. "It's gonna give you a bellyache."

She lifted her body up, standing on her knees and waved her hooves in the air. She whinnied loudly and I couldn't help but laugh. "Be careful, one of the neighbors might throw a saddle on you."

"Nuh-uh!"

"Yes-uh," I said.

Grant and Paulie came over from behind me. They were stiff and awkward, their lips turned in uncomfortable smiles.

"How are the cocktails?"

Grant lifted a champagne flute to his lips. "I opted for bubbly, all that sugary shit gives me a headache."

"Speak for yourself, old man." Paulie threw his glass back, emptying it of its contents. "You think I'm going to let Sam go through the trouble of buying me this much alcohol without getting wasted in her house? Ridiculous, man. Be a good guest."

Vera laughed along too, it was a little joke of hers, to laugh along with adults, pretending she was in on it. "Go find your mother," I said. "She probably wants some help now that Paulie's made it his personal mission to drink us dry."

"Okay, *dad-dy*," she said, exaggerating her syllables to sound more babyish. I ignored the impulse to correct her, to remind her that she was no longer a baby.

"She's growing up so fast," said Paulie.

"That's what they keep saying."

All our eyes met, six black discs reflecting each other's somber expression. "What's wrong?" I said.

Grant smiled—more of a grimace, really—and put a hand on my shoulder. "Enjoying the single life, Jim?"

Paulie patted me on the back, hard. "Free at last!"

"No kids," said Grant. "No wife. No car payments. No responsibilities. Must be good to be you." His voice cracked when he said it, he looked at me expectantly.

I kicked at the animal and shook my head. "Sure is nice," I said. "I'm thinking of going on a trip to the woods. I just bought a cabin. You guys in?"

* * *

Another version of me stood somber, watching the scene. I wasn't sure which interpretation of myself that I was.

I was back in the cabin. I looked out the window. The black earth stretched across mountaintops, presumably across the whole world. And there we were, drinking and laughing.

"We don't know everything," said Paulie finally. "But, we think you can stay, if it helps."

I turned away from the window. "Do you think if I died here, I would stay?"

There was no answer. The mushroom men outside laughed loudly at a joke we couldn't hear.

I sighed deeply. Lost and confused, alone in the company of others. "What if I want to go back?"

Grant shook his head and looked down at his boots. "What do you mean 'go back'? This is your home."

"Fine house you have here. Real bachelor's pad."

I left the two of them, traipsing over to where the dead animal lay, all horns and truncated snout, predator teeth, black eyes, hooved feet, large clawed paws, covered in short dog-like fur—torn apart. The others walked away, I could smell the booze on their breath. I sat beside it, stroking it, thinking about deadly nightshade and burnt earth.

I saw Vera, her hands and knees stained with charcoal, eating a lonely weed. The only one to grow out of our scorched yard. Then, in a matter of seconds my mind built the narrative. *We'd just had a bonfire, we had a permit. It got out of control. This was a week before. Sam and I were drinking these mango juice cocktails and Vera kept saying it looked like juice but we wouldn't let her have one.*

It was *real*. But, it stood in defiance of my other reality: *Vera, playing pony in the yard, munching on grass and roots while I was turned away.* And then the other reality: *there is no Vera.*

I grabbed at my head, which felt full of blood and air and I silently begged for a reconciliation. I was clinging to a dream, a dream of my dead daughter.

The animal stared up at me with those shiny black eyes and I saw the sky reflected in them. My heart started galloping. The sky was red, apocalyptic, as scorched and endless as the earth. I heard more animals in the trees cry out. Calls I didn't recognize.

The animal was dead and now I was wondering what killed it.

(If it was killed at all. If it was ever alive.)

The sky above was crimson, an eternal sunset. I couldn't remember if it was like that before.

We sat by a fire. It was night. The sky had a faint maroon glow. The animal was the fourth member of our group, an anchor to what we knew was real. Paulie brought whiskey and Grant told stories that we'd never heard, but all remembered. We laughed and laughed and laughed. We shifted as the world shifted around us. I stopped trying so hard. I stopped fighting. They told me to float and I floated with them.

At one point, I wanted to tell them something, something important, and I felt this sadness, deep inside. I opened my wallet and I found nothing. When the sadness passed, a fleeting feeling, I laughed at my empty wallet. "Guys," I said, "I have no money."

"You and me both, brother."

We slept outside until I woke up and realized I was alone, except for the animal. The cabin behind me, and in front of me: thousands of miles of burnt black earth, blistered with an eternity of fungi. Somewhere in the distance, I heard the soft purring of a vehicle growing more distant by the second. I took a step towards the trees, cleansed.

4633 MEMORY STICK (PHONE USE MODEL 6A)

To: Oversight Board
Re: Security Breach

As far as we can tell, the whole thing started as a prank. The accused was known to be unpopular in certain circles and the footage suggests that the contraband was slipped into his pocket as a joke. From there, he must have decided to use it by his own free will.

Our hearts are with the victims. From here on out, expect our full support and cooperation.

Sandra L. Connors (pronouns: she/her)
 WAVE Manufacturing
 Public Relations
 <u>Please take our survey!</u>

* * *

Interview with Brandy Wastersteen

Conducted by Mike Clark and Rick Delgado, by the power of the WAVE Manufacturing Oversight Committee

Clark: Can you state your name for the record here?

BW: Brandy Wastersteen.

Clark: Your age?

BW: Thirty-nine.

Delgado: Feel free to answer these at your own pace. You're not in trouble. We're just collecting information. We work for the feds, but we're not here to bite.

BW: Okay, got it.

Clark: Can you tell us how you first met Joshua Prukgaard?

BW: He was my neighbor. I was smoking on the porch—they were duplex style so we were connected. I would go out there and smoke at night, look at the stars. Jayden had just had a nightmare.

Clark: And Jayden is your son?

BW: Yes.

Delgado: In the pre-interview, you said that your son suffers night terrors. Did these happen prior to the incident?

BW: He's always been a troubled sleeper. Still is.

Clark: How did your first meeting with Josh go?

BW: I remember that he was shy. And he worked two jobs. I remember that too. He was always talking about how much he worked. He said it like it was a point of pride, but it didn't really come off that way. It seemed sad. I mean, he was just a kid.

Clark: Did you know where he worked?

BW: I didn't think about it at the time. Now, everyone

knows that he worked for the manufacturer—for the, you know—the chip. I think the other place was a grocery store. Or maybe a warehouse. I just know he worked something like eighty hours a week and barely slept. I guess that's the other detail I should add. It was like three in the morning when I was out smoking, but Josh was already there.

Clark: So you both introduced yourselves, talked about what you did for a living, and then parted?

BW: No, more than that.

Delgado: What else?

BW: He asked if he could bum a smoke.

Clark: Did you give him one?

BW: Yeah. He was hacking up a lung. I thought it was kinda funny, kinda cute, like when you see little kids try to sound grown up. It made me think of Jayden.

Clark: Did he know you had a son?

BW: Yeah I told him. I didn't think anything of it at the time. Of course, if I could go back...

Delgado: Hindsight is 20/20, right?

BW: Ain't that the truth. I didn't know he was going to kill anyone. I didn't know that he would latch on like that, to us. How was I supposed to know that?

Delgado: Of course. Of course. We know that. No one knew that was going to happen but Josh.

BW: Right. Right.

Clark: Are you okay? Do you want to continue?

Delgado: We can break for a moment. It's fine. We're in no rush.

* * *

Clean Start Biohazard—Bill for Service
For Resident: Brandy Wastersteen

Carpet removal...............$199
Carpet reinstallation.......$199
Wall scrub......................$59
Ventilation.....................$129
Lab work......................$86
Displacement...............$112
Labor fee.....................$99 (special!)
Patented Fiber Bio-Cleaning ($0)
Clean Start Guarantee ($0)

Total: $783

Please make payments to Clean Start Biohazard or pay online at our new Clean Start payment portal. Thank you for your business!

* * *

Deposition, WAVE Manufacturing Oversight Committee

Lawrence Jackson, first responder to the death of Joshua Prukgaard

I don't want to talk about that shit, man. I don't want none of that shit in my head. He looked like he went through a thresher. And I don't know what all the black stuff was. And also, I don't want to know. I'm not gonna answer any more questions about this. I'm done.

* * *

Interview with Brandy Wastersteen

Conducted by Mike Clark and Rick Delgado by the power of the WAVE Manufacturing Oversight Committee (continued)

Clark: Did he ever come over to your house? Before his death, I mean.

BW: Once—well, no—twice. Twice if you count the last time.

Clark: Tell us about the first time.

BW: We'd talked on the porch a couple times, in passing. He seemed like a nice enough kid and I felt like he wasn't super threatening, you know? So, I asked him if he wanted to come by and have a couple drinks. It was my Friday and I hadn't met anyone in town except my co-workers. I'd just left my ex, Jayden's father, but that's a whole other story. Josh seemed suspicious, like he'd never been over to a woman's apartment, but I didn't hold that against him. He was just a kid, after all. That's why I invited him over—I felt safe, like I could handle him if he tried anything. But, anyway, he came by and I offered him a drink. He told me he'd never drank before with the biggest doe eyes I'd ever seen. We ended up just talking all night. He got very drunk. I didn't drink that much at all. At one point, Jayden woke up screaming. Just screaming his little face off. I went in there to comfort him and Josh was kinda standing a couple steps behind me, like he wanted to be involved but didn't know what to do. I think that's the problem with Josh— he always *wanted* to be involved, but he never knew how to do it. He wasn't good at that sort of thing. So, I look to the doorway and he's just standing there, frozen. I told him it was okay, that I'd be back in a minute—but something must have snapped in him. He went quiet. He told me he had to leave, that he had work in the morning. And that was it. That was our one night together. I didn't see him for a couple days after.

Clark: Did you think he was angry?

BW: No, I think he was embarrassed.

Delgado: Embarrassed?

BW: Yeah. Like he felt useless and it embarrassed him.

Clark: And from what you know, he didn't like to feel that way?

BW: No, no. I think he liked to feel like he was good at things. I mean, we all do, don't we?

Delgado: Sure, of course.

BW: I think he felt it more strongly, though. Like it was all he had to offer. He believed it too; he had that kind of air of superiority, like he always thought he knew something other people didn't.

Clark: Do you think he did?

BW: No, not really. I think he was just a kid.

Clark: Sure.

Delgado: You said you didn't see him for a couple of days. Can you remember the last time you spoke to him, before the end?

BW: I had seen him come and go in passing for a couple days, just by nature of being neighbors, then suddenly I noticed he stopped going out all the time. I remember because we worked opposite shifts. He was usually just leaving when I was getting back, so I almost always saw him. We just exchanged pleasantries, I guess. He'd ask about Jayden, about his night terrors. I think he was trying to erase the last time he was over, when he got scared and ran. He was trying to prove to me that he understood the problem and would try to fix it. He told me he was reading up on it, that he knew stuff about them now, and that if I ever needed any help just to call him. It was strange, but it was before anyone got hurt, so I didn't think about it much. But then the weird thing was that he just stopped coming and going. He was never usually stuck in that apartment for longer than eight hours. But for two whole days

I didn't see him come or go. What did they say on the news—you know, that it lasted for three days?

Delgado: If the news said it, it's probably true.

BW: Well, I think that's when it happened. Because here's what I remember: I didn't see him on the second day, but I heard him. It was the early morning, like five, and I was fast asleep when I heard banging on my door. I was so tired I couldn't get up, but I heard him yelling at my front door. He was screaming. I thought it was Jayden at first, having one of his night terrors. But no, I recognized his voice. He was yelling at me. Josh was at my door and just screaming his throat raw.

Clark: What was he saying?

BW: He said something like: "I saw it! I saw it!" But I could be wrong. Now, I think he probably said, "I saw you."

Delgado: Did you get up?

BW: I did, but maybe not as quickly as I should have. By the time I got to the door, he was gone. Like he was never there. That was the day that—what happened happened, right?

Clark: We'd have to have a date to match the times, but it's possible.

Delgado: Can you tell us about the day he died?

BW: I can try.

* * *

Video Interview

Subject: William R. Lanz, Webmaster of The Thought-Shifter Conspiracy Forum

No one saw the boy coming, because they didn't know the boy existed. He was just some kid who worked at some place. He was putting together pieces of plastic. Soldering circuit boards.

Nothing big. Nothing big at all. So, they didn't see him coming. When they heard a microchip went missing, they wrote it off as a clerical error. What else could it be? No one knew about the chip, no one cared about the chip, no one thought the chip had any practical use outside niche military operations. And not combat operations, either. Boring shit—intelligence, you know?

The point is—we don't know what he saw when the chip did what it did. The theory is that the mind kinda just wanders about, like it's not as easily glued to a time and place. I don't know, not really. It's all just hearsay. Here's what we do know: there's security footage of him at the WAVE manufacturing campus. He's using his mind, maybe. That's when the murders happened, the three guys who were smoking outside. I mean, we all know the story at this point. These guys played a prank on Josh and it really fucked his shit up, so he came back to get revenge. I mean, we didn't see any of that on the camera, of course. The angle's all fucked up. But we do know that Josh was there, we see him walking toward the gates—or no, floating—floating toward the gates, and from the timestamp, we know it's about thirty minutes before the bodies were discovered.

Everyone wants to know about the carnage. I get that. I'll tell you: it was horrific. I got a source, man. So yeah, I've seen the crime scene leaks. There's a reason that shit won't ever see release, like ever. I'd never seen anything like that shit in my life, man, and I've been all up and around the internet. That's the truth. I'm not lying at all about that. I heard they had to have a full week just to clean the bio-matter from the place. And that's another thing too—the bio-matter wasn't the usual kind of stuff you'd expect. There was this black, inky stuff there as well. We enthusiasts don't know what to call it, so we call it ectoplasm. We don't think it has anything to do with ghosts, but it just sorta stuck. What else are we going to call it, you know? Anyways, all the bodies were coated with it. But this shit isn't about any of that. The carnage, I mean. Everyone wants the carnage. I just want to know about the chip. If he was slipping from time and place to time and place, what else did he see? I'm sure some patriot in intelligence is pitching a tent right now, thinking about what could be if we could transcend time. But I'm worried about how much of that has already been done. We don't know what the kid's done, we don't know what he'll continue to do. Those might have been the three longest days in fucking history. We can cheer now that he's dead, but let's be honest—that doesn't mean shit now.

* * *

To: Oversight Committee
Re: Re: Security Breach

I hope the day is finding you well. I've included a copy of the pertinent security footage from the locker room and parking lot.

It appears that an employee (ID: 723506) took one of the finished memory sticks (containing the 4633 microchip) from the packaging bay at 12:36am while a supervisor (ID: 943601) was distracted by another employee (ID: 884326). We believe they were working together and the distraction was orchestrated. Employee 723506 then excused himself to go to the breakroom to make a call. Our cameras show that he goes directly to Prukgaard's locker, which is usually unlocked, according to our interviews. We cannot see exactly what happens on the camera, but we assume he slips the memory stick from his sleeve into one of Prukgaard's pockets.

At best, we can guess it was meant to result in disciplinary action for Prukgaard, as leaving the WAVE facilities with any of our client's patented materials is strictly prohibited in our Employee Handbook. As Prukgaard was known to be extremely considerate of rules and guidelines, it's possible they were hoping this would bring about a reaction, from both their target and upper management. Prukgaard left early that night and the opportunity to reveal the chip was missed. If the prank had gone as planned, it is unlikely that WAVE would have disciplined Prukgaard, as it is company policy to thoroughly investigate claims of gross misconduct before administering punishment.

Please let us know if there is anything else we can supply you with.

Sandra L. Connors (pronouns: she/her)
    WAVE Manufacturing
    Public Relations
    <u>Please take our survey!</u>

* * *

Deposition, taken by WAVE Manufacturing Oversight Committee

[REDACTED], former engineer on the 4633 Memory Stick project (project title unknown)

I don't know why the kid thought he should use it. Anyone who knew anything about it knew that it wasn't meant to be used like that. But I guess it makes sense if you think about it. It had a relatively common input device. He probably didn't think anything of it. Curiosity killed the cat sort of thing, you know? He must have just plugged it into his phone and then that must have triggered the call.

Once you get the call, you're pretty much done for. Nothing's ever the same after the call. Even in testing, we never actually answer the transmission it sends.

Poor kid. I couldn't imagine.

* * *

Interview with Brandy Wastersteen

Conducted by Mike Clark and Rick Delgado by the power of the WAVE Manufacturing Oversight Committee (continued)

BW: So, the day he died, it wasn't anything too special, not at first. I came home and found my door unlocked. Jayden was in school, thank God. I knew that much. I'm so glad he didn't have to see any of this, not that it matters. I know now that he's seen more than I can imagine. He was in school and I was just worn out, tired. I usually take a nap for a couple of minutes between work and picking Jayden up from school, because I'm usually up at night with him too. So I planned on just dropping out for a little bit.

Delgado: Besides the door being unlocked, was there any sign of forced entry? Anything amiss?

BW: No, I don't think so. It was normal. Even with the door unlocked, I didn't think anything of it. I just thought I forgot to lock it. That might've been what happened. I sometimes forget to do that, you know?

Clark: Got it. So, what did you see when you entered your apartment?

BW: I just walked in, took off my coat, and put my keys on the key hook.

Clark: And Josh was in there.

BW: Yes.

Delgado: Take your time if you need to.

BW: Jesus Christ.

Clark: That's alright. Slow.

BW: It was the worst thing I'd ever seen.

Delgado: Take as long as you need to.

BW: Oh fuck. Okay. Jesus. Got it. I'm here. So, I turned the corner and there he was, just sitting on my floor, just kind of running his fingers through my carpet, looking sort of out-of-it. He looked awful. Like he hadn't slept in days. He looked—like—how do I say this? Like he was coming apart at the seams. Unraveling. Like a spool of thread spinning loose. You know what I'm talking about? Like he had seams in his skin, and parts of his body weren't as tight as they could've been. Like, imagine every person has a big magnet inside of them, and their bodies are held together by this magnet in a thousand little pieces. Well, Josh looked like that, only his magnet was weak, and you could see all the tiny lines on his body, slowly drifting apart. He was oozing with this—I don't know—wispy stuff. It was like black ink that turned straight to vapor once it sat on the skin for a while. His pupils were big as frisbees. I tried talking to him, said a word, maybe his name or something and he looked at me, and it was like he was waiting for me to see him, because then he started falling apart. Or not falling. Maybe blooming? He looked as if he were turning inside out, and all the black stuff on his insides just sort of shot out of him. His body was all contorted-like. He just fell apart, right in front of me. I couldn't look at what was left. I ran out of the apartment and called the cops, and that was that.

Clark: I know this is hard, but you know what's coming next, right?

BW: Yeah.

Clark: Are you okay with us talking with Jayden?

Delgado: Just for a couple minutes. You can be there too, if it helps.

BW: Sure, okay. Fine.

* * *

Interview with Jayden Wastersteen

Conducted by Mike Clark and Rick Delgado by the power of the WAVE Manufacturing Oversight Committee

Delgado: Alright, little man. Can you state your name for the record?

Jayden Wastersteen: Jayden Wastersteen.

Clark: And how old are you?

Jayden: Seven.

Delgado: Seven years old. Great age. Do you like school?

Jayden: Yeah.

Delgado: Oh yeah? What's your favorite subject?

Jayden: I like drawing.

Delgado: Is that right? Are you an artist?

Jayden: I don't know. But I like to color.

Clark: We like drawing too. Keep at it and you might be the next Picasso.

Delgado: You never know.

Clark: So, Jayden. We just want to ask you some questions. Do you think you can answer our questions?

Jayden: I'll try.

Clark: That's all we ask. So, first off, do you remember one of your mom's friends? A guy named Josh?

Jayden: Yeah, I know Josh. I don't like him.

Clark: When do you see Josh?

Jayden: At night, usually.

Clark: So, does he come with your mother? Or does he visit you alone?

Jayden: He was here with Mom, but other times he was here alone. I don't like him. He tells me stuff.

Clark: What kind of stuff did he tell you?

Jayden: Weird stuff.

Clark: Can you remember any of this weird stuff, Jayden? It could be really important.

Jayden: Headaches. He said he got lots of them. His head always hurt. He also said that he could hear voices and I asked him if it was like my voice, and he said, no, it was like radio voices in his head that no one else can hear. He said a bunch of stuff. He said he was always listening.

Clark: Did Josh say what he was listening to?

Jayden: Everything.

Clark: Why do you think he said that?

Let the record show that Jayden Wastersteen shrugs.

Delgado: Do you think Josh was in pain?

Jayden: Yeah.

Delgado: Did he ever mention why he was in pain? Besides the headaches, I mean. Did he think someone did that to him —you know, give him headaches?

Jayden: Sometimes he would talk about how it wasn't supposed to be for him but it happened anyways, like an accident.

Clark: We've just got a couple more questions, that's all. Do you remember the last time you saw Josh?

Jayden: Yeah.

Clark: And when was that?

Jayden: Last night.

Delgado: Do you see him every night?

Jayden: Most nights. Sometimes I think he goes to see my Mom.

Clark: And how do you feel when he comes to visit you?

Jayden: Scared.

Clark: How long have you known Josh?

Jayden: Forever. He looked different when he came over with Mommy though. He used to tell me that we would meet for real one day, but neither of us would know we were friends. But we were never friends! I could never be friends with him! He's scary! I just want him to go away but he won't go! He keeps coming and he won't leave!

Delgado: You've seen him every night then? Before you met him with Mommy, after you met him with Mommy? Every night, forever?

Jayden: Mm-hmm.

Clark: Thank you, Jayden. We appreciate it.

Delgado: Stay safe, little man. That helps a lot.

* * *

The Wave Manufacturing Oversight Committee aims to document and corroborate the events that led to the fatalities at the WAVE Manufacturing Plant and the residual "haunting" of Jayden Wastersteen. If you have any information or whereabouts regarding the post-death situation of Joshua Prukgaard, especially in matters of national security, please call our tip line urgently.

NO MORE BODIES, NO MORE PITS

The man on the television reported that the world would be ending. Someone, it turns out, was dreaming. This dreamer was more capable than the rest, better equipped. He had dreamed everything that ever was, everything that ever will be. He dreamed the television and the newscaster and the family watching at home. Now, scientists were claiming that this dreaming would soon end and the slumberer would wake. And Manuel, his mother, and his father would all be nothing.

In the living room, Manuel's parents argued. They pointed fingers and asked questions of each other and then turned to the television and asked questions of it. Sometimes, they would see Manuel staring, and their rage would begin anew and they would ask questions of him. "What are you doing?" they'd ask. "Go to your room."

Manuel, frozen in place, did no such thing, and his parents soon forgot their command altogether. In the tense shadows of a lavish living room, he stared with his parents at the screen.

Manuel's father paced back and forth, growing angrier by

the second. His mother pursed her lips and was indignant at the dreamer, like she'd been ripped-off at the counter of a grocery store. The whole ordeal was an insult, an outrage.

"Well, I don't know how they can get off like this," said his father, after he'd finally decided to sit.

"There's no way this can be allowed to happen," said his mother.

Manuel sat on the stairs and wondered if he should say something also, or if his presence would only heighten their outrage. He did not fully understand what was at stake, but in a simple, child-like way, he knew that they would have to die —and while that scared him, he also remembered church and remembered what the priest told him about death, that it was a chance to see his family on the other side. For Manuel, dying as a family was as awful as moving from one townhouse to another.

His father turned the television off and suddenly looked over to the stairs and there were tears in his eyes. The way his face was contorted, the way his lips tightened into a straight line, Manuel could not tell if he was still enraged. When the older man got up from his chair and started toward the boy, it took all his strength to stay still. His father grabbed him roughly and embraced him, squeezing him in a way that made Manuel feel like his bones were being crushed to dust, that his eyes would pop out of their sockets. And when his father ended the embrace, his face contorted again, now with embarrassment.

Manuel sat confused, a confusion that continued for several days. His parents had locked all the doors and closed all the windows. His mother had sent a maid to the market to get food for a month. Manuel did not know how this would help, because on the television they kept replaying footage of a white lady with a candle demonstrating how things would end. She'd hold the candle in a dark room, and they'd see her flickering in the orange and yellows of the candlelight and then, suddenly, she would blow forcefully and everything would go black. Somewhere, in the darkness, she would then say in accented Spanish, "See? Nothing."

Surely, Manuel thought, locks were useless.

But this demonstration only prompted more rage from his parents, and when the stations replayed this segment, they would start yelling again.

These chaotic outbursts forced Manuel to stay in his room, where it seemed like he was a world away. His parents did not come up there, they did not call for him to eat. They stayed in the living room and watched the candle's extinguishment a dozen times a day. Sometimes, Manuel wished for the dreamer to wake suddenly. He would close his eyes and brace for it and say in his head: *now!* But nothing would come.

He spent his time looking out his window, where the mania was present but subdued. There were people in the street, but they looked agitated. They went about their business with a frustrated restlessness. They bought food from the carts, but threw money at the cashier. They bumped into each other with the sole purpose of cursing loudly. Mothers hissed at their children to stay close. Manuel felt that the whole world was trying to keep it together, to keep its stitching in place before it was ripped apart at the seams.

The next day, he woke up to his father shouting. His face was red and his eyes were watering. Manuel's mother was close behind him, wearing sweatpants, staring at the floor.

"Have you seen the woman?" he asked.

Manuel shook his head.

"You have to tell us if you've seen her," he said.

"Please," said his mother, dry and listless. "She's here to help."

They looked as if they hadn't slept in days. "Okay," he said, not quite sure what he was agreeing with.

His father grabbed him by the arm and pulled him out of his blankets. "Get up, get up, get up. You need to know what to look for."

Manuel yelped as his father tore him easily from the warmth of his bed. "Kid's got to know what's going on in the world," his father muttered.

When they reached the downstairs, his mother and father sat in their chairs and pointed at the television screen, urging Manuel to watch. As if he hadn't understood the full weight of the situation, his mother said, "They say he's going to wake any day now."

"We don't know that it's a he. It could be a woman."

Manuel nodded seriously. He sat in quiet unease, waiting for another outburst.

There were still commercials at the end of the world, and to fill the time, his father said, "They say whoever it is might be an American. Something to do with what they call a 'pervasive worldview.'"

"Yes," said his mother. "They say it's probably an American."

Manuel thought of the movies he'd watched with his friends. Loud, full of spectacle and costumes. Manuel did not understand the finer points of what an American was or wasn't, but he had his own vague associations and he could see how one could be the dreamer.

His father piped up again. "We don't know for sure though. There's that woman going around and I think she has something to do with it. They don't know where *she's* from."

Manuel sat, still as ice, watching the screen. He hoped that it was going to show him what they wanted him to see so that he could go back to his room and watch the streets in silence.

"There, you see it?"

Manuel did see it. On the television screen, the reporters showed drawings of a woman—in water colors, in graffiti. One after another, images of a woman in a stone turquoise mask flipped by as his parents gasped in zealous awe.

"That's her," said his mother. "That's her. I saw her the other day, outside."

His father nodded violently. "You hear that, boy? Your mother saw her. The woman is here. She's taking people away."

The reporter confirmed these facts solemnly. She told stories of a dozen or so people who had seen the woman in the turquoise mask usher people out of the great collapsing dream.

His father shrieked in ecstasy. "She's our way out! She can save us!"

"I saw her," repeated his mother, as a twitching smile spread painfully over her lips. "I saw her, I saw her!"

As he waited for the candle of his reality to be extinguished, he hid under the covers. When they let him leave the living room, he was shaking. A part of him considered staying with them to watch the television, but every time he turned to look at them, their faces were twisted with rage. He steeled himself early in the evening and quietly said he would be going to bed. They did not say anything in return.

Up the stairs he went, his heart beating loudly in his chest, afraid of what he would see when he opened the door to his room. There was nothing, of course. But the limp dread of knowing he and everything he knew would become nothing was replaced by a more immediate terror. In some ways, this was better. He did not know the dreamer, he did not fully understand the breadth of his dreams. Manuel had pushed himself to understand nothingness, but could not. Conceiving of nothing was as close as he could get to the vastness of the universe. But, the woman was much closer to what he knew of fear. He had seen shadows that looked like people. Only a year ago, he had feared what lurked under his bed. He knew ghost stories, yes—and the woman with the turquoise mask was most definitely a ghost story.

She was there to save them, he reminded himself. But the idea never took hold. It faded into the shadows as he waited nervously to see her standing in the corner of his room, bidding him to an unknown realm. He would repeat his ritual —not constantly, but every hour or so—closing his eyes and waiting for the inevitable awakening, where all of his fear would be rendered null and void. But still it did not come, and the woman remained in the corner of his vision.

In the morning, the light was a welcome friend. It streamed through his window in fat, opaque bars. He sniffed, wondering if there was smoke nearby. Manuel smelled nothing and shifted from one foot to another as he passed his fingers through the rays of thick light. They were so concrete, and in his imagination, or maybe not his imagination, he felt them give slightly. Like sliding his fingers through thin cream.

He shuddered and backed away from the window. When it fell upon him, it seemed to splash, soaking his entire body. It was a sensation that consumed his faculties, and for a moment, he tried scraping the viscous sun from his tissue, but he could not. It remained on him, smothering.

Manuel gasped, deep lungfuls of air that at once seemed to calm him, then struck a new chord of paranoia as he realized he was now letting that creamy light inside himself. He felt the sensation of drowning, of a foreign liquid filling his lungs. He shrieked to himself and fell to the floor, writhing about, half expecting the noise to be a necessary measure for his parents to come check on him, to save him. As the sunlight poured over his body, penetrating his insides, he became accustomed to the new feeling and his racing heart slowed and he wiped the sweat from his brow and got up on shaky legs, like a newborn colt. He galloped down the stairs, as if it was his room, not the sun or the very fabric of existence itself that threatened him. He was relieved now to see shadows and the silvery light of the television. His parents sat in place, watching the screen implacably.

Without looking at him, his mother said, "You felt the sun?"

Manuel nodded. "Yes," he said. "What's wrong with it?"

His mother shrugged. "People have been talking about it on the news," she said, her voice weary. "They say that we can expect more distortions."

Manuel had not heard that word before. "What does that mean?"

"It means that everything is going to shit," his father said. His lips trembled, his cheeks flushed. Whenever he spoke, his hands curled into fists.

Manuel began to back away.

Then, suddenly. "You see the woman yet?"

Manuel stopped. "No," he said.

"If we see her, we'll be alright." His father's eyes shined with a faint glimmer of hope. "We'll be good if we see her. The woman in the turquoise mask is still out there, helping."

Manuel hid his distress at the fact with a cool nod.

His mother spoke next. "I've heard that the Virgin Mary is only a figment of the dreamer. Same with God. We should take down our shrines."

"Never did us any good." He turned to Manuel. "You don't

pray to the Virgin anymore, got that? You pray to the woman in the turquoise mask."

Manuel's palms were sweating. His parents turned their attention back to the television. Outside, the streets roared.

He went back to his room where the silky light had touched everything and he now hung his head out into the late-morning air and felt its residue on his skin. There were hundreds of people in the streets, and they all felt the same stickiness, because they moved as if they were trying to shed their own skin, slithering between each other, absently itching. They carried signs.

Wake up!

Manuel was not sure what they were yelling for, what side they were on, but their voices rose into the air and he thought they were like animals caught in a trap, or bugs who's legs had been plucked. They were clawing for safety, slathering at the mouths. Every move they made was one of desperation, and they made it together.

In the crowd, as the whole mass shifted gradually from crowd to riot, he saw a flash of color. There were men fighting, women pulling switchblades from their purses; he saw a young kid with a lighter burn the edges of a canvas umbrella. And in between these violent bodies, he saw the shape of a woman in robes, her black hair flowing down the middle of her back. Her head was hunched forward, as if with weight, and as the violence swelled, Manuel saw her reach out a surprisingly soft hand and touch a laughing man in the midst of the teeming bodies. She turned her head upward, for just a moment, to look at Manuel. His stomach dropped to the floor. Her turquoise mask was wet with light and when she touched the man, they both blinked out of existence.

* * *

His father began referring to the dreamer as the American. Manuel thought it was curious, if the change had occurred in the night or if it had been gradual and he just had not noticed, but now, everyone on television was referring to the dreamer as the American too.

Manuel hugged the walls, afraid of both natural light and darkness, preferring instead the warm amber glow of lamplight and tinted fixtures. He had moved his blankets and pillows into the living room. He would cower when his father raged, but then he would inevitably quiet and things would move toward a tense normal again. Whenever he closed his eyes he saw the woman in the turquoise mask. She knew what she was doing. It was like in the book they read last year at school, a story. She was the pied piper, she was taking them somewhere. To the American.

"Have you seen the woman, boy?" his father asked fiercely.

"No," he said. "I haven't seen her." His lips were tight with the lie and he held his breath until his father turned his attention back to the television.

"Anyone who sees her is just about guaranteed to leave," he said, absently. "Keep watch. You're our lookout."

In their seclusion, as the woman's heavy mask grew heavier in his mind, he realized he hated his parents. He hated that they were so afraid, so cowardly. They would spend their hours taking caffeine pills and watching the same newscasts, cursing the American and everything the American stood for, and then praying to the woman in the turquoise mask. They did not seem to realize or care that she was his agent. That she was taking them to him.

Manuel's mother pointed to the new altar expectantly. "Make her come to us. Give her your faith."

He did so dutifully, shaking under the visage of the mask nailed to the wall. It had just appeared one day, as so many things seemed to do now. His mother could very well have sent out for it. She could've built the shrine in his uneasy sleep. Manuel gave a side-eye to his parents, sitting like stones in the white light. It was hard to believe that the turquoise altar came from anywhere at all.

As they waited for the woman to save them from a mass snuffing, the streets outside became more hostile. Manuel hid while people pounded on their doors. They yelled horrible things.

Your gold can't save you. The woman won't take you. Come out and see!

His gaunt parents didn't seem to notice at all. They only sat, their eyes yellowed and their lips quivering with quiet prayers.

You're going out with us!

The one that bothered him the most were the loud chants. They came from all directions, and they could've been in front of his door or a block away, but the words felt as if they were being spoken directly to him.

The American dreamed you too!

The closest his father got to a reaction was a nervous shift in his seat. One time, he'd comment, to his wife, an aside. "Just jealous, that's all. Beautiful house. We love the city." And then the words would quiet to murmurs and he would once again turn angry. "The fucking American, he's gonna take it all. The woman, the woman, the woman..."

And then: hours of silence.

It was this silence that bothered Manuel the most, more than the sticky sunlight, or the air that had begun to taste like sulfur and rot. Because it was not just his parents' silence, it was silence all around. There was silence on the streets. When the earth began to shake, rumbling like his father's SUV, a rumble he used to love and admire, he found himself creeping toward the window and peeling back the blinds.

They were still there. But they had found a sort of peace in the proceedings. Their heads were bowed and they all had their hands lifted to a—

Manuel had to crane his neck to get a better look. He couldn't see, they were all in the streets, it looked like it was some sort of mass.

He stood back from the window, the only noise was the woman from the news. She was holding a cup over a candle. Explaining. Everything would end. *Black.*

Manuel ran up the stairs to his bedroom, ignoring the soaking light. The room felt alien, but it was higher up, it had a better view. Back before the dreamer, his dad used to call it the lighthouse. He pushed his head out of the window and felt the sun scrape across his skin. He could see what they were raising their hands toward. Down the street, there was a wooden platform, no doubt built in the midst of the chaos, somehow. Or maybe not built at all. Maybe it was like their shrine, maybe it just happened. Toward the back of it, were three poles that reached high to the sky, each one with a scaffolding that pushed outward to the center of the platform. From the height of the platform, thick rope dangled; each of them were tied in a noose.

He knew the word for it. *Gallows.*

He knew also, somehow, in a distant way, that this was a protest. That they, like his parents, hated the American. But they, unlike his parents, did not want to be taken by the woman in the turquoise mask to meet him. They were opting out. They were protesting.

Three people walked to the platform. They closed their eyes for brief moments, then kissed two fingers and waved to the crowd. One by one, they hung the ropes around their necks, fitting their heads into the noose's embrace. And just as they took a deep breath, the platform fell out from under them and the ropes went taut. Manuel heard the crack of bones as their necks snapped in unison.

Manuel swallowed, his fingernails chipping the paint on the windowsill.

Then, by some odd mechanism, the ropes loosened by themselves, the hinged door went back into place, and the bodies dropped.

Distortions, he remembered. Then: *the bodies.*

Manuel could now see the bodies, the pile of them in a great pit. He could see layers of concrete and plumbing and earth where the great pit had been dug. He could not see the end of it, only its rim. And when the bodies fell into the blackness, where the woman could not take them, three more joined on the platform, and the spectacle repeated.

"Animals," said his father.

Manuel jumped so fast the sunlight raised like droplets off his skin.

His mother and father were behind him. Manuel opened his mouth to speak, but he had nothing to say. He had not seen his parents stand for days now. He had not seen them leave their places in front of the television.

"Life is beautiful," she said. "What a waste."

His father nodded solemnly. "That's why we're going to see the American. We're going to get this all sorted out. You'll see."

His father's rage had dissipated into a sort of persistent malaise. He was tired, there were bags under his eyes. Manuel thought he looked rather like a hound dog with his droopy features.

"Yes, my boy. All will be well. The woman will be here tonight. We've just got word. They said it on the news. That's why we've been watching."

Manuel looked at them both questioningly. "What?" He didn't understand. How would the news—?

"The woman has been talking to us, the good ones. They understand our anguish—over, you know. What's happening. The bad stuff, in the streets." A long, low rumble made their home tremble. "The woman told us that she's coming tonight, to rescue the good ones. Us, we're the good ones. She's going to be in our home tonight."

His father stuck out a finger. "You better look good, be on your best behavior. This is a big deal. An honor." He swept a hand toward the mass grave in the street. "None of this will solve anything," he said. "They're ungrateful."

Manuel could think of nothing to say. Instead, he stammered. "But—but—"

"Take it as a compliment, pal. She likes you."

Manuel nodded, trying desperately not to cry in front of his father.

"This will all be over soon. Just you wait."

With that, they turned away and walked mechanically to their bedroom. Manuel could hear them getting dressed.

Manuel watched the sky fade and was unsure if darkness would fall with time or if it would come with the woman. He was unsure of many things, but as his parents hummed to themselves and whispered conspiratorially, he knew the woman would be here to deliver them to the American, that there was no sense in them lying. She would be here, in his room and he would have to touch her.

Before he fully realized what he was doing, Manuel stretched a leg over the window.

He did not want to meet the woman.

With his feet hanging over the window sill, dangling above the street, he wondered if escape was another dream. His parents were so desperate to cling to what they had, that they would become subordinate to their maker. It was their final stage of grief. Where they bowed down and agreed to play the game as the gamemaster intended. They would delight in his illusions as they followed him to the slaughterhouse, happily accepting whatever comforts he afforded them. They would deny their impending erasure while being dazzled by a turquoise mask.

Manuel reached out to touch the thick air, splashing it with his hands like water. This was not how air was supposed to move.

Bones cracked; ecstatic death rattles punctuated the silence. It was the rhythm of waking.

They were not playing the game any longer. They were denying the American his winners and losers, his grand finale. They were spitting in the face of the woman, their savior, because they knew that one person could not be both at the same time. *Anyone knew that,* thought Manuel, *even a kid.*

He looked below, to the garden his mother so tenderly cultivated. The leaves twisted upon themselves in spirals, their stems lengthening before his eyes. They constricted around each other as if nature had guided them gently to strangulation. They were doing so out of some sort of natural imperative that needed no words or explanation. Manuel watched, the stench of reality filling his lungs. He admired the simplicity of their design.

Deep breath.

He took one last look at his bedroom.

His heart flipped.

Father was tapping his foot, a shell of himself. *How much time had passed?* "Come on, boy. We've got to get going."

Manuel blinked. The sky was black. There were no stars. There were no lights from the city. There was only the sound of necks snapping in the blackness, and the light of his room's bright fluorescents. Somehow, the blackness felt heavier than the sunlight.

Father's skin had turned gray, the lines in his face had deepened. He wore a suit that hung too large on him now. Mother wore a baggy dress and a pearl necklace. She carried a purse on her arm. They looked like they were going to church.

He squirmed on the sill as he saw who stood between them.

Her head eclipsed the door frame; wild black hair snaked out from the sides of her mask. Manuel averted his gaze. The turquoise was more vibrant than anything left in their shared dream.

Except—

Crack!

The bodies fell with a wet crunch. He heard the ropes and wood return to their original positions. New footsteps eagerly awaited their turn.

She beckoned him back into the room with a sweeping motion.

"Hurry up. It's all going to end," said his father, looking at his watch. "The American will be waiting for us."

Manuel shook his head. He felt nauseous. He was terrified. "I don't want to go," he said.

His mother knelt down, her face suddenly bright and cheerful, an imitation of when everything was real. "Manny, baby, we're going to see the dreamer. He made this. Don't you want to meet him?"

Manuel cried out. Everything shook. Rays of light jumped like tracking lines on an old television. His father's face changed shape. His mother withered before his eyes. The woman with the turquoise mask stood taller, her torso elongated, her body now hunched at a right angle to the ceiling.

She glided forward, a sympathetic hand raised outward.

She could not speak, he knew, somehow. But she would take him to the American, the maker. He was hot with sweat and screaming. She could not be stopped, she would take whomever she wished. His fingers danced along the sill. The end could not be stopped. The American would wake. The American would wake and all would be snuffed. Everything gone. Nothing. Nothing. Nothing. She would take them to meet the dreamer who had dreamed everything, who made the sunlight, then made it stick. Who made the people, then made them kill. The dreamer, with his pervasive worldview. She reached out toward him and everything behind her began to unravel into absence. And as everything became nothing, and as the blackness stretched, bones continued to snap and bodies continued to fill the pit; until there were no more bodies and no more pits. And just as everything was nothing, Manuel jumped.

THE FINAL CIRCUS

We heard about the circus from the lips of our brethren. In bars and bookstores, from wide-eyed addicts, tattoo artists, and mordant dreamers. It was on the lips of every angry man, every scorned woman, every screaming child. It started conversations; it ended conversations. For those who were primed for its allure, the very mention of this particular circus inspired conspiratorial whispers, wicked smiles, and earnest, unabashed longing. Irony gave way to sincerity, veins opened. And for those of us who cared for such things, we put our lips to flesh and let the blood rush in.

I was one of these. I was all of them. Knowledge of this impending circus followed me everywhere I went. I found torn handouts on light posts during my midnight walks. The radio crackled to life and I heard advertisements between growling static. On television, the news anchors directed their eyes right at me, staring through the screen, announcing its presence.

The promise of the circus did not offer me any nostalgia, first or secondhand. Still, curiosity gripped me. With repetition, the event slithered to the forefront of my mind. It was no surprise then that when the day came, I put aside my usual nervous disposition and decided to attend.

I arrived in an empty dirt lot. The tent in the center of it was large, black, and weathered. Dust clung to it like mold. I had the immediate impression that this was a traveling troupe, that they likely had been to many cities just like mine, where they had performed for many people just like myself. In line, I saw a small cross-section of these walking hypotheticals. They stood in line with straight lips and wet eyes, murmuring to themselves in one-sided conversation. Every so often, they would look in either direction, to see if anyone was watching them. In a fit of self-consciousness, I realized I was doing exactly as they were and when I made this realization, so too did the rest of the people that were like me. And in our shame, we stood like statues until the box office opened.

The line moved quickly and we shambled forward in near unison. The ticket seller was a woman who spoke in an accent. She had gray hair pulled into a bun, held together with two twin daggers. Her glasses fell to the tip of her nose and she tutted at each of us with barely withheld disgust. "No pay," she said. "Go in."

"How much?" I said, not fully understanding.

But she said the same thing to the person behind me and I was swept up in the momentum of the crowd and unable to argue. I plodded forward into the dark mouth of the circus.

The tent was hot. Inside it, crimson lights magnified this effect. Each of us tugged on our collar, fanned ourselves theatrically. Silently agreeing that we were all indeed very warm. We found seating on hastily erected bleachers that wobbled and clanked from the collective weight of its patrons. There were so many of us—sitting together, huddled tight. Sweat dewed our foreheads and we gazed upon the empty stage while dissonant chords thrummed from invisible speakers.

After everyone was seated, the ringmaster entered the circular stage. He wore a black top hat and a long cloak that dragged on the floor behind him. His face was painted to look like a skull. Between his fingers, a long red cane twirled. He said nothing.

Timidly, we applauded.

A wave of smoke crept onto the stage, and the deathly ringmaster took off his hat. The smoke rose to obscure the bottom half of his body. In an act of submission (to what I could not say), he then removed his cloak. It was now that we saw that the man was nude and that it was not only his face that was painted, but his entire body. Ribs were painted along his flank, bones were painted along his arms. He spun slowly so that we could see him. Again, we clapped.

Then, the mute ringmaster closed his eyes and his face paint became all the more striking. Where his eyes were, were now empty sockets. The performer took a deep breath, and without hesitation, he fell backwards into the smoke.

We all held our breath waiting to hear his impact.

We heard nothing.

We cheered.

This was a place for people like me. It was tailored to us like our very skin.

Next, we saw a series of acrobats. We oohed and awed as they clumsily jumped from one floating ring to another. Their feet were leaden; their faces terror-stricken. So precarious was this display that there were numerous times when an acrobat fell and was never to be seen again. They would leap out into the air, faces twisted with fear, and they would desperately reach for safety and miss it every time. At first, we thought this was a mistake. That the performers had not been trained well, that perhaps they were new or only remarkably unskilled, but it soon became apparent that this *was* the act. That their ineptness was the key to this whole bizarre routine. And soon we began to feel the swell of laughter in our stomachs as we recognized this. We clapped as another scared performer missed their mark and fell into the all-consuming fog. The act culminated with one young woman, probably no more than seventeen, walking on a plank that stood well over thirty feet from the stage floor. Her legs trembled; her expression was one of acute anxiety. Constantly, she looked down and had to steel herself as the height shifted from an abstract to a reality. She would lose her footing and regain it, with no less consternation. Eventually though, she too did fall and her fall was the greatest of them all for it came with an ear splitting scream that ceased suddenly as she disappeared into the swirling fog below.

Our hearts beat in unison, enamored and enthralled by this sudden end and fearful preamble.

The lights went out and we all sat together in blackness, wondering what we would see next. If the lights had come up and the ringmaster returned to say, "Thank you for coming, but that's all for tonight," I think we all would have been dutifully impressed with the spectacle so far. But just as the thought entered our head (*that's it, time to go*), there was a low voice that growled from the blackness.

It said, "We are coming to our terminus. This is our last stop. Can you believe it? This is it for us. This is a necessary sorrow. It is a curse. Farewell."

When the lights came back on, there was a stone pedestal in the center of the stage. On it, a pink infant cried. I leaned in, squinting, as I could not tell if the child was real or merely a prop. It wriggled and whined as infants do, clawing at the air in extended colic. Around it, out of the fog, there emerged a quintet of dancers. We clapped. Their faces were covered in dirty bandages, their bodies were lithe and light. Each of them held a sickle.

The dancers did not move in unison. In fact, they seemed to move in defiance of unison. Each of them adopted their own pace and rhythm, their own jerky movements to correspond with the steadily accelerating beat of manic drums that pounded through the loudspeakers, slobbering out of the darkness.

They swung their blades in wide, wild arcs, each time coming closer to the child whose cries only increased in volume. Then as the drums reached a frenzy, the dancers each touched the tip of their blades to the child's flesh. The child stopped weeping and giggled, batting playfully at the sharp glimmers.

The music stopped. The dancers stood still and from the back of the stage four pallbearers emerged—dour men dressed in black suits who went about their work with grim determination. They carried a child-sized casket.

One of the dancers left their place beside the infant and went to lift the lid of the tiny coffin. The others silently dropped their sickles and lifted the child up high, together, circling the stage, showing its happy face to the entire crowd. When it was turned to us, we cheered.

Finally, they laid the child to rest, in the coffin.

The lid slammed shut and we clapped until the dancers all rushed to the edges of the stage and held their hands up, motioning for us to stop. We fell quiet. We strained to listen. Faintly, I could hear the infant's screaming begin anew.

And just as I heard it, the pallbearers carried the tiny casket offstage. The crying ceased.

The stage was empty and now was the time for the finale. Smoke clung to the stage floor but soon it lifted. It was a normal sort of floor that you'd expect to see at a traveling circus. One made of hastily assembled plywood—designed to be torn down and rebuilt every night. Designed to capture the imagination of a certain kind of person. When the smoke was cleared, we saw a regular floor with no obvious trap doors. It was as ordinary as they come. We all stared in wonder, searching the grain for a trace of the performers. But the more I searched the more I realized the impossibility of this, as the dirt below the stage was perfectly visible. The stage was lifted above the ground only six inches.

The lights went out and we all stood in perfect blackness.

A gravelly voice broke through the crowd again. "Thank you for coming and thank you for leaving. It is always sad to watch someone go. It is always so, so sad." The voice paused and a single sign that read EXIT glowed green in the blackness. "We hope you enjoyed your time with us."

After, we waited in the dark. Surely there was more? Surely there had to be more? But we waited and waited and there was nothing. Soon though, we gathered our things and stood up, a curious malaise overcoming us. A sense of finality, and with that a sense of sorrow.

We moved in droves to the exit, hands on each other's shoulders as we passed in absolute blackness. The sounds of our bodies became silence.

ACKNOWLEDGMENTS

There are always too many people to thank—a couple of pages just doesn't do it justice.

But if I were to start with anyone, it'd be Erik McHatton, who has been perhaps my biggest fan for the longest time, an incredible author in his own right, and a continuous source of camaraderie and inspiration. You're the best, dude.

I'd also like to thank TJ Price, who drove me crazy bouncing ideas around for this collection, but whose perfectionism helped push me to shape the collection into the form it's in now. Thanks, TJ.

In addition, I'd be remiss if I didn't mention RSL and Tim Bloom, who are great friends, advocates, and writers who I truly love being able to shoot the shit with from thousands of miles away.

Thank you to Patrick Barb, who is always down for a beer and an epic dish-sesh on the state of this whole Writing Horror business. You and me: same time, same place?

Thank you to P.L. McMillan and Salt Heart Press for taking a bullet for publishing as a whole and agreeing to release this thing.

Thanks to Jolie Toomajan for being in the same boat at the same time, and providing countless thoughtful encouragements, counterpoints, and commiserations.

And of course, thank you to all the publishers who helped debut these stories in their original form. Publishing is a nightmare grind but it's also where dreams are made reality. Single-person operations run out of an apartment often spark dances across the living room, a flurry of celebratory texts, and happy, happy tears. Without the many publishers who accepted these stories, there wouldn't be a book in your hands in the first place.

If you've ever read, reviewed, reposted about one of my books: thank you too. That means the world to me.

Finally, I'd like to thank my wife, Sarah. What's the point of all this if I don't get someone to snuggle up on the couch with and rewatch *Showgirls?* Love you, babe.

PUBLICATION HISTORY

"The Harried Man" is original to this collection.

"They Always Kill the Dog" is original to this collection.

"The Speakeasy" was originally published in *Howls from the Scene of the Crime* (2024).

"The Museum of Lost Things" was originally published on The No Sleep Podcast, season 16, episode 24 (2021).

"Canonical Victims" was originally published in Seize the Press, issue #7 (2023).

"In Haskins" was originally published in Apex Magazine, issue #127 (2021).

"We Can Only Grown in the Dark" was originally published in Tales to Terrify, episode 614 (2023).

"Zero Boundaries Podcast: Episode 182" was originally published on Signal Horizon (2019).

"Lost Futures, Devoured Pasts" is original to this collection.

"The Sorrow of our Interminable Stasis" was originally published in Chthonic Matter Quarterly, volume 1, issue 4 (2023).

"Alive and Living (Pilot)" was originally published in *AHH! That's What I Call Horror: An Anthology of '90s Horror* (2023).

"By the Grace of Saint Piers, Poor and Dead" is original to this collection.

"A Eulogy for the Fifth World" was originally published in *The First Five Minutes of the Apocalypse* (2023).

"The Children of the Event" was originally published in *Howls from the Wreckage* (2023).

"The Mushroom Men" was originally published in Vastarien, volume 7, issue 0 (2021).

"4633 Memory Stick (Phone Use Model 6A)" is original to this collection.

"No More Bodies, No More Pits" is original to this collection.

"The Final Circus" is original to this collection.

ABOUT THE AUTHOR

Carson Winter is an award-winning author, punker, and raw nerve. His short fiction has appeared in over 20 publications, including *Apex*, *Vastarien*, and *Chthonic Matter Quarterly*. He is the author of *Soft Targets, The Psychographist,* and *A Spectre is Haunting Greentree.*

CONTENT WARNINGS

"They Always Kill the Dog"
    Animal death.

"The Speakeasy"
    Toxic masculinity, animal death.

"The Museum of Lost Things"
    Mass shootings and other wide-scale violence.

"In Haskins"
    Domestic violence/murder.

"We Can Only Grow in the Dark"
    Domestic violence/murder.

"By the Grace of Saint Piers, Poor and Dead"
    Infanticide, animal death, and religious cruelty.

"A Eulogy for the Fifth World"

Graphic sex.

"The Mushroom Men"
Child death.

"No More Bodies, No More Pits"
Suicide.

SALT HEART PRESS

"Invention, it must be humbly admitted, does not consist in creating out of void but out of chaos." — Mary Shelley

We at Salt Heart Press seek the best in horror. We live for it, we crave it, we desire it — nothing gives us more pleasure than the thrills and chills found in the perfectly crafted dark tale. As such, it is our mission to seek out fresh voices in the genre, search out the new and unique, the brave and challenging. We want to be scared. We want to be haunted. And we want the same for you.

So take a look at the books we have and keep an eye out for those to come.

https://www.saltheartpress.com/

www.ingramcontent.com/pod-product-compliance
Lightning Source LLC
Chambersburg PA
CBHW021417110726
47901CB00008B/2196